Perfect Roommate

© Cherry Publishing, 2023,
for the English translation.

ISBN: 978-1-80116-598-3

MRS KRISTAL

Perfect Roommate

Translated from German
by Cherry Publishing

Cherry
Publishing

1

-SIENNA-

After a nearly nine-hour trip from Ellsworth, a suburb of Montana's capital city of Helena, via Chicago to Lincoln, I have arrived at my new home. It is late afternoon, and I will probably fall into bed tired and exhausted after arriving at my new apartment.

The bus stops at the "Lincoln Campus" stop and I get my suitcase and carry bag off. I have been on the road since the early hours of the morning to reach my new home. My parents took me to the airport in Helena. From there I flew to Chicago and from Chicago, I took another bus to Lincoln.

I can't wait to start my studies. All summer I have been looking forward to September and my move to finally be here. This is going to be a new chapter in my life. I am now a college student living in another state, and I will soon be a roommate in a shared apartment. The dorm where I applied for a room sent me a letter saying that they didn't have any rooms available in their dorms. However, I could have the room in an apartment that the college also rents. The previous tenant had moved out because she had graduated.

At first, I was skeptical because I was sure I wanted to live in a dorm right on campus. Getting to classes and lectures would be much faster and less complicated because I could walk. To get to the apartment, I would need an extended bus pass, but the alternative would be even further away. And more expensive. In the end, I accepted. My new roommate is Denver Jones, and she's a senior in college. If we don't get along, she'll move out in a year and a half. Then maybe I can find someone on my own.

Hopefully, I'll make new friends. That's what I'm most afraid of - that I'll be alone all through college. But it doesn't have to be that way because I'm sure Denver and I will get along really well and become friends.

I grab the handle of my luggage and shoulder my carry-on bag, following the signs to the apartment complex. Ever since I got on the bus in Chicago, I've been soaking up everything around me like a sponge. It's all new to me. In the coming weeks, I will have memorized the streets, house numbers, and buildings. Right now, though, I feel like I will never be able to remember it all. I follow the directions on my iPhone, played through my AirPods.

I turn into "Abbey Street" and see the apartment building in the distance. In front of it is a large white sign that almost reaches my chest. In the middle is the logo of Lincoln College and a notice stating that the complex is owned by them and the city of Lincoln. In smaller print are a few sentences about the house rules, and in the lower right corner is the phone number and address of the dorm administration in case of an emergency.

Finally, after so many hours of traveling, I've arrived at my new home. My heart is pounding and I can't wait to check out my new home.

"You have arrived at your destination," says the female

voice from Google Maps, and I turn off the navigation app. Then I turn around and look up at the pretty beige facade. The windows on the second floor are neatly aligned, while those on the upper floors are bay windows. My apartment is on the second floor.

"Here we go," I say, "Now your college life begins, Sienna Gardner."

I pull the key out of my jacket pocket and walk to the front door. It's not easy with my suitcase and my big carry-on bag. And my handbag. Fortunately, the door opens and a blonde walks out. Relieved, I put the key back in my pocket.

"I'll hold the door for you," she says with a smile, and I nod as I maneuver my suitcase through the door.

"Thanks."

"No problem," she replies, and I look at her. Like me, she has long blonde hair, a slim figure, and a friendly smile. "Are you new?"

"Yes," I mumble nervously, because she has identified me as a freshman. A student who spent the holidays at home would certainly have less baggage than I do. That's despite the fact that my parents are bringing most of my stuff in the family van in two weeks.

I have a furnished room because the previous tenant left a lot of her furniture there. In my bag and suitcase are the basics for a month - clothes, materials for events, and some cleaning supplies. Of course, I could have bought everything locally, but I wanted to be prepared.

"Is it that obvious?" I ask anyway, grinning at her.

"You seem a little lost and you have a lot of luggage."

"Oh," I do. "I guess I am, and you are?"

"I'm a sophomore." She grins broadly at me. "Is this where you are going to live?" She points her index finger down the hall of the apartment building and I nod.

"Yeah, and you?"

"I live in one of the dorms on campus, but my brother lives here."

"Oh, I see," I say. "I'm Sienna."

"I'm Phoenix," she replies, giggling. "Nice to meet you. What are you studying?"

"Economics. And you?"

"Me too, how cool!" She looks excited that we're in the same major. She gives me another friendly smile. Then Phoenix raises her hand in greeting. "I have to go. It was nice to meet you, Sienna. Maybe I'll see you again."

Before I can say anything in response, she spins around and runs down the sidewalk. She waves at me again before disappearing from sight. I wave back and then go inside to take the stairs up to my new apartment.

I got the key to the apartment in the mail, which I thought was a little unusual, but I don't mind. I wouldn't have wanted to pick it up today or drive all the way to Lincoln for it.

I am even more excited to see the apartment from the inside. I have only seen it in pictures. Some landlord, and I'm not excluding the dorm administration, took photos of the rooms years ago and

haven't put any new ones online since. It is possible that the apartment I will have to live in for the next few years is totally crappy.

Arriving at the second floor, I fear I will need some oxygen. It's doable without luggage, but hell with it. Besides, I'm so out of shape and hate exercise so much that it dragged my final grade in high school down. Panting, I pull out my key again and unlock the door. Next to the door is a small sign that says *Denver Jones*. This is it! Again, my heart beats in my throat as I enter the apartment. Dragging the suitcase behind me, I drop the carry bag on the floor.

"Made it," I sigh and look around. I'm standing in a large living room, the central room of the apartment. This is where I'll spend my evenings, maybe even chill out with Denver for movie nights. If she's the type. What she doesn't seem to be the type for, though, is tidiness. T-shirts are scattered on the couch, along with an empty pizza box and a beer bottle. I purse my lips. I hope she doesn't leave her stuff all over the place and that this is just a one-time thing. Otherwise, I'll end up cleaning up after her. I take a deep breath to stop the negative thoughts and slip off my jacket to hang it on the coat rack. As I do so, I realize that Denver must be pretty big and bulky. The jackets are huge. Also, a lot of them are from the college football team, the Lincoln Tigers. I found a few things about them on the Internet but didn't bother to read up on them. Of course, I know that football is a cultural thing and that the players are not only the kings of the college, but also pretty good-looking. A lot of girls would lick their lips to be seen next to one of them. But I'm here to learn, not to end up in a quarterback's bed. I'm here to get a good education. A football player certainly won't help me with that.

I leave the coat rack behind me and continue into the living room. The decorating seems rather sporadic and not like she has a knack for it. In addition to a large couch and a wing chair, there is a huge flat screen TV in the living room. With each passing minute, I feel more and more uneasy about my roommate. I came to Lincoln with a clear image of her. She is a little shy, neat, and naturally curious, and she takes her studies as seriously as I do. Not a party girl or a person who leaves her stuff lying around. The much too large football jackets that might belong to her boyfriend don't suit me either. I don't want the guy around all the time. What if we can't lock our bathroom and he catches me in the shower?

I shake my head.

It's way too early to be thinking about my roommate's boy-friend barging into the bathroom. I don't even know if she has one. Maybe someone just forgot their jacket.

The click of a door makes me jump, and before I can figure out where the sound is coming from, I'm confronted.

"Who are you?" The voice, which doesn't sound female at all, makes me jump. "And what are you doing in my place?"

I turn around and yelp as I see the guy in front of me. He's tall, at least eight inches taller than me. He has broad shoulders, muscular arms and legs. The six-pack is nothing to sneeze at either. And he is only wearing a towel around his waist. It wasn't until I took a second look that I noticed his short blond hair was wet, and that little drops of water were running down his chest and stomach to the edge of the towel, where a fine strand of blond hair was visible. Holy Mother of God, who is this hottie? I look away from the center of his body and face him again.

Suspiciously, he raises his eyebrows and folds his arms across his chest. This makes them look even more muscular. I'm sure the temperature in the room has risen considerably in the last few minutes. "I... so I... so I..." I was completely at a loss for words. "I'm Sienna."

"Okay," he replied, still skeptical. "And what are you doing in my apartment, Sienna?"

"This... this is your apartment?" I look around helplessly, but other than the pizza boxes and the beer bottle on the coffee table, there's nothing to indicate that this isn't his apartment. I remember the jackets on the coat rack that I thought be-longed to Denver's boyfriend. Panic spreads through me as it dawns on me that these are his jackets and Denver's boyfriend doesn't exist. Did I mix up the doors? No, that's impossible. The sign on the doorbell said *Denver Jones* in big, bold letters, and the key fit the lock. "But the... the sign said *Denver Jones*."

"So what?" he wants to know. "I'm Denver."

"What?" My voice cracks again, sounding much squeakier than it really is. My heart is pounding in my throat and the knot in my stomach is growing. At first, Denver doesn't react, but scrutinizes me meticulously. Slowly but surely, his stare makes me uncomfortable, so I turn around and go back to my luggage. Denver follows me. He's not even holding the towel, which sits very low on his hips. Doesn't it occur to him for a second that the knot could come loose and I could see his dick? Surely none of this is happening.

I reach for my purse and search for the dorm paperwork. It's silly, I know, but I can't believe he's Denver. I was expecting a young woman like me, not this sex god. Denver is incredibly hot.

Also, I can't believe that co-ed housing is provided by the dorm administration. Nervously, I pull out my notes and read through them. But again, they only confirm that I'm in the right apartment.

"So?" He clears his throat when I still haven't turned around. "Did you find what you were looking for?"

I don't miss the mockery in his voice, but I don't let it get to me. This must be a big misunderstanding. There's no way I'm sharing an apartment with this guy. Did I mention how hot he is? And if I think he's hot, other girls think so too. Girls who may not have as much self-esteem as I do and who like to be spoiled by him. God, just the thought of him having sex in the room next to me makes my head spin.

"You're Denver Jones?" I ask again, just to be sure.

"Yes, I'm Denver Jones," he says, unfazed. "And you're Sienna - what else?"

"Gardner," I reply. "Sienna Gardner. The ... dorm administration assigned me the spare room."

"What?" he asks, reaching for my papers. "May I see?"

13

I nod and hand him the papers. When his hand touches mine, I flinch and look at him. Denver meets my gaze. Close enough that his aftershave wafts over to me now. His blue eyes stare at me and his lips curve into a smile.

"Thank you," he says as he takes the papers. He starts to read them and snorts. "They're so stupid. Denver is a unisex name. They thought I was a girl. Which I'm definitely not."

Denver looks at me and grins. Then he slides his eyes down his muscular body and I follow him like a chick to its mother.

"Not a girl," I confirm. "Definitely not a girl."

He laughs and hands me the notes back so I can wrap them up and put them in my bag. "So, what now?" I ask. "I... there's no way I can live here."

"Why not?" He looks puzzled. "I mean, I would have preferred a guy too, but..."

"Well, thanks."

"I thought you said there was no way you could live here."

"And you're not even dressed!" I point at his body, and he raises his eyebrows. Denver laughs softly and licks his lips.

"I'd be happy to take the towel off if you-"

"Don't you dare." Threateningly, I raise my index finger to point at his half-naked body. "You wouldn't. We... we have to stay calm. I'm really tired today, but we have to deal with this tomorrow.

I can't live here. He's a man, and I don't need to see the final and clearest proof of that. It would never work between us. Just seeing how messy he is. It would relegate me to being his cleaning lady, which, by the way, is something he desperately needs.

"What do you want to sort out?" he asks, turning on his heel and heading for the bathroom. "I'll be right back."

He disappears into the middle of the three doors on the opposite wall and I shake my head. This can only happen to me, right? Denver Jones, my nice and sweet roommate, has turned into an incredibly hot, funny, and kind of charming guy. I can't live with him. It's not going to work. Denver and I just aren't right for each other.

"I'm back." I look up to see that he's sadly changed into sweat shorts and a t-shirt. "Back to our conversation. You won't find another room. Everything is pretty much full. And the ones that are available are disgusting."

I look around and he groans.

"I had some buddies over yesterday," he says, actually starting to clean up. "I was going to take a shower and then get to work. You arrived too early."

The corners of Denver's mouth rise mischievously.

"I guess I should have thought of that myself, that I'm just early, huh?" I reply sarcastically and he grins even wider.

"Exactly," he says. "And like I said - it doesn't always look this messy around here. I do clean up."

"It's late afternoon," I point out, but Denver just shrugs.

"Yeah, so? It ran a little late yesterday. So Sienna, how do you think you and I are going to get along for the next few months?"

"I'm sure I can clear up the misunderstanding with the dorm administration and..." He raises his eyebrows and I let out a pained groan. "Come on...at least give me some hope."

"Yes, Sienna!" He grins and winks at me. "Tomorrow you'll find a new room, ideally right on campus, so you won't enjoy any of your student life, but will spend the next few years stuck between your books and lectures. While here, with me, you would experience real life."

"Are you making fun of me?" I ask, and he can't help but grin again.

"Just telling you how it is," he says with a shrug. "You're definitely not getting a new room. I have no idea how the mix-up happened, but at this point we should make the best of it."

This guy really drives me crazy.

"You have no problem at all with me being your new room-mate?"

"No," Denver says, reaching for the pizza boxes on the cof-fee table. "I'll be gone in a year and a half. I don't care who I live with for the last few months as long as we get along. Besides, I'm rarely home anyway."

"Well, I for one don't appreciate you telling me that you don't care if I live here or with some disgusting smelly guy who... never mind. Anyway, where are you usually?"

I'm clearly more interested in that now.

"At practice, in meetings, occasionally at a lecture, and out with the team."

"What team?" I ask, and he looks at me in surprise.

"Didn't you read up on the college?"

"Of course I did." I'd spent weeks comparing colleges and reading everything, literally everything, about Lincoln College that was relevant to my major. Admittedly, I wasn't particularly interested in the college beyond that. I planned to get involved in extracurricular activities and clubs. Maybe make some new friends and spend some time with them. But Denver doesn't need to know that. "I wouldn't be here oth-erwise."

"And you don't know who I am?" He raises his eyebrows and gives me a look of disbelief. I do the same to him be-cause it's a really stupid question. I have no idea who he is, and frankly, I don't care.

"No," I answer his question. "But I'm sure you're going to tell me."

"I'm Denver Jones and..."

"Oh, you're Denver Jones, I knew that-"

"I'm the quarterback of the football team, Sienna," he con-tinues, a bright smile forming on his face. It's one of those hundred-watt smiles that make every girl weak in the knees. "People know who I am."

"You're the..." My jaw drops as I let his statement run through my head. He's the fucking quarterback. The guy everyone idolizes and wants to be like. "Holy shit."

Denver laughs and puts his hand to his chest. I have to admit, he has huge hands. Otherwise, he wouldn't be able to hold those huge egg-shaped balls. Still grinning, he raises his eyebrows.

"Is that good or bad?"

"I have no idea," I sigh. "Which one is my room?"

I change the subject to avoid thinking about the fact that I'm going to be rooming with the quarterback from now on.

"Hang on a second," he says, holding up the pizza boxes. "I'll take these into the kitchen and then show you around."

"Oh okay," I say, looking around, "thanks."

Denver goes into the kitchen, which I haven't seen yet, and I stare after him. Somehow, I have to agree with him. A voice tells me that I'm in the right place to spend my time in college.

It was my wish to get away from my parents and do something completely new and on my own. Even though I never imagined that my roommate would turn out to be the quarterback of the football team, I like it. It's a big change from everything I knew in Montana.

Who knows? Maybe we'll even become friends.

2

-SIENNA-

Denver comes back from the kitchen a few minutes later and smiles at me. I still can't believe he's going to be my roommate for the next year and a half. Normally, the college is meticulous about assigning apartments and rooms to the same gender.

Denver is well known on campus and it should have been obvious that he was a man. And what a man he is. I still can't get over how hot he is. Even now, in a shirt and sweat shorts that almost reach his knees, he cuts a good figure.

"So," he says, clapping his hands. "Here we are in the heart of our apartment. The living room. Parker, your previous tenant, and I spent a lot of time together. We'd play games, watch movies, or have friends over."

I wonder if he expects me to do the same. I'm not a party animal and I really want to focus on my studies. That's important to me. Besides, I don't know anyone in Lincoln except him and the blonde girl I met at the entrance. It doesn't surprise me at all that Denver has a large circle of friends and acquaintances.

"You don't have to do this, of course, and you can stay in your room. It's just a suggestion. Sometimes my teammates will come over and we will have our team meetings here."

"Okay," I mutter, wondering if they're all as hot as he is. The football players at my high school were good-looking, but I was never their collar, and I didn't want to be. I was definitely not athletic enough for cheerleading. Those guys weren't interested in anything beyond that anyway. "I guess that's okay with me. But I'm here to study, not to party."

I smile at him. Denver raises his eyebrows and nods slowly. But his expression tells me there's more to be said on the subject. Something - probably a sharp comment - is on the tip of his tongue.

"What?" I ask. "I care about my studies."

"I'm not saying anything," he says, raising his arms. "I just think you should take advantage of all the opportunities that student life has to offer. That includes getting drunk and laid."

I gasp and look at him with wide eyes. Our conversation is about to go in a completely different direction, which makes me nervous. I cross my arms over my chest and wait for him to say something else. At nineteen, I'm officially not allowed to drink at all. And sex ... well ... the offer would have to be really, really good for me to get involved in something meaningless. Denver, for example, would be one, but now that he's my roommate, that would just lead to problems. Not to mention that we would sleep together and not be able to look each other in the eye afterwards.

"First of all, I'm nineteen years old and I'm not allowed to get drunk and-"

"Seriously?" he cuts me off. "As long as you don't end up in the hospital, no one will know. Why don't you come with me later?"

"You're going out again today after ... well, overdoing it yesterday? I'm super tired and-"

"Nothing strong coffee can't fix. My sister's coming too, you'll like her."

I'm surprised that he already thinks I'll like his sister. After all, he's only known me for half an hour, and in that time we haven't found anything in common. Why in God's name would he think I would get along with his sister?

I remember Phoenix from down the hall saying that her brother lives in this house. But what kind of coincidence would that be if Phoenix was Denver's sister?

I laugh out loud, which makes Denver raise his eyebrows again. "What's the matter now?" he asks. "Why are you laughing?"

"When I came in earlier, a girl held the door open for me. Her name is Phoenix and she said that her brother lives in this house."

"Oh man!" He laughs out loud. "Phoenix is my sister."

"No kidding?" I inevitably laugh too. "Coincidences do happen."

"She woke me up," he says, his face contorting as if he'd rather still be in bed. "I had given her a key - to use while I lived here alone, but, of course, I'll take it back from her."

"Okay," I say. "Can we get on with the apartment?"

"I thought we were still talking about sex." Heat immediately shoots into my cheeks as he says this and he lets his eyes slide down my body. "Or don't you do that because you're only nineteen?"

Something flashes in his eyes and he doesn't seem to want to drop the subject.

"I'm going to have to disappoint you, player," I reply. "I have sex."

"You have sex?" Denver licks his lips and grins at me. "Who with? Do you have a boyfriend? Will he come in and out of here?"

I purse my lips and shake my head. Apart from the fact that it's none of his business, even though I've been completely honest, he doesn't need to ask me that. It's my private business. I've never asked him about the girls he's been with. Honestly, I don't even want to know because I'm sure they're all flawless.

"It's none of your business, but no, I don't have a boyfriend," I answer. "Do you have a girlfriend?"

Denver laughs again, as if it's absurd that he's spoken for.

"I don't have a girlfriend," he replies. "I don't have time for that."

"You call a girlfriend a that?" I raise my eyebrows. "Interesting."

"I guess you're a bit of a feminist yourself, huh?"

"No," I say. "But you have time for sex and drinking?"

"It's a lot less stressful, isn't it?" Denver grins and shrugs.

"Less stressful?" His arguments are getting better and better. "Let's leave it at that. Can you show me the place now?"

I don't want to discuss relationships, sex and alcohol with him anymore.

"Of course," he says, smiling at me. "This is the living room, as I said. Let's move on to the bathroom."

I nod and follow Denver to the middle of the three rooms along the far wall. The fact that the bathroom is between our rooms is a good thing. If we were right next to each other, we'd be able to hear each other better, but it would also be distracting, I think. Not to mention that I would have to listen to some moaning or hear him and his conquests go at it so wildly that his bed hits the wall. Pictures of Denver hovering over me flash before my mind's eye. His blue eyes staring at me lustfully as he thrusts himself into me. I shake my head.

Oh God, I've never thought about sex so much, in such a short time, as when I'm in his presence. This can't be happening. This is the guy I'm going to be living with for the next few months.

"Here we are."

I flinch and look at Denver, perplexed. He seems irritated that I haven't been listening to him. I nod and walk past him, looking around the bathroom. It's bigger than I expected. As you might expect, it's as messy as the living room. His clothes are scattered around the room. Shampoo and shower gel are scattered on the floor of the shower, and the towel he tied around his waist earlier is lying on the floor. I don't even dare go near the sink. I'm sure his hair is there, and the remains of his toothpaste stuck to the porcelain. I grimace in disgust.

"What is it now?" Slightly annoyed, he looks at me and shoves his hands into his pockets.

"Well," I muse. "It's not that ... neat."

"Of course not," Denver says. "I didn't have time for it."

"Denver!"

"Sienna!" he imitates my voice and I roll my eyes. "I would have cleaned up if I knew you were moving in."

"Why do you need a reason to clean?" I ask, walking over to the sink after all. Next to it is a shelf for his razor and aftershave. One shelf is open for my things. Next to the door is another shelf for towels. There is space here as well. The bathroom is sparsely furnished, but, in my opinion, absolutely fine. The shower is large and above the sink there is a shelf for my toothbrush, toothpaste and creams. There is also enough space for my makeup. I am happy with the bathroom.

"Housework isn't really my thing." Denver grins. "But it seems to be yours."

I roll my eyes, because this reeks of gender roles at its worst. Denver laughs and comes up beside me. He nudges me with his shoulder, touching me directly for the first time. Even though I'm wearing a hoodie, the warmth of his skin immediately penetrates the fabric. I immediately step aside to break the contact. The mischievous look in his eyes tells me all too well how he envisions us living together. I cook, clean, and do the laundry while he goes to practice and is king of the college.

"You should see the look on your face," he says. "I can clean up if it's that important to you."

"Don't make fun of me," I say mouth agape. "It's important to me that the place is clean and that I feel comfortable here. I'm not overly fussy, but I do expect you to be able to tidy up at your age."

"Yes, Mom," he sighs. "Kitchen?"

"Sure," I mutter and follow him. I have to stop reacting to his teasing. It's what he wants. Even though it's admittedly fun. It goes to show that we can be casual and comfortable with each other. "I can't wait to see what it looks like in there."

I grin at him and Denver rolls his eyes.

"You caught me on the wrong foot today," he admits. "I'm not dirty. Besides, we have a cleaning lady."

"Hang on!" I stop and he does the same. "We have a ... cleaning lady?"

"Yes," Denver says, as if it's the most natural thing in the world for two students to have a cleaning lady. "She comes in once a week and sweeps the common areas. I thought it made sense."

"Oh," I say, nodding. "Cool."

He laughs and goes into the kitchen. I follow him.

The kitchen is - against my expectations - tidy. Sure, there are empty beer bottles and two glasses on the counter, but otherwise it is very neat and big. Much bigger than in the photos sent to me by the dormitory administration. I can't help but feel that the apartment I was supposed to get and the one I ended up in are not the same. This kitchen is bright, thanks to the window opposite the door, and has an open design, with an island in the middle of the kitchen. In no way is this the kitchen of a normal student apartment.

"This is not the right apartment." I point at the kitchen island and the large window. "I mean ... it ... it's great, but the photos were of a different one. I didn't really notice it until I saw the kitchen. In the bathroom, I thought I just didn't appreciate the square footage."

"What do you mean?" asks Denver, leaning his butt against the counter.

"Wait a minute." I run back into the living room and to my bag. From it, I pull out my iPhone, unlock it, and pull up the dorm management email, which shows the floor plan of the apartment and photos of the rooms. I am eighty percent sure that this apartment is different from the one the administration suggested. And most of all: the one I agreed to.

"Look at this," I say, handing Denver my iPhone. "This isn't the kitchen, and this isn't the bathroom. It's much smaller. But the address and the key are to this apartment."

He looks at everything calmly as I sit down at the kitchen table.

"This is indeed a different place." Denver nods in agreement. "Be glad you ended up here."

"What if the person who was supposed to move in here feels cheated?"

Denver looks at me questioningly and hands me the iPhone. He does everything with a calmness that drives me crazy. He has lived here for years, so no one will think he should move. I groan in frustration because I have no desire to move. I like the apartment and, contrary to my initial fears, Denver seems very nice and I think we'll get along well. But I don't want to get in trouble and look like a fraud.

"Well," he says, pointing his index finger at me. "We should find out who they mixed you up with. It must be a girl, because they thought I was a girl. Maybe you'll get lucky and she'll be glad she's got a roommate."

"What if she wants to move in with you?" I ask and Denver laughs.

"I wouldn't blame her."

I roll my eyes again and stand up.

"Oh, come on." Denver gently punches me in the shoulder. "You had to expect that."

"Kind of." I grin too. "Will you show me to my room?"

"Sure," he says with a sweeping gesture. "Follow me, please."

Laughing, I throw my head back and follow him.

Two hours later, I have unpacked most of my things and settled into my room. I put pictures of my parents and friends on the dresser. Then I made my bed and organized my closet. I sit on the bed for several minutes, not daring to take a shower. It's stupid, I know, but somehow I feel self-conscious. Denver's nice and I don't think he'd barge into the bathroom. Besides, I'd lock the door. Annoyed at myself for worrying so much, I get up and leave my room.

The TV is on and Denver is sitting on the couch.

"Hey," I say and he turns to me.

"Hey. Want to take a shower?" He points at the towels in my arm.

"Yeah?" I answer more hesitantly than I'd like. "Is that okay with you?"

"Sure," Denver says, putting his arm on the back of the couch to rest his chin on. Smiling, he looks at me. "You live here, Sienna. It's your apartment too."

"Yes, of course," I reply. "It's still a little unfamiliar to me. It's my first time living in a shared apartment."

"I understand." He grins. "If you need anything, let me know."

"Thanks." I smile at him again and go into the bathroom. I lock the door and test the lock again. There's no way I want to face Denver naked. Sighing, I put my towel on the shelf and get undressed. Then I get in the shower and turn on the water. As soon as the hot water trickles down my body, I groan. It feels so good and I feel better right away. The day was long, filled with tons of new impressions on the flight and later the drive from Chicago to Lincoln. Then the first meeting with Denver and the shock that he was definitely not a girl. For the first time in hours, I can really relax. I wash my hair, soap up and rinse off again. Afterwards, I step out of the shower stall and reach for my towel. At home, I would have gone to my room wrapped in it and changed there, but I don't dare do that today. Instead, I do everything in the bathroom. Drying off, changing, and getting my hair ready to air dry and form light waves.

As I step out of the bathroom, I hear voices coming from the kitchen. Curious to see who it is, I walk toward the door and push it open.

Denver is sitting at the kitchen table and another guy is standing by the counter. They both have a beer in their hands. Denver has traded his shirt and sweat shorts for a pair of ripped jeans and a black hoodie with the football team's logo. His buddy is wearing a similar outfit. A cloud of aftershave hovers over them.

"Hi," I say, making my presence known. Denver and his friend look up, the corners of their mouths tug into smiles, and I feel like I'm being scrutinized for the second time that day. This time not only by Denver, but also by his friend. His brown eyes sweep over my body and finally stop on mine. Nervously, I put one foot in front of the other because I can't fathom his gaze. Like Denver, his confidence oozes from every pore of his well-trained body.

"Hey," Denver speaks up. "I thought the shower had swallowed you." I feel a blush rise to my face and shake my head. A feeling of unease creeps up my spine at the look on his buddy's face. I don't want him to imagine me in the shower. I glance over and notice that he's still watching me intently.

"Uh, yeah," I stammer. "So, you're ready to go out?"

With a nod, I motion to his outfit and smile at him. His buddy's presence makes me nervous, and even though I've loosened up around Denver, I still don't feel as confident as I should. I can handle his hints and teasing, but I still have to figure out how to handle a second guy of his ilk - and that's obviously his buddy.

"Absolutely," he says, looking over at his buddy. Denver's eyes flashes as his buddy grins broadly and points at me with a nod.

"Are you going to introduce me or should I do it myself?" He winks at me. "Denver's not a gentleman, you'll have to excuse him."

Denver rolls his eyes and takes a swig of his beer before finally introducing us.

"This is Jake, my best friend. Jake, this is my new roommate, Sienna." Denver points at me, then at Jake, and back again. "That should get you acquainted."

I raise my eyebrows and look at him questioningly. Am I wrong or does Denver not want me getting to know his best friend? Amused, I notice that he actually makes no further effort to tell me anything about Jake or vice versa. I offer Jake a friendly hand, which he immediately accepts.

Jake is also very handsome, but the exact opposite of Denver. Brown hair, noticeably more muscular, and a few inches taller.

"Hi," I say. "Nice to meet you."

"The pleasure is all mine."

Jake is flirting with me, even I can see that. His lips curl into an adorable grin, and when he looks back at me, he licks his lower lip with his tongue.

It was definitely the right decision not to show up in a towel. I don't even want to imagine how embarrassing that would have been and what Jake would have thought. He's already going on the offensive. Denver doesn't seem to miss it either, because he clears his throat loudly.

"You want to come with us?" he asks with a smile and I shake my head. I'm really tired and just want to go to bed. The day has been exhausting and as much as he means well - I really need to sleep.

"I'll stay in, but thanks for the offer," I reply, yawning demonstratively. "I'm incredibly tired."

"Too bad." Jake grins. Of course he's grinning. It seems to be his permanent expression the whole time he's around me. His attempts at flirting don't really interest me. Guys like Jake and Denver are out of my league and I'm not dumb enough to get involved with either of them. Denver taps him on the shoulder and puts his beer bottle in the sink. Jake does the same.

"I'll clean this up tomorrow. We have to go."

"Okay," I say, making a dismissive hand gesture. "Have fun."

"Thanks," Jake replies, and Denver rolls his eyes and walks past us into the living room. Jake and I follow him. "Take care, Sienna." Jake's still flirtatious undertone is starting to amuse me. He doesn't seem to be giving up. But I haven't responded yet.

Of course, they're both wearing college jackets with the football team's logo on them. "Do you play football?" I ask Jake, pointing at his jacket. He grins broadly and nods. I grin and realize he has the same passion for the sport as Denver. The twinkle in his eye when he told me he was a quarterback was incredible.

"I'm a running back. Are you into football?"

"Not really." I shake my head. "Sorry."

I sit sideways on the arm of the couch and watch them get ready. If I thought Denver's physique was big and intimidating, I was wrong. Jake is so much bigger and has a much wider back than his friend. My knowledge of football is limited, but as a running back, Jake probably docs more muscle work than Denver.

"We'll fix that," Denver interrupts our conversation with a grin and winks at me. "See you tomorrow."

"See you tomorrow," I say, waiting for the apartment door to slam behind them.

What a first day.

3

▪SIENNA▪

The next morning, Denver isn't awake when I get up. With my MacBook and a cup of coffee, I sit down on the couch and turn on the big flat-screen TV. It must be Denver's, and he kindly left it in the lounge so I can use it, too. After finding the right remote and clicking through all the pay-TV sports channels, I get stuck on the Disney Channel and watch the 90s sitcom "The Nanny". Besides, it's nice to watch and the jokes always make me laugh out loud. I haven't seen or heard from Denver and it's almost eleven.

While he sleeps, I use the time to check my schedule against the college's class schedule. I want to be able to find the right classrooms on Monday, because I don't want to be late for my first week of college. Now that things have gone wrong with the apartment, I'm a little worried that things might go wrong with my classes. My friend Clara, who is studying in Helena, told me not to worry. Everything would work out. Besides, I should consider myself lucky to be living with Denver. I told her about the dorm management's mistake.

To my amazement, there are all kinds of pictures of Denver

Jones on the Internet, and I found him on Instagram. But I don't dare follow him because I didn't know how that would look. Sure, he's nice to me and invited me to a party right away, but we're still not friends. Clara was of the opinion that I should get involved with Denver quickly and go to bed with him, because nobody knows me here anyway. In her opinion, I should not miss this golden opportunity.

I asked her if she was out of her mind. Denver is my roommate and I don't think having sex with him will help our relationship. Clara also said I should bring him to Helena for Thanksgiving so she could meet him. I told her that I would see what I could do. Deep down, though, I know I would never invite Denver to my house. The looks on my parents' faces when they see him would speak volumes. He is not the kind of man they envision for me. My family is not overly conservative, and my parents liked my first boyfriend, Patrick, who I dated until a few months ago, but Denver is the exact opposite of him. He was quiet, level-headed, focused on studying, didn't go to parties, and wasn't a jock. Physically, they have very little in common. Both have blond hair and light eyes. But that's about it. Patrick's body wasn't even close to being ripped. He was just thin.

Sounds from Denver's room filter into the living room, and it looks like he's finally woken up. I'm surprised he didn't wake me last night. No doubt he was drunk. But as exhausted as I was, a steam engine could have driven through the apartment, and I would have continued to sleep.

"Fine by me," I hear him grumble, and I snap to attention. I immediately turn off the TV and sit up. "Just get out!"

Confused, I look at his door and can only guess who he's talking to. The next thing I know, the door is yanked open and a girl about our age appears in front of me. She is wearing a short dress that barely covers her bottom and breasts.

Her brown hair resembles a bird's nest and her makeup is smeared. Her deep panda eyes stand out and her lipstick is halfway down her cheek. I unintentionally curl my lip when I see her. She looks terrible. Then a realization hits me that almost causes me to gasp.

Denver didn't come home alone tonight; he came home with her. They had sex. It can't be true that he would pick up the first available girl and bring her home with him. My first night here, the least he could have done was skip it, right?

So much for him at least giving me a little grace period before he shows his true colors. I don't even want to know how many women he hooks up with in a week and how many he makes out with at a party.

Why did he even bother to invite me yesterday? I wasn't going to spread my legs for him. Not for him and not for Jake!

Of course, ladies' man Denver Jones and roommate Denver Jones can be completely different. I get to see the roommate. Although I'd be tempted by the ladies' man, too.

"Morning," I mutter and look at her.

"Mo- ... morning," she replies, biting her lip. She seems uncomfortable with the situation. "I ... I was just leaving and I didn't know... he didn't say he has..."

Jesus. She thinks I'm his girlfriend. Which I find pretty funny, because then I would have been in his bed, or at least Denver would have known I would run into his one-night stand.

"She's not my girlfriend." Denver's voice is hoarse and still slightly sleepy. Pretty sexy, to be honest, but the situation is far too absurd to dwell on the sound of his voice any longer. "Morning Sienna."

I look at him with wide eyes and can't help but stare at his body. Denver is wearing only a pair of tight black boxers. Although I saw him in a similar state of undress yesterday, the towel did a much better job of hiding his penis.

"Good morning," I reply, looking him in the eye. There's a look of amusement on his face that I find completely inappropriate. He's putting us all in an awkward position. "Slept in?"

Denver grins at me as the girl blushes.

"Envious?" he wants to know, and her face resembles a tomato. Judging by her outfit, I assumed she was used to situations like this, but she looks like she is so embarrassed she wants to be swallowed by the ground.

I begin to feel sorry for her. Maybe she thought it would be the night of her life and Denver would realize she was the one for him. This, unfortunately, is total bullshit because he made it clear not five minutes ago that he wanted her gone. No one who spent the night with the love of their life would do that.

Denver seems to be more of a "laid once - and done" kind of guy.

I keep watching them, slowly raising my eyebrows when they don't move.

"Envious?" I pick up his words again and laugh. "Of what?" Chuckling, I can't help but let my eyes slide between his legs. I don't know where I got this confidence all of a sudden, but exposing Denver in this situation feels way too good. He follows my gaze, registering what I'm hinting at, and his expression hardens.

"You should go," Denver barks at his mate. "Now!"

She meets his gaze and bites her lip. "Are you still going to give me your number?

I have to admit, she has a lot of nerve. He's giving her a pretty nasty time right now, and he's doing it in front of me. On top of that, he kicked her out a few minutes ago and she's still asking for his number. I'm impressed. For me, it would have been time to leave as soon as possible so as not to embarrass myself any further.

"No," Denver replies angrily. His expression is hard and he

is about to explode. He wants to get rid of her. "You know the rules, Hailey. I'm going to take a shower and when I get back, I want you gone."

Well, I have a few questions about those rules. If only to tease him further. But unfortunately, I don't get to ask my questions because he turns and disappears into the bathroom. But not before the door slams shut with a loud bang.

Stunned, I look back and forth between Hailey and the closed door.

"I should go," she mumbles, looking down at the floor in dismay. "I'm...sorry."

"It's okay," I reply, smiling encouragingly at her, "have a good day."

I have no idea what to say. This is the first time in my life that I've had to walk a one-night stand to the door. Hailey nods and quickly leaves the apartment. What about me? I want to kill Denver for putting us in this position. Especially me, who has absolutely nothing to do with it.

I get up from the couch and walk around it. I lean against it with my arms crossed and wait for Denver.

It takes less than ten minutes before the shower stops and he comes out, freshly showered. Once again I have to pull myself together not to stare at his torso. He just looks so good.

"Is she gone?" he wants to know, heading for his room.

"No, I offered her coffee and she's in the kitchen," I answer, and his eyes widen. "Of course she's gone. What was that all about?"

"What do you mean?" he asks, his eyebrows furrowed. His lips are pressed together and he looks tense. I follow him to his room. Once there, I stop talking for a moment and look around. After all, he didn't show it to me yesterday. It has the same layout as mine, but is two to three square meters larger. It's clear that Denver has lived here for a long time. Unlike the rest of the apartment, this room has a personal touch. Posters and jerseys hang on the wall, and on a dresser are photos of him and Phoenix, whom I recognize, and their parents. Next to him is another girl who looks like Phoenix.

I tear my eyes away from his family and the questions in my head and look at him again. "What do I mean?" I ask. "Do you think it's funny that I ran into your lover?"

"I never said I thought it was funny," Denver replies irritably, looking at me. "I just don't care. It was stupid, but I didn't know you were sitting on the couch."

"It's you-" I shake my head. "Did you forget I was here when you slept with her?"

He raises his eyebrows and looks at me questioningly.

"Honestly, I don't care if you're here or not. This is my apartment and most importantly my room. I can do what I want in here. And if I sleep with a different girl every night, that's none of your business, Sienna."

I gasp and want to say something in response, but I can't think of anything. The audacity of this is beyond anything I can think of. I admit that he's right that it's his room and he can do whatever he wants in it. I'm going to have friends over sometimes and I don't want him to kick them out. But it was my first night in Lincoln and I would have liked him to show a little consideration.

"Is there anything else or do you want to see my dick too?" asks Denver with a grin. He seems to have completely forgotten our discussion and is in a great mood.

I jump and he actually puts his hand on his towel to open it. My cheeks start to glow and I shake my head violently.

"No," I say in a firm voice. "I ... I'll wait for you in the kitchen."

Without waiting for his answer, I turn and leave his room. I don't want to see Denver naked this morning either. I pick up my empty coffee cup from the coffee table and head for the kitchen.

"I'm back!" Less than five minutes later, he's standing in front of me. Denver walks past me, grinning, and grabs a coffee as well. "You want another one?"

"No thanks," I say. "I thought we could ... set some rules?"

Rules will make living together a lot easier. They will prevent situations like this morning or yesterday, after he threw a party that left the apartment in a mess. At least that's how I imagine it. I doubt it will work. The way Denver is looking at me makes me doubt it even more. He raises his eyebrows and leans against the counter as I sit down at the table.

"What kind of rules?" he wants to know with a mocking undertone that makes me want to lash out.

"Well, a garbage schedule or maybe a coffee schedule. You know ... rules like that." My voice trails off at the end, and I get noticeably hotter. His gaze is probing and I can tell he doesn't like it. From his point of view, everything seems to be going well so far.

"If you insist," he says with a shrug. "Write something down."

"Don't you think it would be useful?" I ask, looking at him. Denver doesn't look hungover, which kind of surprises me. His friend looked pretty wrecked. But who knows how much sleeping with Denver has knocked her off her game. I press my lips together and try to block out the images that come to mind. The last thing I need is to imagine him having sex. Which I'm afraid I'm going to have to deal with a lot more over the next few months.

Back to my rules. They are more important. They will help us if we ever butt heads. I'm also going to write down some one-night-stand rules, because I think they're necessary. Otherwise, Denver will be on my case.

"No," Denver says. "We don't need anything like that. We each put our stuff away and..." I raise my eyebrows and he groans. "That was an exception yesterday. I didn't know you were moving in."

"If we ever have a dispute, we can go back to the rules and-"

"That's bullshit, Sienna," he retorts, putting the empty coffee cup in the sink. "What have you got planned for today?"

Confused that he's asking me about my plans, I look at him. "I have to go back to the administrator's office, but otherwise I have no plans."

"Do you know where it is?" he asks, smiling at me.

"I checked Google Maps, so I'll be able to find it," I reply. "Maybe I'll get a bike to get to campus."

Denver snorts and I look at him questioningly. Why is the idiot laughing? I think a bicycle is a good idea. It will help me get around faster while saving me money on stupid bus tickets. "Biking during the winter semester in Illinois. Are you from California?"

"No. From Montana."

"Then you should know that biking is out after the first snowfall." I press my lips together, reluctant to agree with Denver. He's still laughing.

In a way, I understand. Riding a bike in the snow is really not a good idea.

"How do you get to campus?" I ask casually. "I saw that the number five and nine buses go there."

"By car," he replies. "I don't take the bus."

As if it's the most absurd thing in the world for a quarterback to take a bus, he starts laughing again. I start thinking he's laughing at me.

"You have a car?" I ask in amazement, and he nods.

"Of course I have a car," Denver laughs. "Do you have a driver's license?"

"Yes, and I've been driving accident-free ever since, if that's what you're going to ask."

A little miffed, I look at him, but he just grins amused.

"Actually, that would have been my next question," he says. "I'll drive you to the dorm."

"Really?" I look at him, more than a little surprised that he would offer. Surely he has his own plans for the day.

"Sienna," he sighs. "If I offer, I'll do it."

"Then I'll change, grab my stuff, and we can go?"

"You do that," he says. "See you in a bit."

I nod and leave the kitchen, not wanting to keep him waiting too long.

4

-SIENNA-

Denver and I leave the apartment building and he unlocks a dark blue Ford Maverick pickup. I whistle through my teeth when I see the vehicle. Not bad, it must cost at least $20,000. "Not bad," I say, and he looks at me with a grin. I guess my praise for his car goes down well. "How can you afford a car like this?"

Denver is a college student. He probably makes a little money playing football, but not enough to afford a brand-new Ford Maverick.

"The Ford dealer is a fan of the football team, and he lets me use it." Denver shrugs like it's the most natural thing in the world.

"Wow," I say. "And that's just because you play football?"

I'm aware that players get a lot of privileges in college. That was true even in high school. They were allowed to skip tests or write a class paper a week later because of a big game. But to be given a car is beyond my wildest dreams.

"Yeah." He grins and holds the passenger door open for me. "Get in."

I oblige and get into the passenger seat. Denver closes the door behind me and walks around the car. The beige seats match perfectly with the black center console and the steering wheel, which is also black with all kinds of buttons. The large monitor in the center serves as the car's control center. Denver takes the driver's seat and closes the door behind him. After buckling up, he starts the engine. There's a roar and the monitor lights up. "Is it okay if we listen to some music?" he asks and I nod.

"Sure. It's your car."

"Okay," he says, plugging in his iPhone. Then he puts it in the center console and drives off, after double-checking that I'm buckled in.

Somehow, it's strange, everything that's happened since yesterday. Sometimes I feel like pinching myself. Having Denver as my roommate is really incredible.

"Tell me about yourself," Denver says, looking over at me. "Where are you from? Do you have any siblings? What brought you to Lincoln?"

"I'm from Ellsworth, a small town near Helena, Montana," I tell him. "The courses available at Lincoln appealed to me the most. What about you?"

"I'm from Chicago," Denver says, grinning at me. "Not from Denver. And I'm twenty-one years old." He winks at me and I can't help but laugh. I didn't think his parents would be crazy enough to name him after the city he was born in. Although I do find the question of how he got the name intriguing.

"So?" I ask. "How did you get that name?"

"My parents met in Denver and named me after them."

"That's cute," I sigh, and he laughs and leans back. Denver cuts a decidedly handsome figure while driving, too. He's wearing jeans and a white t-shirt. Over that, a turquoise lumberjack shirt. He looks insanely sexy.

"Cute." He laughs. "That could only come from a woman. Do you have any siblings?"

"My dad has a son from a previous relationship," I say. "His name is Lawrence and he's ten years older than me. He lives in Ohio with his family. I don't have any contact with him, how about you?"

"I see," Denver says. "I have two sisters. Phoenix, whom you already know, and Madison."

My head jerks up, and Denver groans as if he's caught on to my realization. "Yeah, they're named after cities too."

"What's the deal with that?" I chuckle. "Denver, Phoenix and Madison."

"We lived in Phoenix, Arizona for a couple of years and then in Madison, Wisconsin. My dad worked there. We moved three times in the first seven years of my life. From Chicago to Phoenix and then to Madison. My parents named Phoenix in honor of the old home, and Mad-" He sighs. "You know the drill now."

I chuckle and nod.

"How old are they?" I continue and Denver smiles. "Phoenix is nineteen like you and Madison is fifteen. We've been living in Chicago ever since because my mom didn't want to move with three kids."

"What does your dad do?" I ask with interest. My parents are politicians and both were a constant presence in our home. My dad was the mayor of Ellsworth for many years until he went into teaching political science. Mom devoted herself to the duties of an upper-middle-class homemaker - her daughter, that is, me, and prestige charity projects.

"He was in the Army," Denver says, his voice now noticeably more subdued than before. Gone is the affectionate way he spoke about his sisters. "When I was five and started school, I went to Madison for pre-kindergarten and first grade.

43

Then Phoenix started school too, and my parents decided they wanted to make their permanent home in Chicago, which meant my dad was just going to be away from us until he got a permanent station in the Chicago area."

"And he has one now?" I ask.

His expression changes completely and I get the feeling he's turning pale. I say nothing more, just stare impassively at the street in front of me. I don't like the fact that Denver's emotional state is changing like this.

"My father died five years ago, or fell, as they say among soldiers." Denver's eyes are blank, but he glances over at me anyway. "In Iraq."

"Denver, I..." I don't have the words to express what I really want to say. I am so sorry for his loss. To be half-orphaned so young is terrible. Especially since he has two younger siblings.

"It's okay!" He tries to look composed and hide his true feelings from me, but he can't. "It's part of life. My mother has had a new partner for three years and is happy with him."

"Do you like him?"

"Yes."

I realize we're not getting anywhere with the conversation. If Denver wanted to talk about his stepfather, he would. But since he doesn't, I don't really know what to talk about. I feel it would be tactless to tell him about my parents. It feels wrong, but changing the subject completely might make him feel like I don't value his story. I don't know what to do and just hope he picks up the conversation again.

"What about your parents?" he asks me after a few moments, thankfully. "What do they do? What are their names?"

"My parents are former politicians," I tell him. "My mom was on the city council and my dad was mayor. Now he's in education. Mom takes care of the family. I don't think I need to say any more about that. My mom's name is Esther and my dad's name is William. And what's your mom's name? What does she do? What was your dad's name?"

For a moment, I'm unsure if I should ask Denver about his father so directly, but he's a part of his life. I don't want him to think I don't care about him.

"My mom's name is Lori, and she's a nurse, but she didn't work for a long time when we kids were little. My dad's name is Frank." He says.

"So, politicians...you must be the model daughter then, right?"

Grinning, Denver looks over at me and I laugh. I should be, yes, but I'm not. After all my mother's attempts to force girly hobbies on me failed, she realized that I'm different.

"Once I failed at ballet and thought horseback riding was stupid ... well ... that's when they gave up on me being the model daughter."

"Riding?" he asks, wiggling his eyebrows.

"On a horse, Denver," I answer. "Not on a ... " I deliberately don't finish the sentence and am glad I can't see myself in the mirror. My cheeks must be burning with shame. How does he manage to get me into these situations?

"Man?" he asks. "Too bad."

"Idiot," I grumble, but still have to grin and am glad that our conversation has lightened up again. Even if I had to put my foot in it to get there. It was clear that Denver wanted to steer the conversation towards sex. "Do you have any other hobbies besides football?"

"I like sports in general," he said. "Going out with friends or spending my free time in front of the TV sometimes. When the season starts next week, I'll be on the road a lot. You'll like having the place to yourself." He grins and looks at me. "What are you studying and why haven't we talked about it yet?"

"Economics, and you? Why we haven't talked about it, I don't know. There seemed to be more interesting topics."

Denver laughs and nods in agreement. We both know what topics I'm talking about.

"Sports science," Denver replies, and I have to laugh. It suits him. "Phoenix is also studying economics."

"I know." I look at him with a smile. "She told me in our two-minute conversation at the door."

"The next time we go out, you should come with us," he suggests. "Then you'll have a chance to really get to know Phoenix and my other friends. You already met Jake."

"You're going out again tonight?" He can't be serious. He's been partying the last few days, if I can believe his stories.

"No." He grins. "I have to be at the first official practice for the new season tomorrow morning. I can't be drunk or tired then. I'll probably spend the evening on the couch."

"Oh, of course!" How silly of me not to have thought of that. Embarrassed, I look out the window so he won't notice how uncomfortable I am. "I'll be in my room."

"Why?"

"So you can have some peace."

"Did I say I wanted peace?"

"No, but..."

"Then why do you think I do?" he replies, glancing sideways at me for a moment. "You're welcome to sit with me. I don't mind. We live together now, Sienna. My place is your place, and if something bothers me, I'll tell you. So - will you watch TV with me?"

"We'll see," I answer evasively, not sure if he really wants me to or if he's just being polite.

46

Denver parks his car in front of the dorm and we get out together. I look up at the aging 1970s facade and set my jaw. It's clearly seen better days.

"Nice, huh?" asks Denver as we walk up the steps to the front door.

"Totally," I agree, following him. He holds the door open for me so I can walk past him and into the building. Smiling and burying his hands in his jeans pockets, he follows me.

"Do you know where you need to go?" asks Denver, and I pull the note out of my pocket and read it.

"It doesn't say where the administrator sits."

"Okay," he says, looking around the first floor. "Usually, the administrators are assigned by the first letters of our last names. Your name is Gardner, right?"

"Okay," I say, following him to the large information board next to the stairs. "And yes, my name is Gardner."

I'm glad that Denver is with me and knows how everything works. Without him I would be hopelessly lost. Too many corridors and rooms. The idea to arrange them alphabetically would have occurred to me at some point, but this way it saves me a lot of stress and, above all, time. We stop in front of a big sign and Denver points to the name under "M" for "Gardner". "Here. Mrs. Lawson. She's in room fifteen."

"Perfect!" I look at him, pleased. "Let's see what she says."

I'm about to walk off when Denver grabs my arm and stops me. I immediately stop at his touch and turn to face him. We've never really touched before and a strange electric shock runs through my body. I look at him wide-eyed and he looks back at me for a moment.

"Do you really want to draw her attention to this?" asks Denver in a calm voice and I raise my eyebrows.

Of course I do. I could get into trouble if I don't report the mistake. I don't think they'll be very sympathetic to the fact that I took a fellow student's room, not to mention the fact that I misled the dorm administration by not reporting it.

"It's not the right apartment, and I don't want to end up being charged with fraud and kicked out of college."

He raises his eyebrows and looks at me like I'm blowing things out of proportion. Maybe I am because the key and the address match. Besides, they told me Denver would be my roommate. So, the blame is on them, but in the end I guess they have the upper hand. "Nobody's going to sue you for fraud, but..."

"I don't care if they kick me out for cheating or because they don't like my face. The reason doesn't matter. What matters is that if it happens because I wasn't honest, I won't have a place to live. Now come on!"

Denver sighs and follows me down the hall to room fifteen. It doesn't take us long to find the right door. Stopping in front of it, I take another deep breath and knock. "Yeah, what is it?" an unfriendly voice says from inside and I look at him. He shrugs and I turn the doorknob and slowly step inside.

"Good afternoon," I say pleasantly, putting on my best smile. "My name is Sienna Gardner and..."

"Do you have an appointment?" Before I can speak, she cuts me off. I shake my head.

"No, but I..."

"Make an appointment and-"

"I have a question and-"

"Everyone who knocks on this door has a question and, in the end, want to discuss their rental with me. Make an appointment."

Completely taken aback by the woman's rudeness, I shrink back and close the door. There is no point in arguing with her. I would end up on the losing side, and if she sees the mistake, she might really kick me out. She might even accuse me of trying to cover something up. I really don't need that.

"I'm supposed to have an appointment," I tell Denver dejectedly. It could be days or weeks before the matter is resolved. The more time that passes, the worse my chances are that they'll believe I was being honest in the first place. Denver raises his eyebrows and sighs. He is acting like I am stupid for even trying to talk to the administrator.

"Let me try," he says, pushing me aside to get to the door. Panicked, I look at him as he reaches for the doorknob.

"What are you doing?"

"I'm going to sort it out for you." He looks at me with determination and a straight face.

"But she said I have to make an appointment." I look back and forth between Denver and the still closed door. This could cost me my college career if he approaches her now. I can't even think about it. How would I explain it to my parents? I wouldn't put it past my mother to be happy if I went home. Annoyed, I shake off the thought of my mother and focus on Denver again.

"You do." He grins cockily. "I don't need one."

What's that supposed to mean? Denver is a college student just like me. Sure, he's a senior, but the same rules apply to everyone. Before I can stop him, he knocks on the door and Mrs. Lawson invites him in just as rudely as she did me.

"Good afternoon," he says, so overly friendly that I can hear him smile. "Denver Jones, my girlfriend has a request."

I gasp when he calls me his girlfriend. Because if there's one thing I'm not, it's his girlfriend. Well, it would be nice if I were. Especially after meeting his conquest this morning. And now that I think about it, he was right and I should never have come here.

"Denver," I hiss. "Let's go."

"Oh, Mr. Jones," the stupid floozy says in her brightest voice, and I widen my eyes. I must have misheard. "Why don't you come in, and, of course, I have time for your girlfriend."

Excuse me? Surely she's not going to let me skip making an appointment to kiss Denver's feet.

"Come in," he says, holding the door open for me. I give him another uncertain look, and then walk past him into my administrator's office. Mrs. Lawson's eyes widen when she sees me. She is obviously surprised that I am Denver's girlfriend. Then she seems to think about how to avoid falling out of Denver's favor. Thanks to him, she is now doing damage control.

"Oh, Ms. Gardner," she says pleasantly. "I didn't know you and Mr. Jones were dating."

Neither did I.

"Yes ... uh ... we are ... dating," I mutter, for lack of anything better to say, and look at Denver. He just grins and points to the chairs in front of her desk, so I walk over and we sit down. Mrs. Lawson sits at her desk as well.

"How can I help you?" she asks, but only looks at Denver.

"Sienna was assigned to the wrong room and we'd like to clear that up with you."

"The wrong room?" she asks, looking at me in confusion. "Do you have the paperwork?"

"Of course." I pull the paper out of my pocket, still stunned that she's being so nice to me. If it weren't for Denver, she'd have left me in the hallway, but she's kissing his ass. I hand her the papers and she looks at them with a furrowed brow. Cautiously, I look at Denver because I'm nervous now. If there's really something wrong with the room assignment, I'll have to move out. I don't have an alternative. I don't think

Mrs. Lawson will do anything to help me. Unless she's doing it for Denver's sake.

"What exactly happened?" she asks, looking at me. "The address is right, and the key must have been right, too, right?"

"Well ... Denver was assigned to me as-"

"Look, the photos from the e-mail-" Denver cuts me off and I gasp. It's nice of him to get me this far, but I can handle my own business. "And the photos on her phone are different. We don't want the person who got the photos of our apartment to complain."

He hands her the iPhone, and she compares the photos.

"Just a minute," she says, turning to her computer.

"What are you doing?" I hiss at Denver. "We need to tell her the truth."

"And then what?" he asks quietly. "Will she kick you out? Let me handle this." I look at him for a moment, but don't answer. I don't want to get thrown out of the room, so it's probably better that he talks to the woman. She likes him.

"We actually made a mistake here," she says, looking at us with wide eyes. I tense up and look at Denver, who remains calm. "You got the room because we registered Mr. Jones as Ms. Jones. I don't know how that happened. I can't figure out the photo thing either."

"And what does that mean?" I ask worriedly. "Do I have to move out?"

"Do you want to move out?" she asks, looking at me expectantly. "It's not customary to give rooms to the opposite sex." She smiles kindly at us. "I can give you a room in another house and..."

"No!" Denver and I exclaim in unison, making us both laugh. "I want to keep the room," I repeat my request. "If that's okay, and no one else will be negatively affected because of me."

"As it stands, no one else is registered for the room or has complained to us," she says, glancing briefly at the screen. "You can keep the room."

Relieved, I look at her and then at Denver, who smiles at me. I pretend that I didn't want to live with him at all, but the truth is that I don't want to leave him. I like him far too much already and I think we'll end up having a good time living together.

"Thank you very much," Denver says exuberantly and stands up. I do the same. "You've really helped us out."

"You're welcome," she purrs, and I want to point out that she wouldn't have even heard me out, had it not been for Denver. But I refrain from commenting and leave the room behind Denver. But I don't say goodbye. There's no need to be any friendlier than necessary.

"Unbelievable," I mutter as he closes the door. "If it wasn't for you, she wouldn't have even heard me out."

"Being a football player has its advantages," he says with a grin. "And you're definitely not going to hear from her again. She won't mess with me."

"It's reassuring how powerful you are." The irony is hard to miss. But knowing Denver, he takes my statement seriously. Damn - and in a way he is. Within seconds, he gets an appointment with the administrator that would take others days.

Denver laughs and puts his arm around my shoulders to pull me close. With my body pressed against his, I can feel his hard muscles through my sweater. He's quite a bit taller than me, so my head barely rests on his chest. Again I feel that strange electric shock that I felt when our hands touched.

"If you only knew." He grins. "Are you hungry?"

"A little," I answer honestly, rubbing my stomach to emphasize my words.

"Well, let's get something to eat."

5

-DENVER-

Two weeks later

I walk out of my room and find Sienna in the kitchen. She is standing at the stove with ground beef and tomato sauce sizzling in the pan and pasta cooking in the pot next to her. She is a real homemaker. For the past week, I have been enjoying her exceptional cooking. She usually cooks for us every other day, so we can eat for two days. She looks at me with a smile and I look back at her. The first day I noticed that Sienna was hot, but now it seems like she's trying to torture me. She's wearing short shorts that barely cover her butt and a tight top that shows off her body. She's not 90-60-90, and I'd go so far as to say she'd still look amazing with a pound or two less. But she has curves in all the right places. I am beginning to wonder if it was a good idea to let her continue to live here. I could have easily had the administrator make her leave. But what did I do? I passed Sienna off as my girlfriend, used my college status to help her out, and now I realize that I think she's way too hot to keep my hands off her for the next year and a half.

I liked Sienna from the first moment I saw her standing in the apartment with no idea where to go or what to do. It was actually kind of cute the way she stood there embarrassed because I wasn't wearing anything more than a towel around my waist. I couldn't help but notice that her cheeks were flushed, or that she didn't like to talk about life's vices. Sex, alcohol and drugs - okay, drugs are out of my league - but sex and alcohol are definitely not her scene. Which is a shame, especially when it comes to sex.

In the last two weeks, we have hardly seen each other. Sienna's classes have started and she attends them diligently. Every night she sits in the kitchen and goes over her schedule for the next day, making sure she gets to each class on time, while still getting a cup of coffee first. I found out that she prefers her coffee with a little bit of milk. It's something she takes very seriously, commenting on the amount of milk she takes when she doesn't make it herself. A loud "Stop!" when too much is poured is not uncommon. By God, after fifteen years of friendship, I still have no idea how Jake drinks his coffee, let alone my sisters or my mom.

When Sienna comes home in the afternoon, she cooks something, we eat it together, and then she goes straight to her room. I think her dedication to her studies is remarkable. I will never be like that and only do what I have to do in my studies between training and games. I get good grades and I've never neglected my classes and seminars for football, but I don't bust my hump like I would for football.

I don't want to work as a sports scientist anyway. I just need to study something.

My goal is clear: the NFL. And that goal is even more of a focus this coming semester than it has been in the past. Unfortunately, we lost to Ohio last Saturday and are in last place in our division. Of course you can say that it was just one game and we still have a chance, but that's not what I want.

I want to win all the time - everything.

"What are you cooking?" I ask, setting my iPhone down on the kitchen counter. Sienna turns to me and grins. "Are you hungry again?"

"Maybe," I reply with a grin, crossing my arms over my chest. "Do you want to come over to Darren's tonight?"

"What's going on there?" Sienna takes two plates from the cupboard and sets them on the table. Then she gets silverware and two glasses to go with them. I stay where I am, waiting as if ordered, and let her do it. It's not that I don't want to help, but last time she grumbled at me for messing things up for her. So, this time I let her do it and dutifully sit down at the table.

We'll just hang out, have a drink, and chill."

She nods and puts two coasters on the table for the hot pot and pan. "Can you drain the noodles, please?"

"Sure," I say and stand up. Smiling, I stand next to her, grab the colander she's already taken out of the cupboard, and set it in the sink to drain the pasta. Sienna watches me with a smile. "What's wrong?" I ask, as the corners of her mouth turning up until she can no longer hold back a laugh. Although I can tell she doesn't want to laugh.

"Maybe you're turning into a homebody after all."

"Let me remind you, you didn't want any help last time."

"Okay, okay." Laughing, she raises her hands. "You win."

I grin at her and put the strained pasta, still in the colander, back in the pot and on the table. We sit down together and Sienna puts some on my plate. "Thank you." I accept it and wait for her to help herself to some as well. "Enjoy."

"You too." I look at her again as I dip my fork into the noodles. It smells delicious. The tomato sauce is just the right consistency and the pasta is al dente. "You seem a little off the last few days. Is everything okay?"

I've noticed that she's been quite introverted and not as

cheerful as the first few days. Of course, I could be wrong and it's just the stress of studying. In the first semester, you take everything so much more seriously.

"My friend Clara says that I hardly keep in touch with her anymore. Surprised that I noticed, she puts down her fork and looks back at me. Sienna buries her teeth into her lower lip. "It's true, but I'm not doing it on purpose. Everything is still new to me and I'm trying to fit in. She, on the other hand, is still at home and has some of our old friends around her."

"And now she's accusing you of not caring about her anymore?"

"Something like that," she replies with a sigh. "I don't understand why she blames me. I'm the one who has to start over, not her."

"Maybe she regrets not making the move," I speculate. "And now she's jealous that things are going so well for you."

"I don't think so." Sienna looks at me thoughtfully and fills her fork with pasta again. She looks at me steadily as she chews. "She'll calm down. Do you have plans for today?"

"Yes," I answer, leaving the subject alone for now. "Tonight, like I said, we're all meeting at Darren's place. Do you want to come?"

"I don't know," Sienna mumbles and I try not to roll my eyes. For the past two weeks, she's always found an excuse not to meet my friends. I think it's a shame. I'm sure she'd like to meet them, and my sister has been asking about her, too. Unfortunately, Phoenix hasn't seen her since the day she moved in and they meet at the front door. "Don't you think it's strange?"

She raises her eyebrows and I do the same. What's strange about me wanting to introduce Sienna to my friends? It can only be good for her to build a network of people at college as soon as possible. They don't have to be her best friends. But for a nice evening out, it's all right, right? I don't think she's made so many new friends that there's no room for any more.

"Why should I find it strange? I'm inviting you. You're not forcing yourself on me and you're not expecting me to take you with me." I shrug.

"Hmm," Sienna does. "I still don't know. I have a class tomorrow and-"

"Are you just looking for another excuse not to go?" I look at her indignantly, raising my eyebrows. Sienna bites her lower lip, which looks incredibly cute and hot at the same time. The way she slowly sucks it in with her teeth and then lets it go is so damn hot. I reach for my water and take a big gulp to stop staring at her mouth.

"I'm not looking for an excuse," she replies, sticking the fork in her mouth. She chews and swallows the bite. "It's just that I want to focus on my studies and not go out partying in the middle of the week."

"We have practice in the morning," I take the wind out of her sails. "We're not getting drunk. It's a nice evening with friends."

"If you say so." Sienna picks at her food. I can tell she's running out of excuses. Grinning, I lean forward and seek her gaze. It takes a moment for her to raise her head and look directly at me with her blue eyes.

"What else do you have to say in your defense?" I lean back and cross my arms over my chest. Sienna's eyes flick over my biceps and I grin.

"When are we leaving?" she asks, the corners of her mouth slowly turning up. "I don't want to hear any more. You win."

I laugh quietly and lick my lip. "At seven!"

I park my pickup in front of Darren's apartment building and turn off the engine. Sienna is sitting next to me. I almost want to say that she is looking forward to this evening. Sienna is wearing a pair of tight jeans that accentuate her cute butt. She is also wearing a skin-tight dark red long-sleeved shirt with ruffles on the collar, the hem and the ends of the sleeves. Over it a denim jacket. Her long blonde hair falls in soft waves over her shoulders. Looking at her, I'm not sure it was a good idea to invite her over and introduce her to my buddies. Those idiots will pounce on her like a horde of ravenous hyenas. Fresh meat. I take a deep breath to push these thoughts away and tuck my keys and wallet into my jeans. Especially Darren wouldn't hesitate to get her in the sack.

"Shall we?" I ask, looking over at her.

"Sure," she says with a grin. "You know Denver..." Sienna pushes open the door and continues to grin at me. "Thanks for letting me come along. I'm sure it'll be good for me to meet some new people. Maybe you have some hot buddies."

She gets out of my car and my jaw drops. I quickly jump out as well, slamming the driver's door behind me to follow her. She can't be serious, can she? Of course, I know my buddies are popular with the opposite sex. Jake with his brown eyes and hair and a much more muscular body than mine. But he needs those muscles to take down the defensive players on the other teams. Darren is a Southern boy with more tattoos on his body than I can count. I know every part of his bare body. That's the downside of communal showers and large locker rooms. Like Jake, he has dark, almost black hair and eyes. Many people even think that Darren has Mexican roots.

This appeals to the girls. And both are not averse to flirting with a conquest for the night. It makes me sick to think that this could be Sienna. Luckily, she doesn't seem too interested in dating anyone yet.

"What do you mean, I might have hot friends?" I ask again, just to be sure.

She giggles and I tense up even more. Giggling is never good, I know that from my sisters. Phoenix also giggles when she likes a guy and then it ends in a fiasco. Madison is thankfully too young to cause me that kind of grief.

"I'm in college now," she says, "nobody knows me here, and my friend Clara thinks I should have a good time."

"The one who's mad at you?" I ask with a furrowed brow. "Interesting. And you want to follow her advice?"

I don't know why I don't like the fact that Sienna isn't averse to noncommittal dates. At nineteen, she's a grown woman and can do whatever she wants. Still, I have to admit that it would bother me if she made a pass at one of my buddies. Just like it bothers me with Phoenix, who is a no-go zone for all my buddies. They stick to that too.

"Come on," Sienna says in a good mood, wiggling her eyebrows to draw me in. "Didn't you ask me during our first conversation if I was having sex?"

Of course I did, but it was a joke, a fucking joke. Besides, I had only known her for a few minutes at the time. Stupid jokes come easily to me. Today, two weeks and many conversations later, I see it very differently. Sienna and my buddies - that's a red flag for me. It only leads to trouble that none of us need.

Arriving at the front door, I ring the bell and the buzzer sounds, allowing us to enter the house.

"Ladies first!" Gentlemanly, I let Sienna go first. She walks past me, the perfume she's wearing tonight wafting around my nose. In the car, I thought it was Hailey's sweater in the backseat that she left behind after one of our meetings. But it smelled way too intense for a piece of clothing that has been sitting there for over a week. Now I know why. It's Sienna's perfume. I close my eyes for a second to collect myself. It's just damn perfume, no reason to freak out. Then I follow her up the stairs and enjoy the view of her ass.

Darren lives with Ethan and Julien. Ethan studies psychology and spends most of his time in the library and Julien studies business English. He also plays football.

"Who does Darren live with?" asks Sienna, as if she can read my mind, looking at me curiously.

"Ethan and Julien," I answer. "Ethan spends ninety percent of his time in his books, studying psychology, and Julien-" I look up the stairs, "is standing in the doorway."

She grins at me and turns to Julien.

"Hey Denver," he greets me and we high-five. "And you're not alone."

It doesn't take a second and his whole focus is on Sienna. Almost greedily, his eyes glide over her beautiful body, lingering a little too long on her breasts for my taste.

"Hey!" I clear my throat louder than necessary to draw his attention away from Sienna. "This is Sienna - my roommate."

Even though I try to sound neutral, I have little hope that Julien doesn't notice how much his looks bother me. He's known me too long not to know how I react when I'm interested in a girl.

"Your roommate?" he asks, the corners of his mouth turning up. Confident that something can still work out with Sienna, he goes on. "With her own bed?"

I almost choke on my own spit and give him a sour look. That was a totally unnecessary comment, although I have to admit that I usually don't mind when my buddies make jokes like that. The girls we take to parties or these evenings are just there to warm our beds the next night. So his reaction is perfectly normal. He can't smell the fact that Sienna is really my roommate, even though our relationship has been purely platonic. Jake met Sienna on the first night and asked me about her. Darren was there when we talked about her.

"Yeah, with her own big bed," Sienna answers before I can answer, grinning at Julien. "Nice to meet you."

"I ... Nice to meet you too," he stutters, looking at her wide-eyed. "Come ... come in."

Sienna walks past him into the apartment. Julien looks from her to me, waving his hand as if he'd burned his fingers. I fix him with my gaze and refrain from commenting. She's not Phoenix and I'd only make a fool of myself if I told him to keep his hands off her.

I follow Sienna into the living room where Darren, Jake, Gary, Phoenix, Joy and Gary's girlfriend Hannah are already sitting. The boys' apartment is similar in size to ours, but with an extra room and a guest bathroom, which I find very convenient. Darren, Ethan and Julien rarely use the small kitchen. They usually eat in the dining room or grab something on the way. While Julien's and Ethan's rooms are to the right and left of the bathroom, Darren's is a little off to the side next to the guest bathroom. In typical bachelor fashion, most of the furniture is thrown together and the decor on the walls is not cute houseplants and family photos, but empty special edition whiskey bottles - nicely lined up on a small shelf - and football jerseys of our idols.

"Hey guys," I greet the boys with a handshake and my sister, Joy and Hannah with a kiss on the cheek. "This is Sienna."

"We already know," my sister informs us. She will also have told Joy that I have a new female roommate instead of a male roommate. She's her best friend, after all. "She introduced herself."

I look over at Sienna and she shrugs her shoulders. I can't help but notice how she keeps surprising me. At home, she acts like a demure and dedicated college student, and now she's introducing herself to my friends, striking up conversations with them, and acting like they've known each other forever. Jake hands me a Coke because I am driving, and I sit down next to him on the couch.

Sienna sits down across from me next to Phoenix and starts talking to her and Joy.

My sister and Joy have been friends for the past year. Joy studies psychology, but she doesn't spend half as much time in the library as Ethan does. She's twenty and a real looker with her Asian roots and the blue-dyed tips of her waist-length black hair, but not my type. Her style is very feminine and short. Really short. Most of her skirts don't even reach halfway up her thighs, which makes her legs look endless. She always dresses sexy and knows what she has and how to show it off. But she never looks cheap, like some of the other girls on campus trying to get our attention. Today, Joy is also wearing a short black dress with spaghetti straps, black silk tights and Doc Martens on her feet. Her eye-catching makeup with perfect black eyeliner completes her look. Next to her, Phoenix and Sienna, both with long blonde hair and light makeup, look almost boring.

"We thought you were going to hide her from us forever," Darren says, nudging my shoulder. "Hey Sienna, why didn't he let you out before?"

I roll my eyes and Sienna looks up. She meets Darren's gaze and her mouth twists into an amused grin.

"I didn't feel like it," she says with a shrug and looks at me. "Denver kept asking me to come."

"I would have kept you locked up at home," Darren says with an obvious flirtatious undertone. I roll my eyes in annoyance. "There are so many dangers out here."

"Dangers?" She laughs heartily and takes a sip of her beer. "Like your bad pickup lines?"

A roar echoes through the living room and the girls toast Sienna. Darren next to me suddenly falls silent and seems to need to collect himself. I guess he didn't expect Sienna to blow him off. I'm also surprised that she can dish it out so well. But most of all I am surprised that she can resist our Casanova. Darren's flirting and hookups are legendary. At least for a defender.

"My lines aren't bad!" He exclaims like a little kid, which makes us laugh even harder. "I mean, you live with the king of bad lines."

"Hey!" I punch him on the upper arm. "What's that supposed to mean?"

"Oh, come on... I lost my number, can I have yours? Seriously, Denver?"

Admittedly, the line is bad, more than bad, but I had to say something.

"I only said it once," I immediately justify and roll my eyes. I wanted to get the girl in the sack as soon as possible, I couldn't think of anything better. And she jumped right in. "And it worked, as you know."

"I'm surprised," Sienna said, wrinkling her temple in mock astonishment. "Considering how obnoxiously forward you are."

The boys spit out their beers, and Phoenix nearly drops her cup. The Coke spills onto the fluffy beige carpet under the coffee table. Joy makes an indefinable squeak, the way only a girl can. All eyes are on Sienna, and I know exactly what they're thinking. I have to stop myself from snorting out loud.

Sienna looks back and forth between us before turning bright red.

"Oh my God," she shrieks, her face contorting. "It's not

like that! I ... I mean, we... we didn't... well, we... we didn't have sex. I have my own bed! Denver, say something!"

She looks at me in panic, and now I can't help but laugh, too. I'm sorry, but I allow myself these few seconds of pleasure now that she's put me in this situation.

"Sure." Jake wiggles his eyebrows meaningfully. "Like you two don't..."

"Say something," Sienna cries, looking at me urgently. "Please!"

"Talk is silver, silence is..." Jake rambles on, and now I feel sorry for her.

"Jake," I growl. "We didn't have sex."

Sienna's complexion slowly returns to normal. She smiles at me gratefully.

"We didn't have sex," she confirms my statement. "But I did have to show his one-night stand the door."

"Seriously?" asks Joy, rolling her eyes. "You didn't offer her coffee?"

"Of course not," I reply, annoyed. "Nobody does that."

I look around and hope that at least Darren and Julien are on my side. Jake is still loyal and offers us coffee.

"Denver, that was Hailey Sanders," Hannah says now. "She's very nice."

"Nice she was," I reply, thinking about how she blew me without hesitation. Sienna looks at me and raises her eyebrows. I'm not scoring any points with her right now by making light of what was an embarrassing situation for her back then. I avoid her gaze and clear my throat. "I, like everyone before me, didn't force her to do anything."

While the boys nod in agreement, the girls roll their eyes. I'm getting tired of this conversation. I didn't bring Sienna to embarrass myself in front of my friends, even if the guys think my behavior is normal. They're no different, all of them.

"Anyway," Julien says suddenly, turning his attention back to Sienna. "Tell us about yourself. Where are you from, why are you studying at Lincoln, and why the hell are you living with Denver?"

I'm grateful to him for changing the subject and indirectly saving me. But I also look at him warily to see if he wants something more from Sienna. She laughs and brushes her hair back. Then she looks at me and smiles.

"I'm from Ellsworth, a small town near Helena in Montana, and Lincoln is a long way from my parents. I really liked the course offered and now to the part you're really interested in -" Sienna glances around the room, amused. "Why I live with Denver."

"There's only one answer to that," I interject. "I'm..."

"Now please don't tell me you're a great guy," she interrupts me with a mischievous twinkle in her eye. "You intimidated that poor dorm lady so much, there was no way I could move out."

I roll my eyes, but when I see Sienna's grin, I know I did the right thing.

6

-SIENNA-

Today I'm meeting with Phoenix at our house. She's a semester ahead of me, but she has to repeat a class from the first
semester. She failed the final exam. While I sort through my
transcripts and printed slides, Phoenix keeps looking at her
cell phone.

"Phoenix," I address her in a firm voice, and she flinches.
"Shall we get started?"

"Do we have to?" She gives me a serious questioning look
and I raise my eyebrows. "Let me put it another way - can we
stall?"

"Why would we stall?" I sigh. "The sooner we start, the
sooner we'll be done."

Phoenix groans and throws herself back against the cush-
ions. She looks at me like a petulant child. I can't help but
laugh and lean back as well. Then I look at her again. She
looks at me with blue eyes as though she's already finished the
course. But this semester has only just begun. Something is on
her mind. We've only known each other for two weeks, maybe
less, but I can tell that something is bothering her.

"You don't really want to study, do you?" I just ask out loud, trying to get an answer out of her.

"Is it that obvious?" she wants to know, biting her lower lip. I nod curtly and she sighs. "I didn't want to go to college after high school, I wanted to travel and find myself. I wasn't ready, and unlike Denver, I don't have sports to save me. But my mom and John, her boyfriend, thought I was wasting my time."

Looking at her thoughtfully, I recognize my parents' point of view. They wouldn't have understood if I wanted to work and travel for a year. In their eyes, it would be a waste of time.

"So, you picked a course and enrolled?"

"Yes," she says matter-of-factly with a groan. "The other classes were easier for me, and Jake has been helping me study, so I'm getting pretty good grades, but this-" She points at my papers. "It's pure torture."

I'm tempted to ask if Jake is really just helping her study. After all, he's Denver's best friend, and he wouldn't be happy if he was tutoring his little sister in other areas, too. But I don't think Phoenix is in the mood for that. Besides, it's none of my business.

"Oh man, Phoenix," I sigh. "Have you talked to Denver about this?"

"Oh, for God's sake," she exclaims, and I can tell this is not an option for her. "He feels the same way, and now I've wasted all this money from my college fund. I don't have a scholarship like Denver's to buy me time."

I look at her with compassion and think about what would be the best advice to give her. Talking to her mother and John again doesn't make much sense. They both seem set in their opinions. They probably just want what's best for her and Denver, which is why they insist that Phoenix go to college. Not having her big brother on her side either must make her feel very lost.

"What about changing majors?" I suggest after a few moments of silence. "Of course, you'll lose time that way too, but if you keep failing, you'll get kicked out."

"I know that," she replies, sinking deeper into the pillows. Phoenix lowers her eyelids and plays with the hem of her sweater. "What do you think I should do?"

"Figure it out." I sigh and look at Phoenix. "If you're unhappy, you have to tell your mom. There's no point in studying something you don't like."

"Of course not." Her voice is bitchy and she takes a deep breath to calm herself. Then she continues in a much softer voice. "But I don't know what I want to study instead of business. Maybe I'll get knocked up by a potential NFL buddy of Denver's and be set for life."

Stunned, I look at her, searching for the humor in her statement, but unfortunately, I can't find it. She's deadly serious.

"Phoenix!" My voice cracks several times. "No way!"

She rolls her eyes and leans toward our papers. "I was joking!" She tries to make light of the statement, but I'm not buying it. As down in the dumps as she was a few minutes ago, I can just imagine her actually letting a football player impregnate her.

"Although I should really think about it."

I knew it! She's serious!

"You definitely shouldn't," I reply, rolling my eyes. Then I turn to face her. "We'll study together, prepare, and you'll pass the exam."

Phoenix still doesn't look convinced, but I don't give up. She has to stick it out this semester so she can convince her mother to let her change majors. After all, she gave business studies a shot.

But before we can get started, the doorbell rings.

"Did Denver forget his key again?" asks Phoenix with a

laugh and gets up to open the door for her brother. I haven't made that many friends at college yet, so most of the people I deal with are Denver's friends or haven't asked for my address.

"Hello?" Judging by her questioning voice, it's not Denver, one of his friends, or the mailman.

"Hello!" I jump as my mother's voice rings out. This can't be happening. How could I forget that my parents were bringing the rest of my stuff in the van? This is such a mess! Especially since I haven't told them yet that Denver is a guy and not, as they assume, a girl.

"You must be Denver, Sienna's roommate."

I run to them as fast as I can and manage to cut Phoenix off at the last second before she blabs to my parents. "Mom, Dad," I exclaim, hugging them in turn. "What are you doing here?"

"We're bringing the rest of your stuff," my mom replies irritably, pushing past Phoenix and me to get into the house. I give my friend a warning look.

"Hi honey," my dad greets me with a smile. "And you must be Denver."

Phoenix points to herself and I give her a meaningful look that I can only hope she understands. There's no way my parents can find out I'm living with a hot football player. Who also regularly has sex with his conquests in the next room. The day before yesterday I had to kick another one of them out the door. I can't think of anything better to do early in the morning.

"Yes!" Phoenix sounds a little too exuberant for my taste. I can't let her mess this up. "I'm Denver. Denver... Sienna's roommate, Denver!"

"They get that your name is Denver," I hiss at her and push her behind me.

She gives my dad an exaggerated smile and I do the same.

70

I have no idea how I'm going to get out of this mess. If my parents find out that Phoenix isn't Denver and the real Denver shows up here, I'm going to be in big trouble. "Would you like something to drink, Mr. and Mrs. Gardner?" asks Phoenix with a smile and points to the kitchen. "How nice of you to visit."

Phoenix leads the way, my parents follow, and I bite my lip, wondering how I'm going to get out of this mess. It would probably be best to tell the truth and do it before Denver shows up and I have to drag him into my lie as well. It's bad enough that Phoenix has to pretend to be her brother because of me.

"Sienna!" I wince. "Where are you?"

"Coming, Mom," I call, following them into the kitchen.

Once there, I look at my parents with a smile and spread my arms to welcome them. Instead, I try to do some damage control. "I'm sorry I'm so surprised by your visit, but I've been pretty busy the last two weeks."

Phoenix raises her eyebrows, and I shrug - as if there's nothing wrong with lying to my parents about everything.

"How long are you staying?" asks Phoenix and hands them a coffee. I look at my parents, tense. Hopefully not longer than the next two hours, because that's the maximum time Denver will be at practice. The last few days he's had problems with his adductors and had to leave practice early. I don't have to mention that this frustrates him and he has been in a really bad mood since. So, it is possible that he will be in the kitchen at any moment and I have no idea what to do.

Let's not speak of the devil. He's not here yet.

"We got a hotel room in Chicago. So, a few days to see the city and Lake Michigan."

"So you're not staying here?" Phoenix points her index finger at the kitchen floor as if to mark the spot.

71

"There's no room here," my mother says, and I nod immediately.

"Of course there's no room," I retort, "There's..."

"Sienna?" I jump and Phoenix's sugar falls out of her hand and onto the floor from shock. Luckily, it distracts my parents enough that they immediately want to help her. This in turn gives me time to leave the kitchen and rush into the hallway. I have to catch Denver before he sees my parents. And more importantly, before they see him! I'm turning red and my heart is pounding in my chest. I hate lying to my parents and dragging the people I call my friends in Lincoln into this, but I have no choice.

Oh man, I'm in so much trouble. Denver will never approve of my white lie and go along with the charade. Why should he? I should have just told my parents the truth. What are they going to do other than cut off my money, stop paying the rent and-.

Fuck!

There is no way I can tell them that Denver is my roommate and the person they think is Denver is his little sister Phoenix.

"Hi!" He's standing in the living room, completely relaxed, smiling at me. "Is that Phoe's bag?" He points to his sister's bag and I nod.

"Yeah, she's in the kitchen and I..."

"Sienna!" My mom flings open the kitchen door and looks at us in surprise. Her eyes dart from Denver to me and back again. Over and over again. "I didn't know you were expecting company." With her best two-hundred-watt smile, the one that won her many an election back home, she walks toward us, and Denver's eyes go wide.

"Visitors?" He looks at me, then back at my mother. "I'm not-"

I ram my elbow into his stomach, making him shut up, but not so conspicuously that my mother sees it. Then I smile angelically and walk over to her. "This is just... Phoenix-."

I could slap myself for not thinking of a better name for him. Phoenix? Seriously?

"Denver's brother!" I explain quickly, so that Denver doesn't ask any stupid questions.

"I'm sorry, what?" he blurts out. "Denver's brother?"

I overestimated him! He didn't get it.

My mother looks at him skeptically, then at me. If she doesn't want everything to fall apart now, she's going to have to swallow this story. My God, am I glad their parents gave them gender-neutral names. If Phoenix had been named Claire and Denver Michael, my white lie would have looked very different, and the name mess would have been even bigger!

"What did you want, Mom?" I distract her with a smile. I ignore the fact that my heart is pounding in my throat. "Is everything okay with the sugar?"

"There's nothing wrong with the sugar." My question irritates her, I can tell. She doesn't really believe that everything is okay. But she doesn't seem skeptical enough to keep pestering me with questions. "Your dad wasn't sure how we were going to help him with the big shelf, but that doesn't seem to be a problem now." Her eyes are still on Denver, and if I didn't know better, I'd say she was checking him out. He looks delicious again, though, in that tight t-shirt and his short sweatpants. "I'm Esther - Sienna's mom."

"Phoenix," he mumbles, and I can tell how weird that makes him feel. "Nice to meet you. May I borrow your daughter for a moment?" Denver points at me. "Our washing machine is broken and Sienna and Phoe- Denver offered to wash my workout clothes here. Then I'll be happy to help your husband."

"No problem," she almost whispers, spinning around again

to go into the kitchen to tell my dad and Phoenix the good news. Keeping up the charade, Denver grabs his gym bag and drags me behind him into the bathroom.

Oh God, oh God, oh God. I really haven't thought this thing through. But the last two weeks have been so exciting and wonderful that I completely forgot about my parents' visit. Denver has made me feel welcome after the initial difficulties and we have become a good team. Although the stereotypical roles are true that I do a lot of the housework and he brings home the bacon - after all, he pays our cleaning lady - we still get along well. I have made friends with Phoenix and Joy. It's all happened so fast and been so exciting that I haven't given my parents or my white lie a second thought. Now it seems to be coming back to haunt me.

Denver pulls me into the bathroom. He literally pushes me in before following me and slamming the door behind him.

"Can you explain this?" he hisses, pointing at the now-closed bathroom door. "I thought they knew we lived together."

"They do, but-" I blurt out. "But they don't know your gender."

Denver impressively crosses his arms over his chest and raises his eyebrows. "Are you kidding me, Sienna?" he snarls.

"They know my roommate's name is Denver Jones."

"So what?"

"I didn't tell them you were a guy," I meow, feeling Denver corner me. Surely, he must understand that I couldn't tell my parents the truth. At least not for a little while. "I ... I couldn't tell them. They pay my rent, and they weren't thrilled that I took the room that was two hundred dollars more expensive anyway. The only thing that made them lenient was the fact that I have a nice roommate."

"Phoenix isn't your roommate," he snarls and starts pacing. "What are you going to do when they want to see my room?"

"It'll work itself out somehow," I dodge his question and he rolls his eyes. "What was I supposed to do? They're going to be pissed and they might take me back to Montana."

Just the thought of it makes my breakfast slowly creep up. I don't want to go back to Ellsworth where all the neighbors will be talking about how I couldn't make it in Illinois. A few years ago, our neighbors' daughter came back from New York because her boyfriend cheated on her. All summer long, the talk of the town was that people like us couldn't make it in the big city and she should have stayed. Lincoln is not a big city, and no one cheated on me, but the gossip wouldn't be any less.

"You'd deserve it," Denver growls. "Sienna... I ... I can't pretend I don't live here. My stuff is all over the place ... my clothes are in the bathroom. I hardly think Phoe uses *Hugo Boss for Men*."

The more Denver talks, the more stupid I feel. Of course the apartment is full of his stuff. We have to come up with a good reason why.

"Then we'll say it belongs to Phoe's boyfriend."

"And who would that boyfriend be?" Denver raises his eyebrows, crosses his arms over his chest, and straightens himself in front of me.

My head literally rattles.

"Jake!" I bite my lip. I couldn't have come up with a more stupid example.

"Jake?" asks Denver, confused. "How did you come up with Jake?"

"Darren or Julien then." Hastily, I try to think of more examples so as not to cause problems for Phoenix and Jake. Annoyed with myself, I throw my hands up in the air. "It doesn't matter, okay?"

"No, it doesn't," he says, pacing again. "Jake and Phoenix?"

I'm getting more and more flustered, struggling to find the

right words to get him off the subject. Phoenix will kill me if I tell her brother what I don't really know myself. She has never talked about Jake before. I just assume there's more going on between them.

"That was just an example," I sigh. "Can we please get back to the real issue?"

"Which is?" He focuses his gaze on me. "How you manage to do more damage in fifteen minutes than an entire army does in a year?"

"Very funny," I reply pointedly, pressing my lips together. "Denver, please! Focus!"

"Sienna, this is getting out of hand. I can't lie to your parents about everything and-"

"Of course you can," I cut him off indignantly. We've been in the bathroom way too long. My mother will be looking for us soon. "Please Denver. Just until they leave, and when they come back tomorrow or the day after, you'll be at practice and..."

"What about Phoenix?" he asks, raising his eyebrows. "What are you going to do if they want to have dinner with you and the supposed Denver?"

Honestly, whether my parents want to have dinner with Phoenix - aka Denver - and me is the least of my problems. As long as they don't see his room and realize that I've been lying to them, then everything's fine, right?

I meet his gaze, though I almost dare not. Denver is very angry with me and I can totally understand. I should have told him that my parents didn't know he was my roommate. Even more, I should have told them on the first day when they called me to see if everything was okay. Maybe even the second day after Denver helped me with the administrator. I should have acted after a week at the latest. But I didn't, and now I'm in a huge pickle. Besides, I should never have put him and Phoenix in the position I did by switching their identities.

"I'm sorry," I half-mumble, looking at him with my lower lip pushed forward. "So, so sorry."

"Do you have anything to offer in your defense besides that ridiculous puppy-dog look?" Denver wants to know, raising his eyebrows. "Or is that it?"

"For starters, that's it." I try for a grin. "Please, please don't blow my cover."

He sighs and points to the door. "All right. I'll put in a load of laundry to make it look real, and then I'll make sure they don't know I'm changing in my room."

Relieved, I jump up and throw my arms around his neck. "Thank you, thank you, thank you."

Denver seems surprised and staggers back a step at my little assault. But he quickly catches himself and wraps his arms around me. As he does so, he presses me against his muscular body and his tangy aftershave rises to my nose. Wow. Not only does this guy look outrageously handsome, he smells it too.

"Thanks, Denver," I whisper against his chest, hugging him a little too tightly. "I owe you one."

We stay in this position longer than necessary and finally it's him who pulls away and clears his throat. With heated cheeks, I let him go and smile at him one last time in thanks before disappearing into the kitchen to join my parents and Phoenix.

Just as I open the bathroom door, he pulls his shirt over his head and reveals his six-pack.

This sight alone is worth every lie!

"Go on," he says with a grin. "Otherwise, your mom will get the wrong idea about us."

He's right. My mom would go crazy if she caught me in the bathroom with a half-naked Denver. Granted, she knows I've already had a boyfriend and that I had sex with him. In fact, she had to take me to the gynecologist to get the pill. But I had been with him for almost a year before I asked her to take me to the gynecologist. I left out the fact that we were already having sex at that point. I am her only child and she is always very concerned about me and my reputation. Seeing me in an intimate embrace with Denver, the quarterback of the football team would set off all her alarm bells. In her opinion, I should only exchange such affection with my boyfriend. My mother is very conservative in that regard.

Without answering Denver, I turn on my heel and mentally prepare myself for my parents' questions.

7

-DENVER-

After throwing my workout clothes in the washing machine and turning it on to keep up appearances, I go to my room. Going is an exaggeration. I sneak into my room because it officially belongs to my little sister. I can't believe I'm getting involved in this nonsense. I'm Phoenix Jones?! The fact that I have to go through this really sucks. I'm pretty much anything but my little sister.

Well, better Phoenix than Madison. She's obnoxious at fifteen. I shake my head at the thought of my other sister.

I change into a hoodie with the Lincoln Tigers logo, jeans, socks and sneakers. Then I take one last look at myself in my floor-to-ceiling mirror before I leave my room.

"Oh Denver," I hear Sienna's mom say. "We are so happy that Sienna has found such a great roommate."

"Hello Mr. Gardner," I greet her father warmly. "I'm Phoenix."

I can tell by my sister's devilish grin that she is enjoying this little game and has no problem playing along. Sometimes I think there is a great actress lost in Phoenix. But Phoenix in

Hollywood, I don't even want to imagine that. I'd rather have her do something practical. Not that I couldn't finance her failed existence as an NFL player, but better safe than sorry.

"Hello," Sienna's father replies, shaking my hand. "William Gardner. Nice to meet you. My wife said you'd help me with Sienna's furniture?"

"Of course," I say, looking over at her. "As a guest, I'm happy to do it, right?"

Sienna's eyes narrow to slits, and I could swear she'd like to punch me in the face right now. But she has to take these jabs now.

I'm fucking pretending to be my sister and my sister is pretending to be me.

God, it's confusing.

This is all Sienna's fault. I hope none of my boys ever find out about this. They'd tease me until the end of my college days for putting up with all this for Sienna. After all, I've only known her a few weeks. If they had their way, I would have banged her by now anyway.

I shake my head. These thoughts are completely out of place right now.

"Then we can carry the boxes," Sienna says. "We'll be done in no time and I'm sure you're so tired you'll want to go straight to your hotel in Chicago."

Her desperation is so palpable that I can't help but grin. Maybe I should play this game and get back at her that way. Because apparently nothing is more upsetting to Sienna right now than a long stay at our house by her parents.

"You almost sound like you want to get rid of your parents," I say indignantly, raising my eyebrows. "That's not nice."

Sienna presses her lips together and clenches her hands. Of course she wants to get rid of her parents because she's afraid she'll spill the beans.

"That's not true," she retorts, crossing her arms. "I would never want to get rid of you. I just thought you..."

It's on the tip of my tongue to tell her to stop thinking, but I think that would be going too far.

"The sooner we get started, the sooner we'll be done and the sooner we can figure out what to do with the rest of our time."

Sienna gives me another dirty look while Phoenix grins at me.

"It's really good that you're here, Phoenix," Sienna's mother says. "We were thinking about asking a neighbor to help with the heavy furniture."

"Yeah, it's always good to have a man around the house." I wink at Sienna. "Where are you parked, Mr. Gardner?"

"In the house, yes," Sienna replies devilishly. "In the apartment, no."

I'm about to raise my eyebrows, but I let it go. My impression now matches her stories from the first days. Her parents don't seem to know what makes their daughter tick, but that's not necessarily a bad thing. My mom doesn't know everything I do either. She doesn't need to, because then she'd worry. It's enough that my sisters worry her regularly with their behavior.

Madison is completely out of control right now and dresses in gothic style. God, she even dyed her blonde hair black. I almost fainted the last time I saw her. And Phoenix can't get her butt in gear at college. Mom tells herself it's just a phase with Madison. After all, she's about to turn sixteen. When Phoenix was sixteen, she got a belly button piercing and her skirts couldn't be short enough and her necklines low enough. That wasn't any better. When I was Madison's age, our dad died and I immersed myself in football so I wouldn't have to deal with his death. Which, to this day, I've only done sporadically. Although I hate to admit it. We started family therapy at that time, which helped my sisters and mom more than it helped me.

I couldn't participate in the conversations with the psychologist. I was sixteen when my dad died. Seventeen when I started therapy. My father was everything to me - he was my hero. It was incomprehensible to me that a strange woman would want to know how I felt and tell me how my mother, my sisters and I should deal with our loss. So, I boycotted therapy and stopped going. Mom, Phoenix and Madison finished it on their own. Also, I think the loss of our dad hurt me more than my sisters. I was older than them and a boy. This may sound silly to some. But because my dad was in the Army and we had our permanent family home in Chicago, my time with him was always very limited. He was deployed most of the year. So, I was all the happier when he finally came home. We played sports together, he taught me how to drive, and he watched me play football whenever he could. His deployment before he died would have been his last. After that, he would have been stationed in Chicago and with us permanently.

I push thoughts of my father aside and focus on the here and now.

"Shall we get started, then?" Sienna breaks through my thoughts visibly annoyed and I nod absently.

"I've made a list - of everything we have in the car and in what order we should bring it into the house so that Sienna, Denver and I can put it away immediately. This strategy will help us avoid chaos," Sienna's mom explains.

My gaze flies to my sister, who declares Sienna's mother crazy with just one look, and then to Sienna herself, who is visibly embarrassed by her mother's behavior. Her cheeks turn a bright red as I meet her gaze. On the other hand, it's convenient that her mother has everything planned. Less work for us.

"And all we have to do is carry?" I ask, pointing between her father and me, who nods curtly. "Great!"

"Let's go downstairs and get the furniture and set up." I follow her father out of the kitchen and downstairs, out of the apartment.

"And you spend a lot of time with Sienna, too?" he asks. I look at him and think about what I'm going to say. For a moment I'm afraid he's smelled a rat in our white lie, but Mr. Gardner seems completely at ease.

"Yes," I say calmly. "She lives with my sister and that's where we run into each other."

"What do you study, Phoenix?"

"Sports, sir!"

"Sports," he replies, giving me an approving look. His gaze slides down my body and finally lands on my face. "Do you play football?" He points at my hoodie. I nod. "Position?"

"Quarterback."

"Quarterback," he mutters, and together we leave the apartment building and walk to the white van. "Do you have NFL aspirations?"

"Yes," I answer, beaming at him. "I want to join the draft in a year and a half."

"The NFL is tough, kid," he says, and I nod. I know the NFL is tough, and college is child's play by comparison. If I'm not a first-round pick, I'll probably start out on the bench. Even then, nothing is set in stone. A lot of good teams upgrade behind their starting quarterback to think about the future.

"I know that," I reply, and he opens the trunk of the van. "Do you like football?"

"Yes." His face lights up and he smiles at me. He is genuinely interested in my sport, and that pleases me immensely. "My son Lawrence played in high school."

I remember Sienna telling me that he was from a previous

relationship of her father's. She has little contact with him and can count on one hand the number of times she's seen him in her life.

"And after that he didn't want to go on?" I ask with interest. I know a few guys who quit after high school. Places on college teams are fiercely contested, and scholarships aren't easy to come by. Many don't have enough talent or just don't want to play sports professionally. For them, it was great while they were in high school, but after that, they have other plans.

"His mother, my ex-wife, didn't think it was worth it." Sienna's father looks sad. His expression becomes more closed, and I can see how hard it must have been for him to bow to his ex-wife's wishes. "He had to do something practical."

"That's a shame," I say, helping him lift the outer panels of Sienna's shelves out of the van. "My parents have always been supportive, and my mom and sisters come to my games whenever they can."

"It's nice that they support you. I would have loved to do the same with Lawrence," he says with a sigh. "Unfortunately, Esther and I were not blessed with any more children. And Sienna will hardly know a football from an oversized egg."

I laugh out loud and can barely contain myself. Sienna made it clear early on that she wasn't interested in football. She didn't seem to know the rules either when we watched a replay of one of my games from last season a few days ago or when I tried to analyze my running routes. I couldn't because she kept interrupting me. She didn't know how many possessions I have before a play ends, or why a field goal is worth three points, but the extra point after a touchdown is only worth one, even though both are made by the kicker. I tried to explain it all to her, but in the end all she understood was that there are two teams and the sport is brutal. I'd love to tell her dad that, but I'm afraid I'll blow Sienna's cover.

We have a home game this weekend and it would be nice for her to come to the stadium with Phoenix. I haven't asked her yet because I'm sure she'll find some excuse. It's pretty stressful.

"Sienna's here to study, not watch football," I answer instead, and Mr. Gardner nods.

"Of course she is," he says, looking off into the distance for a moment. "It was hard for us to let her move - especially for my wife - but Sienna has to make her own way. Make new friends and experience things for herself."

"So you don't want to take her back to Montana?"

"Me?" he laughs. "My wife would, for sure, but not me. I have a hobby room now since Sienna's room in the basement is unoccupied."

Her dad is becoming more likable by the second and doesn't seem as boring and strict as Sienna described him. But we always see our parents in a different light than everyone else. He makes a very open and friendly impression on me. Smiling, I think about how well he would have gotten along with my dad. Maybe he would get along with Mom's boyfriend, John, too, although something in me keeps preventing me from accepting him with her. It's still impossible for me to imagine any man other than my dad being there. I make this all too clear to John. Our conversations over the past three years have been kept to a minimum. I would have preferred it if Mom had stayed alone longer after Dad's death. We've argued about it many times, and my sisters have made it clear that it's not up to me. Deep down, I know she's happy with him. They've been together for three years, living in their house and building a life together. My mom will never forget my dad. Even if only because she has three children with him. Besides, my mom was in her early forties when she was widowed. I don't want her to be alone for the next thirty or forty years just because I can't imagine another man by her side.

"I would have expected a different answer," I say honestly.

"Because I think my daughter should grow up and live her own life?" he asks, shaking his head. "Of course I don't want Sienna to get involved with the wrong people and get into trouble. But she's nineteen years old and happy here."

"Yes, she is," I say with a smile. In fact, Sienna hasn't seemed unhappy once in the last few weeks. Yes, she said that her studies were stressful and that she needed to settle in, but she never sounded unhappy. Her eyes always lit up when she talked about her studies, which often made me want to ask if we were having the same conversation. "Are we going to take the pieces upstairs and put the shelf together?"

"That's what my wife's plan says." He laughs and turns to me. "So, is there a team you want to join, Phoenix?"

I ponder his question for a moment. My wish would be to be drafted by the Chicago Eagles. That way I can stay in my hometown and be close to my sisters and my mom. But the NFL is not a wishing well, and the Eagles don't have any problems at quarterback right now. Instead, I worry about having to go to Florida or New York.

"I have no illusions about going to Chicago," I reply with a shrug. "Even if I wanted to. Then I'd still be close to my family."

He nods in understanding and we enter the hallway and carry the things upstairs. There we are met by Sienna, her mother and Phoenix.

"This way," Mrs. Gardner tells us and I glance at Sienna. I'm not sure if she's comfortable with her mother's tone. After all, she is dictating how her room should be decorated.

"I want the shelf in this corner," she says, and I look at Sienna again. I don't know what to expect from her. Maybe a confirmation that this is okay with her. But she remains silent. Almost indifferent, as if she's done arguing with her mother's decorating wishes. "Maybe we'll move the desk and the bed."

I look at Sienna again, but again she doesn't answer. Lost, she stands in the middle of the room, giving her mother free rein. The Sienna standing here and the Sienna I've gotten to know over the past few weeks just don't match. She's not a shy little mouse who puts up with everything. My God, she regularly throws my one-night stands out the door, gives me a piece of her mind, and even beats Darren to the punch. I don't like seeing her like this at all.

"Anyone else want a drink?" Sienna asks, disappearing from her room before we can say anything in return.

"Oh, Denver!" I lift my head to answer Sienna's mom when I remember that I'm Phoenix now. "What do you say we hang some more of the curtains we brought?"

I look at Phoenix, who is standing a little awkwardly next to Sienna's mother and clear my throat. "I'll be quick..." I mumble. "I need the little boys' rooms."

I leave Sienna's room and look around the living room.

"Sienna?" I call softly. "Where are you?"

Turning around, I see that the door to my room is ajar. Sighing, I go to it and knock. "Hey," I whisper and step inside. "Are you okay?"

She is sitting on my bed, completely unnerved, throwing her hands in the air.

"I don't know," she sighs, "Yeah, I forgot they were coming, but I..." She stops in mid-sentence.

I walk over and sit down next to her. Sienna gives me a quick look and then goes back to staring at her feet.

"Is your mom always so-" I think about how to put this into words. I don't think 'exhausting' is the right word. "Motivated?"

"Yes," she says, rolling her eyes. "And she won't be satisfied until the room looks the way she likes it. Because she thinks I will like it too."

"So tell her you don't like it," I suggest. "And that she can't move everything around."

"You aren't serious?" Sienna looks at me like I'm out of my mind. Unlike her dad, her mom seems pretty annoying. I really hope they go away soon. I don't like this Sienna at all. She looks intimidated and helpless. More and more I can understand why she wanted to put as many miles and flight hours between her and her mom as possible. Perhaps she would have preferred to go to Florida. Mrs. Gardner couldn't get there in her van, at least not as fast as she could to Illinois.

"Of course I'm serious, and if you hadn't lied to her, I'd kick her out."

"No way," she cries, her eyes wide. "You can't kick her out. She's my mother!"

"I can't anyway, because Phoenix lives here." I wink at her and stand up. Inspired, I clap my hands together and then reach down to her. "Come on," I say quietly. "Let's get this over with."

"Thanks Denver," she grins, "you shouldn't have to do this.

"I don't want to lose my cook and housekeeper," I retort indignantly, and she gives me such a venomous look that I almost laugh. "Come on, you know I don't see you like that."

"I hope not," Sienna grumbles and starts to walk past me when I stop her and pull her back. She stumbles into my arms. Her body bounces against mine and I enjoy the feel of her soft breasts pressing against my torso. In general, I enjoy her touch far too much.

"Sienna," I sigh. "I've had plenty of chances to get rid of you. I got through the last few years of college without you."

She has to stifle a grin and narrows her eyes to slits.

"I don't know, Mr. Jones," she chuckles, "maybe you only have one thing on your mind."

This is the moment when the common sense in my brain

shuts down. I don't have only one thing on my mind with Sienna, but I wouldn't push her off the edge of the bed either. It would be easy to bend my head toward her and kiss her. To press my mouth to hers and taste her flavor for the first time. I risk a fleeting glance at my bed as I'm slapped across the chest. I guess that was a little too obvious.

"Denver Jones!" Sienna puts her hands on her hips. "You're a lecher."

"So?" I ask with a grin. "Weren't you the one who liked to have sex?"

Sienna wants to get indignant and throw something at me, but I ignore her and quickly make my escape.

8

-SIENNA-

I'm relieved that my parents left a few days later and didn't find out that Phoenix isn't Denver. My mom insisted on taking us out to dinner, but we gallantly talked our way out of it. I really hope they don't come back to Lincoln in the next few months. Otherwise, I'll either have to tell them the truth or continue to resort to this little white lie.

It's not easy for me to lie to my parents, but if they cut off my rent money, not only will I be out on the street, but I'll have to quit my studies because it's hard to study for exams while living under a bridge.

I walk into the college lecture hall and look for a familiar face. I have business management every two weeks. It's easy and interesting for me. Even though the demands are very high and the length of the texts unbelievable.

At a table in the front row, I recognize Millie. I've taken other classes with her, but never sat next to her. She doesn't strike me as someone who reaches out to others on her own. She is very shy.

"Hi," I say when I arrive at her desk. "May I sit here?"

91

Surprised, she looks up at me and adjusts her glasses. Admittedly, the word "temptress" doesn't jump out at you when you see her. Her simple pink blouse and jeans are complemented by her glasses and her severe braid. There is no make-up on her face. But she doesn't need it. She has bright brown eyes, rosy cheeks, and absolutely perfect skin. Other girls would kill for that kind of naturalness or spend thousands of dollars on beauty treatments.

"Of course," she greets me in surprise, putting her backpack on the floor. "Have a seat."

"Thanks," I say and sit down. I unpack my MacBook, notepad, pen and iPhone.

While her outward appearance is unassuming and her demeanor shy to others, she has the latest electronic gadgets in front of her. Her MacBook is the latest model, and her iPhone is the latest model with three cameras. "Millie, right?" I ask and she nods.

Her glasses slip down and I chuckle. "Sorry," she says, "they won't stay put." Millie pushes her glasses back up and grins at me again. "Yeah, I'm Millie and you're Sienna?"

"That's right. We have some classes together."

Millie's expression brightens at my statement. She seems happy that I've noticed her, too.

"Are you from Chicago?" Surprised at how talkative she is, I shake my head.

"I'm from Ellsworth, a small town near Helena, Montana," I explain. "And you?"

"I'm from Minneapolis."

"Oh," I mean, raising my eyebrows. "Cold."

Millie laughs and nods.

I open my MacBook and log on. I haven't found the right solution for my notes yet. Writing everything down by hand is too much work for me, but I learn better with handwritten notes to help me memorize the material. Digital texts, on the other hand, are quicker to revise and share with my classmates. The cloud would be another option for storing the data.

"So?" Millie says suddenly, and I look over at her. It's still disconcerting to me that a few minutes ago she was like a shy deer and now she's chatting away. "Have you met a lot of new people?"

"A few," I answer, looking around the room. "Mostly through my roommate and you?"

"So-so," she mumbles, playing with her pen. She seems nervous and uncomfortable with her answer. But she doesn't have to be. I know all too well how hard it is to make new friends. In fact, she's the first person I've actually struck up a conversation with who isn't friends with Denver. "I'm not very good at meeting new people." She smiles at me and shrugs shyly.

"You met me," I reply, smiling openly at her.

"Yes, that's right," she says, "Where are you staying? I got one of the last rooms in one of the dorms on campus."

I can't help but laugh, thinking that she could have gotten the room I wanted so badly - but then it wasn't available, which is why I'm living with Denver now. I still like it much better and I'm really grateful for the mistake.

"I live in one of the apartment complexes on Abbey Street," I explain. "The administration mistakenly listed my male roommate as a female roommate. In the end, all the rooms in the dorms were taken, and I couldn't move."

"You ... you live with a guy?" Millie looks like she's been kicked by a horse.

"Yeah," I say, shrugging. "There was no other available room, like I said."

"Oh, I see," she says, "is he nice?"

"Sure," I reply, trying to be casual. "Denver's all right. We get along great."

"Denver?" she gasps, "You don't mean Denver Jones, do you?" Millie laughs hysterically. Is she serious? After all, Denver isn't a god.

"What does everyone think is so special about him?" I ask, blowing a strand of hair from my forehead. "He doesn't wash his hands after touching his balls just like any other guy."

I shake my head in amusement while Millie's turns bright red. She seems to have either no sense of humor or no experience with men. I suspect the latter.

"Do you have any hobbies?" she gallantly changes the subject. "I was thinking about joining the college newspaper."

"Joining the college newspaper isn't a hobby, is it?"

"It isn't?" She gives me a confused look and I shake my head.

"Oh," she replies, playing nervously with her pen. "Maybe we can have lunch sometime."

"That's not a hobby either, but I think it's a good idea," I reply, winking at her as our lecturer enters the room. I look at Millie again and give her a warm smile.

When we leave the room an hour and a half later, I feel completely exhausted. It feels like a huge bucket of information has been poured into me which I can't even process. How in God's name am I supposed to keep up with all this without completely losing my personal life?

"Wasn't that interesting?" babbles Millie next to me. "Although there's a lot to cover before next week."

"A lot of material?" I say indignantly. "Surely she doesn't think I'm going to read fifty pages on corporate law and apply and compare it to Amazon and Apple. In my head!" Completely horrified, I look at Millie, but she doesn't flinch in the face of my tirade.

"We can do it together. You read one text, I'll read the other, we'll tell each other the information, and then we'll write something together."

"I don't even want to read one of the texts," I whine, and she laughs.

"You're going to have to, Sienna. The more you do now, the less you'll have to study later."

"I think that's a myth," I reply, sighing. "Let's get something to eat first."

We enter the cafeteria together, each taking a tray to get in line. As we do so, I let my eyes wander around the large room. Here, college is no different than high school. There are the jocks, the cheerleaders, the nerds, the musicians, and those who don't feel like they belong to any of these ultra-groups. And then there's me, who never hung out with the jocks and tended to avoid them in high school. Now I live with the quarterback. Denver sits in his usual spot and looks in my direction. I raise my hand and wave. He waves back, and the girl who has the honor of being glued to his ass today puckers her mouth when she sees him greet me. This regularly drives me crazy. He just wants to shag her. Why does he always have to put on such a show in broad daylight? We're not in high school anymore.

"Did he wave at you?" asks Millie, wide-eyed as she grabs a plate from the waiter. I do the same.

"Yeah," I reply curtly. "He's only human."

"Hmm. Do you know his buddies well, too?"

"Define *well?*" I echo, and Millie blushes on cue. "I mean ... yeah, I know Darren, Julien and Jake."

"Ah, okay." I can't tell if she's disinterested or doesn't know how to answer. "I like football. We have an NFL team in Minneapolis, the Minnesota Warriors."

"You like football?" I look at her wide-eyed and hand my money to the cashier. I would have guessed that everyone here liked football, but Millie - never. At first glance, she doesn't seem like a woman who would be into such a brutal sport. In fact, I could imagine her keeping her eyes closed for the several hours a game lasts.

"Yeah," she says with a smile. "I even know a rule or two ... it's fun to watch."

"Wow," I groan. "I never expected that from you."

"Most people I tell say that," she laughs, pushing up her glasses. "Do you like football?"

"Not really, but if you do, go to the stadium for me," I joke. "Denver really wants me to go this weekend." I sigh.

"The game is sold out," she replies in amazement. "I couldn't get a ticket."

"Why don't you come with me," I suggest. "Phoenix, Denver's sister, will be there. It'll be fun."

"I don't know," she mutters uncertainly. But I can tell by her expression that she really wants to come. "He doesn't even know me and ... and I want a ticket from him."

"Then we'll change that." I grin and cut her off. I grab her free hand and pull her behind me. Denver will be happy to meet her. After all, she's my first college girlfriend. Maybe I'm going a little overboard with the girlfriend designation, but what's not can still be. "Come on."

Millie, however, does not move a step, causing me to stop as well. I look at her questioningly.

"Millie?" I address her, raising my eyebrows. "Are you coming?"

"You... you want to sit with them?"

"Yes," I say as a matter of course. "I told you, Denver is my roommate."

"Yes, but ... but he's also - I shouldn't sit there."

"He breathes the same air as you, he shits in the same ... well, he shits in the same toilet at home as I do, and a hundred times more stupid things come out of his mouth than out of yours," I groan. "You'll be a match for him and the others. They're nice." I smile at her encouragingly.

Millie looks at me again and then at the boys. "All right," she whispers, and a smile creeps across her face. "Let's have lunch with them."

"Perfect." I grin loftily and make my way to the table.

Jake sees me first and gestures for the girl in the chair next to him to get up. She looks at him in total indignation and throws back her hydrogen blonde curls. In a way, I can understand her indignation. It's nothing like the one that's still stuck to Denver. Next to Jake sits Darren. Denver and the girl next to him are in the chairs across from him. Julien and Dan have each taken a seat at the end of the table.

"Hey," I say, smiling across the table. I like Denver's friends and am happy to see them at lunch. Surprisingly, I get along better with them than I thought I would. "Can we join you guys?"

"Sure." Jake grins and immediately goes into flirt mode. I roll my eyes and gesture for Millie to put down her tray. She does as she's told and plops down in the chair that Jake has vacated so that she's now sitting between him and Darren.

"Come over here, Sienna." Denver pulls a chair over from the next table and slides it between him and his conquest. I raise my eyebrows because I can't believe I'm supposed to sit there. Denver, however, makes no move to change anything. He knows I prefer to avoid his flirts and one-night stands. Most of them know by now that I'm his roommate, and they let me feel their envy. Of course, they never say anything to me directly, but I pick up on the gossip behind my back and the rumors about Denver and me. To some people, it seems completely incomprehensible that there is nothing going on between us. Even in high school, it bothered me to be the center of attention when false truths were told.

"Before I forget." I straighten my chair and turn to my new friend. "This is Millie. Millie, this is Denver, Jake, Darren, Julien, and Dan." I don't know the girls' names.

"Hey guys!" In a good mood, Phoenix comes over to us, accompanied by Joy. "Everything okay?" Blessed with a confidence that makes me envious, Phoenix pulls up a chair for herself and Joy at our table and sits down. Phoenix wears her blonde hair in a high ponytail. To my surprise, she's wearing a football team hoodie that's at least two sizes too big for her. I wonder if it's Jake's. I have to grin. A pair of gray jeans and black sneakers complete her outfit. Phoenix is, as so often, without makeup. Joy, on the other hand, has applied her eyeliner and sexy eye makeup. Meanwhile, the tips of her hair are turquoise. A white t-shirt, simple skinny jeans and white sneakers complete her style today. I'm very happy to see both of them.

"Hey," I say. "Phoenix, Joy - this is Millie."

"Hi," they say in unison, and Millie shyly replies. For her, this situation must be like stepping into another world. To be honest, it would be for me, too, if I weren't Denver's roommate and didn't already know this gang. Phoenix and Joy immediately jump into the conversation at the table.

"Sienna, are you coming?" Joy asks me and I look at her questioningly.

"Where?"

"To the party tonight," Joy answers, blowing a lock of her hair from her forehead. "It'll be fun."

"She won't have time," Denver chimes in before I can answer. "I'm sure she has to go back to studying."

I look at him indignantly. Apparently, I'm the only person

at the table, Millie excluded, who takes her studies seriously. Although, after today's Business Management seminar, I don't see it that way either. The lecturer is really out of her mind if she thinks I'm reading everything.

"Oh, I'm sorry I don't have it all shoved up my ass already, Mr. Quarterback," I counter.

"No false envy," he retorts, grinning mischievously at me. "And the cleaning lady we have doesn't pay for herself either."

"Uh," Darren laughs, "this round goes to Denver."

"Shut up," I grumble at him. "And you shut up, too." I point my fork at Jake, who immediately raises his arms.

"Do you like football, Millie?" he asks her instead, and she immediately blushes, probably not expecting to be the focus of attention. She looks like she'd rather vanish into thin air than answer him.

"A little," she says, picking at her food. "I happen to be familiar with it."

"I'm afraid she didn't get a ticket for Saturday's game," I interject. "I offered her mine."

Denver gives me a quizzical look and I shrug.

"I told you I can't take it," Millie says, shaking her head. "I'm not going, it's okay."

Only an idiot couldn't see how much she wants to go.

"Oh nonsense," Darren interjects now, smiling at her. Millie looks back at him and her cheeks turn another shade darker. "We'll get you another ticket."

"No," Millie says, waving him off. "That... that's really not necessary."

"It's no big deal. We each have a number of tickets. I have a few left."

"See," I say with a grin, pointing at Millie. "Now you have a ticket."

She's still not comfortable with the whole thing, but neither I nor the boys are deterred from our plan. "Thanks," she whispers, smiling shyly at Darren. He nods unconcernedly and turns his attention back to the conversation at the table.

"Can we talk about the party again?" asks Joy, looking at me. "Are you coming or not?"

"I-"

"She's coming," Denver decides, and my head whips around so I can look at him. He seems completely pleased with himself and his answer. Even though he knows full well that I don't want to go and that I have an important class in the morning. "And it's not open for discussion."

The boys laugh and Phoenix and Joy can't hold it in either.

"What?" Denver and I ask, looking at them.

"Oh man," Jake says, rolling his eyes in amusement. "You should have seen the way Brittany and Tiffany took off when Denver only had eyes for you."

At least now I know their names. I try to ignore the rest of Jake's statement, but I can't. Everyone is looking at me - at us.

Heat shoots into my cheeks as the attention makes me feel uncomfortable. Denver keeps looking at me, grinning, and puts his arm around me. "That was my plan," he says smugly. "Sienna's the perfect alibi for annoying chicks."

I roll my eyes and slap his arm away.

"Get your hands off me," I hiss, but he's unfazed and just pulls me closer. "Denver, damn it!"

9

▫SIENNA▫

One month later

I've been studying in Lincoln for over a month now and have found great friends in Millie, Joy and Phoenix and the best roommate in the world in Denver. We get along very well and have a lot of fun together. My fear that I would have to run the household alone and that he would stand by and do nothing has fortunately not been the case. On the contrary, he always offers me his help and is a pretty decent guy. Of course, we sometimes have arguments and issues where we completely disagree. Denver has a terrible habit of drinking his leftover morning coffee in the afternoon. Cold and with stale milk. I've told him a hundred times that stale milk can build up bacteria. On the other hand, he thinks it's terrible that I go over my schedule for the next day out loud every day, even though I've been doing it for weeks.

Since Denver has officially accepted me into his clique, I have become good friends not only with the girls, but also with his buddies. I especially get along well with Jake, which Denver doesn't always approve of. Sometimes I even think he's jealous of him. Jake also studies economics, and when he is with us, the discussion soon turns to - for him - past courses. Denver can't join in and usually clears his throat loudly to remind Jake that he's visiting him and not me.

It doesn't make sense to me that he's jealous if he really is. Of course.Jake is an attractive guy, but he is not my type at all. Besides, it wouldn't contribute to the peace in our apartment if I started something with Jake. The same goes for Darren, Julien or Dan. Denver always gives me the impression that he doesn't want to see me with his friends. He interrupts our conversations more often than necessary, doesn't let us have any fun with each other beyond a platonic friendship, and usually prevents me from sitting between them. Even when one of them approaches and grins at me, his body tenses. This is especially noticeable when we go to a gathering together.

Denver continues to indulge his terrible habit of wearing as little clothing as possible at home. Especially when it comes to his upper body. The play of his muscles is great when he moves. They twitch slightly and I can easily imagine how they would feel if I ran my fingers along them. How he would tense them and his body would tremble when I trace the furrows of his six-pack with my tongue. Goosebumps would cover his body. Yes, I think Denver is incredibly hot and I think about him too often and too much.

God, what am I thinking? Denver is my roommate and a good friend. For more than a month, I've been struggling with thoughts like these, and they don't help me feel relaxed about living with him. Especially since I know he's no slouch. The number of girls he drags into our apartment is so alarmingly high that I'm not sure he hasn't already fathered children or is carrying STDs. Almost every weekend, and sometimes during the week, he has a new one come over. I never remember their names. I also don't bother to walk them to the door and explain in passing that I'm just his roommate. The longer I live here, the fewer one-night stands think I'm his girlfriend. Word has gotten around that the quarterback lives with a blonde. My understanding is that his girlfriend would never sit quietly at the coffee table and watch his one-night stand walk out the door.

Disgusted by the whole thing, I purse my lips. I have to stop thinking about Denver Jones and start thinking about him as a purely platonic friend. But that's anything but easy - especially since he sometimes looks at me as if he's not averse to there being more between us. There are those looks, we don't have to kid ourselves. I'd be pretty stupid if I didn't notice that he keeps looking at my butt.

"Sienna!" Phoenix snaps in my face and I jump. "Where are you with your thoughts?"

Phoenix, Joy and I have a dinner date at a diner near campus. It's a typical American diner with silver tables and bright red benches. The counter is white and the bar stools are placed at regular intervals in front of it, covered with bright red leather to match the benches. The walls are dominated by merchandise from the Chicago Eagles, Chicago's resident NFL club, and the Lincoln Tigers. Denver's jersey made it to the wall, which makes me proud. I'm glad he's so successful in his sport and that he's going to achieve his dream.

"With your brother," Joy squeals, biting into a French fry. "Right?"

Embarrassed, I reach for my Coke and don't answer. Nothing has happened between Denver and me.

We're just friends.

Besides, he has such a full sex life that he doesn't need me for that.

I open my mouth to say something back when Millie comes over to our table.

Perfect Roommate

"Hey guys!" Out of breath, she sits down next to me. "Sorry I'm late."

"Did you have to check the slides against your transcripts first?" Joy teases her, making Phoenix and I laugh. Millie is definitely the nerdiest of us and the smartest. And she doesn't have to do all this annoying cramming. Even if she only studies half as much as I do, she gets a better grade. She's a natural at economics.

"Not funny," she grumbles, tucking one of her brown strands behind her ear. "What were you guys talking about?"

I'm glad she's become much more open in the last few weeks. Of course, she's still shy about some things, but that's fading with time. Sometimes she even says words like "pussy" or "fucking". Considering that she thought Denver was a demigod when we first talked, that's a step up. Her advantage over me is that she's an ace football fan. Millie knows every position, every play, and sometimes can even predict Denver's play call. At one point, she hesitantly admitted that she loves football.

"About Sienna dreaming about Denver," Joy says with a grin, and I roll my eyes.

"I don't dream about Denver," I clarify. "I'm..."

"I get it," Joy says, throwing up her hands. "You don't think he's hot at all, and he leaves you cold."

My friends know that's not true. But I don't want to talk about it now. Especially not when his little sister is sitting at the table, staring at me. Phoenix has never openly said that it bothers her when her friends are interested in Denver. But I can tell that she stiffens when the subject of Denver and me comes up. Unfortunately, it's come up way too much lately. Joy mostly goes down the "I think he's hot and I want to go to bed with him" route. Millie, on the other hand, takes a much softer approach. She says it's obvious that I like Denver and that I daydream whenever we talk about him. While she would never put it as crudely as Joy, the message is the same: I like Denver!

It's still hard for me to really get emotionally involved with this idea. I like him, yes, and I really enjoy spending time with him. When I come home from my classes in the afternoon, I'm happy to find him already there, or I catch myself leaving my room door open a crack while I'm studying so I can hear him coming home. We spend more and more evenings together. The first two weeks I spent a lot of time in my room, but Denver is pulling me out more and more. We have dinner together and watch a movie. We mess around a lot and ... and there are always these little gestures that make my heart beat faster. When his arm brushes against mine on the couch, or he pulls me close with a grin to make me believe he can lull me to sleep. But there's also the other Denver Jones, the pickup, the heartthrob, the quarterback. I don't like this part of him because it points out that nothing will happen between us because he would have to give up his free single life.

I can't interpret Phoenix's looks. I don't know if she's just annoyed by the subject or if she knows and disapproves of it all. Even in high school, Denver was a girl magnet and many girls just wanted to be friends with Phoenix to end up in his bed. Understandably, this has left its mark on her over the years. Joy and Millie have long since understood that I find Denver more than nice.

While Phoenix keeps quiet and Millie tries to put the best face on things, Joy is just Joy. She always says exactly what is true but that nobody wants to hear.

"Sienna and Denver," Phoenix laughs and rolls her eyes. "That's silly."

It doesn't seem to be on her radar. Good for me.

Joy and Millie immediately raise their eyebrows.

"The only reason they haven't slept together yet is because they don't want to jeopardize their friendship," Joy says, shoving another fry into her mouth as if we were talking about the weather. She's incredible. But she's not entirely wrong. Still, I wonder if we should really be talking about whether Denver and I will ever have sex.

"Don't forget all his one-night stands," Millie adds. "I hope he doesn't have any STDs."

Joy and I snort, while Phoenix rolls her eyes and covers her ears for a few seconds.

"That's disgusting," she says, her face contorting in disgust. "You're talking about my brother's sex life."

"Shall we talk about your sex life instead?" asks Joy, looking at her intently. "Who are you sleeping with, Phoe?"

Phoenix, who had a big mouth a moment ago, becomes very quiet and stares at her burger. Huh? What's going on? She's usually good for a joke, too.

"Nobody," she replies, reaching for her burger. "There's no one."

"Really no one?" Joy asks, and Phoenix shakes her head.

"No," she hisses, annoyed. Her eyebrows are knitted together, a frown line forming between them. She looks at us tersely. It's as if Joy has stirred up a hornet's nest. "Who's Millie sleeping with?" She tries to change the subject.

Millie's face turns bright red. She seems so uncomfortable with the question that she must be silently wishing for new girlfriends. She looks at me, then at Joy and Phoenix.

"I... well, I..." she stammers awkwardly. "It's private."

Once again, we snort. This is anything but private in our girl clique. But since I think Millie is still a virgin and has at most made out with a guy, I leave her alone. Joy also keeps her mouth shut. Which is surprising, since she usually has to go one better.

Secretly I think Millie has a crush on Darren. Which, to be honest, would be an absolute disaster. He doesn't even know she exists and breathes the same air as he does.

"You guys are so boring," Joy says, shaking her head. "I had sex yesterday with-"

"Ethan," I finish her sentence. "I know Denver analyzed it at length."

"How does he know?" Joy frowns. She's not uncomfortable. Her posture is still casual, but she still doesn't seem to be one hundred percent comfortable with what Denver is telling me.

"He was with Jake at Darren's when you guys... well... got busy." Joy groans and I laugh softly. "But Jake was on a date then too."

"I'm surprised Jake doesn't have any STDs," Joy says amused. "He takes everyone, doesn't he?"

"I don't think so," I mutter, glancing briefly at Phoenix, who still hasn't spoken on the subject. What the hell is wrong with her? Normally she loves this kind of gossip and suddenly she doesn't make a sound. According to her, Jake is just helping her with her studies, but I don't know if I can believe that one hundred percent. I could very well imagine that there is more between them. She has already hinted several times that they study together and after some parties I have been to, I also noticed that Jake and Phoenix went home together. I doubt that they each just went to their own bed.

The two of them would make a cute couple. Jake's a great guy, and I can understand why she's hoping for more.

"Maybe we should drop the subject," Millie says, looking back and forth between us. "We can't change it."

She tries to sound diplomatic, and when Phoenix nods vigorously, I have to grin. Millie has an incredibly good instinct for when a situation is too much for one of us.

"I agree," Phoenix grumbles. "He can fuck whoever he wants."

I roll my eyes and pop a chip into my mouth. Of course he can, and judging by her reaction, she doesn't care. Who would have thought.

"Let's face it, guys," Joy says with a serious look on her face. "This is no fun. You..." She points at Phoenix. "Don't comment on the Jake thing and-"

"There's nothing going on between me and Jake," Phoenix shouts angrily. "Why would you even think that?"

"Well. Because it's obvious?" Millie of all people retorts. "You like him, don't you?"

I have to stifle a grin because I never expected Millie to say it to her face like that. Especially since she wanted to end the subject diplomatically. On the other hand, Millie is the only one who believes that there has to be a romantic relationship behind every hookup. The fact that you can have sex with someone just because it's fun is out of the question for her. Actually, I'm not a fan of it either. Only Joy and Phoenix do it. I'd rather share that in a relationship than a quick number after a party, or worse.

"And he likes you too," Millie babbles. "What's the problem?"

"Denver," Phoenix says frustratedly, and I'm surprised to hear her say anything at all. "Jake says he's his best friend and I'm his little sister."

"The bro code," Joy mutters. "Pretty bad move on his part."

Phoenix nods sadly. Millie's eyes go wide as if she'd never heard of it.

"Don't tell me you don't know the Bro Code." Joy raises her eyebrows and Millie shrugs. "Jake won't do anything with Phoe because she's Denver's little sister. You don't sleep with your best friend's little sister. Bros before hoes. Except Phoe's not a hoe."

"Yeah, but if it's consensual," Millie retorts, her eyebrows knitted in confusion. "They like each other."

"You're cute." Phoenix laughs and gets up to go to the counter. The lunch menu here is All You Can Drink. I think she wants to get out of the situation so as not to reveal her true feelings to us. We watch her leave and I sigh.

"She's really letting it get to her," I say and Joy nods. "I could ask Denver if she really..."

"Don't do that," Joy says. "As long as he doesn't suspect anything ... you'll end up waking a beast that should be left to sleep."

"True," I reply as Phoenix comes back to us. She leans back in her seat and massages her temples.

"We never discussed it, okay?" She glances slowly around the room. One by one we nod, "And not a word to anyone."

"Sure," I say, nodding again.

"Denver can't find out about this under any circumstances."

"Then let's change the subject," Millie says, and I turn around in surprise.

Denver enters the diner in good spirits with Darren and Jake. As expected, he looks good enough to eat. He's wearing black shorts, sneakers and a black hoodie with the Lincoln Tigers logo on it. I can't help but notice the other girls in the store checking them out. The guys are eye candy. Their presence is intimidating. Everyone turns to look at them. Many of the female customers wish they could be at their side, and the male customers would like to be friends with them. It's a cliché, but that's the effect. It's pure showmanship and everyone is speculating about which table to sit at, which drink to order and what to eat.

When they see us, they wave at us and we wave back. We immediately move together to give them room at our table. Darren and Jake grab two chairs from the next table and sit down. Darren between Millie and me and Jake between Joy and Phoenix. As if it were natural, they reach for my friends' fries. Only Denver remains standing.

"Won't you sit down?" I ask him and can't stop a smile from forming on my lips. He smiles back and puts his hand on the back of my neck. Immediately my skin starts to tingle where he touches me and I grin at him dopey. About a week ago, Denver started touching me repeatedly, as if by accident, but on purpose. Like now, for example.

"There's no chair," he says. "As you can see."

He grins at me and I roll my eyes. Sometimes he really is a little diva. He could just as easily pull up a chair from a table a little farther away.

"Oh my God," I sigh and stand up. Denver looks at me with wide eyes. Grinning, I point to my chair. "Now you have an empty chair. I'll get another one."

He shakes his head in amusement and sits down. When I turn to get another chair, he grabs my hand and pulls me onto his lap. Surprised, I squeal, causing my friends to laugh. Embarrassed, I look away, although that's not a good idea either, because the alternative is Denver's neck.

"Are you embarrassed to sit on my lap?" he whispers and I roll my eyes.

"No," I answer firmly and he grins at me. Before I can react, let alone protest, he pulls me even closer. His big hands are on my thighs and his aftershave is wafting around my nose. Joy and Millie look at me intently. Phoenix seems distracted and disinterested.

"Hi," the waitress's bright voice rings out as she approaches our table. Like most of the temporary workers in Lincoln's restaurant industry, she is a student. As you might expect, she throws flirtatious looks at the guys before lingering on Denver. Figures. It's really gross that the girls are still flirting with him even when I'm sitting on his lap. It's probably because they know I'm just his roommate and not his girlfriend.

"What can I get you guys?"

"Three cokes, two nachos and three beef burgers," Darren orders for everyone.

Her lips are drawn into a thin line, and I can clearly see that she would have liked to take Jake and Denver's order in person so that she could strike up a conversation with them. Her gaze lingers on Denver for a moment, hoping he will speak again. But instead, she scowls, makes a note of what Darren ordered, and heads back to the counter.

"Tell me, Joy," Jake says, looking at her with amusement. "Are you and Ethan sleeping together more often now?"

All heads turn to Joy and she shrugs her shoulders in amusement. She doesn't seem at all uncomfortable with the question. How can that be? I would be mortified. Millie would probably start to cry and run away. Phoenix is spared such questions because Denver would intervene first.

"No." Her voice is completely neutral - as if she's talking about a shopping list, not sex. "And you? Have you settled down yet?"

Tense, I look at Jake and then at Phoenix. She's clutching her drink nervously, which can't be good. She probably doesn't want to hear Jake's answer.

"Me?" Jake laughs. Darren and Denver join in. This answer is not good at all. "What are you thinking?"

"Yes, what am I thinking," Joy replies tensely, casting a cursory glance at Phoenix. "You are and will remain a..."

"Incorrigible charmer," I interject. "Insanely cute and lovable."

Denver laughs softly and Jake's eyes widen.

"Something you want to tell me, Sienna?" he asks, wiggling his eyebrows. "I mean, if you ever want to get together-"

"Shut up, Jake," Denver cuts him off rather gruffly, his fingers digging harder into my thighs. As he does, I'm pressed even tighter against him, feeling his chest rise and fall erratically. What the hell is that about? Jake and I are just messing around. That's no reason to give me bruises. Jake lifts his hands and laughs softly.

"Sorry, bro. She's all yours."

Now I need a moment to sort out the jumbled thoughts in my head. I know Denver never likes it when I flirt with his buddies. But hearing Jake say that I am all his is a little strange. Denver treats me like a friend, except for a few small gestures every day. A friend, not his girlfriend.

Slowly I turn my head and look into Denver's eyes. He stares past me to Jake. His fingers dig painfully into my flesh and I'm afraid he's going to lose his cool at any moment. Not wanting to provoke Denver any further, I move very slowly on his lap, putting some distance between us. Only very hesitantly does he comply with my request and remove his fingers from my thighs. I immediately notice the lack of warmth and wish he would touch me again and press me against him. Pull yourself together, Sienna. My inner voice tells me to focus on what's important and not on what my body, and worse, my heart, wants - him!

Apparently, there have been conversations between the guys that I'd like to be enlightened on.

"What does he mean?" I search Denver's eyes and it takes him a few seconds to tear his eyes away from Jake and look at me. His jaw is clenched and if arrows could shoot out of his eyes in the direction of his best friend, they wouldn't hesitate for a second.

"What he means is that he has the hots for you, but he gave Denver his word to leave you alone." Phoenix's statement makes me cringe, and now more than ever I'm expecting an answer from Denver. She can't be serious, can she? Jake doesn't like me. This is ridiculous. Almost as ridiculous as the idea that Denver told his friends not to flirt with me.

Phoenix gets up from her chair and storms out of the diner after exchanging a meaningful look with Jake.

My eyes widen and I watch her go as Jake jumps up and follows her. Even though she was referring to me, her words are more a reflection of her own screwed up situation with Jake. Luckily, he goes after her to fix it.

"What the hell..." Denver looks between Joy, Millie, Darren and me. "Can someone tell me what's going on?"

I turn my head to look at him.

"You better explain to me why you apparently told your friends not to date me?" I say. "That you weren't thrilled when we had a good talk, I know. But this..." I point to the exit of the diner through which Jake and Phoenix disappeared. "This is really over the top, Denver. You're acting like you're my... my..." The word boyfriend doesn't cross my lips now, because I don't want to risk him getting stuck on it, and we stop talking about his ban on flirting. "I'm all ears, Denver."

10

-DENVER-

When we decided to go to the diner after practice, I had pictured things a little differently. The missing chair came in handy, but otherwise nothing has gone according to plan. I think I'm in the wrong movie. My best friend wants to bang Sienna, my little sister goes running out of the diner like she's been bitten by a tarantula. Jake follows her and Joy stays silent. Joy is never silent and has something to say about everything. To add insult to injury, Sienna now knows that I told the guys they couldn't go out with her.

What the hell happened in the last few minutes? Of course I told my teammates and buddies to keep their hands off Sienna. Especially since I've already noticed a few of them checking her out. None of those jerks are right for her or even good enough for her. She is so sweet and kind. They just see her bombshell body and want to fuck her. Not that I'm normally any different, but with Sienna, my protective instinct gets triggered. It's similar to my sisters, but somehow different. I don't want anyone to get too close to Phoenix and Madison. That's why I'm even more curious why Jake followed Phoenix.

I don't understand it, but I have other things to worry about than them right now.

I'm sure Phoenix is pissed off because I'm interested in her girlfriend. I used to flirt with her friends all the time in high school, and in the years since, I have had occasional sex with Phoenix's girlfriends. In my opinion, none of them were as close to her as Sienna. They were superficial acquaintances. So, I didn't think it was that bad. If my sister felt differently, I'm sorry. I never wanted to put Phoenix in an awkward position. That's what happens when you're only two years apart and the age difference becomes more and more blurred as the years go by.

I look at Sienna again, who has gotten up from my lap and is standing in front of me with her arms crossed, and then at Darren, Millie and Joy. None of them seem to want to jump in and help me out of this really awkward situation. On the contrary, they look at me with the same questioning eyes.

Explaining to Sienna why I've declared her off-limits to my buddies goes against the grain. She will draw all the wrong conclusions. Whereas -

It's not just that I don't want any of them hitting on Sienna because I want to protect her, but because... because I'm into her myself. Hell yeah, I admit it. I have the hots for Sienna - big time. But not just physically, but because we get along so well. I see it every day we live together. I remember things like her favorite coffee, or I know what days she's home and what time she gets in. I wouldn't care about any of that if I just wanted to have sex with her. I like Sienna and the thought of her sharing all that with another guy drives me crazy.

This whole thing between us is getting more and more complicated. In the last few days, I've gotten braver and started touching Sienna. Not just when we're on the couch, but in our everyday life. Like after we arrived at the diner, when she was still sitting in her chair and I put my hand on the back of her neck, or when I pulled her onto my lap instead of grabbing my own chair. It would have been easy for me to go to a distant table and grab a chair. But I wanted her on my lap. I wanted to feel her body against mine and make it clear to all the guys, including Darren and Jake that she belonged with me.

Sienna has never pushed me away or shown that she doesn't want my touch. On the other hand, she has never taken the initiative. I wonder if it would be uncomfortable for her to tell me that she doesn't like it. That would be terrible, of course, because I don't want to force her to do anything.

"Denver!" Sienna's voice reaches me and I look at her. "What are you doing? Why would you say that?"

"I didn't say anything," I deny. "You better tell me why Jake and Phoenix..." I point my hand at the door and look at her uncomprehendingly. "Left the diner together and..."

"It's not about Jake and Phoenix, it's about you," Sienna grumbles at me. "I get to decide who I date and who I don't. Got it?"

Fuck, this is really hot, the way she is standing in front of me with her arms crossed, demanding answers. Answers I'm not sure I want to give. I'm still waiting for her to make a decisive move, but the way things are right now, that's not going to happen. She's mad as hell. Luckily, before I can answer, the waitress comes over and sets the food down. Darren digs in heartily. I look at Sienna again and reach for my burger when she doesn't react. Instead, she sits down in Phoenix's chair.

"Okay," Joy says, as if completely unaware of what has been going on at our table the last few minutes. "Are we going to Josh's party tomorrow?"

And even though I'm surprised she's changing the subject, I'm grateful to her for doing so. Smiling, I nod at her. She

117

doesn't respond to my gesture, instead focusing on Millie and Sienna.

Josh is one of our teammates. Darren nods and Millie gives a hesitant nod as well.

Honestly, I think she's kind of cute. Not in a sexy cute way like Sienna, but really cute. She's very inexperienced with men and making friends with the girls is also new territory for her. However, she always gets involved and comes along with us. We've all become pretty good friends over the past few weeks.

"What about you guys?" asks Joy, looking back and forth between Sienna and me.

"I'm in," Sienna says, looking over at me with a sexy twinkle in her eye that I'd rather see in a much more intimate setting. "If Denver allows it."

As if I've been shoved into a barrel of ice without being asked, I cringe. She doesn't need my permission to go to a party. I'm not her boyfriend. She made that clear earlier.

"Permission to do what?" I ask, licking the burger sauce off my fingers. "That you can go to the party?"

"Yes," Sienna says, helping herself to the nachos. "Your friends will be there. You don't want me running into them or... falling into their beds."

"Seriously?" I groan. She can stop with these childish provocations. Although I have to admit, I'm on the verge of actually forbidding her. I don't want to see her in any of those beds. "I never said I wanted you all to myself."

Before Sienna can answer, Jake and Phoenix return. My sister looks much better. I breathe a sigh of relief. I'm glad she and Jake are getting along so well and that he was able to calm her down. He would always look out for her and Madison.

Jake grabs a chair from the next table and they sit down. I turn my attention back to Sienna. "You can do whatever you want. And with whoever you want."

I'm kidding myself.

"Perfect." Sienna grins at me with satisfaction. "I've got some really nice offers."

"Good," I growl, scowling as I continue to eat. "Well, have fun."

"I will," she says happily, licking her lips. She looks damn hot - damn. "I'm glad we cleared that up, Denver. After all, you always bring your conquests home with you. Equal rights for all."

And as if the situation couldn't get any worse, our friends start to laugh.

My mood has been at rock bottom since yesterday afternoon. After we left the diner and came home, we both holed up in our rooms for the rest of the day. We didn't even have dinner together. But we always eat together when my schedule allows. Sienna has been avoiding me and I almost didn't expect her to talk to me again. But this afternoon she did and asked if we would go to the party together. Of course I said yes right away.

Now I'm standing at the apartment door, waiting for her to come. How long can a woman take in the bathroom?

"Sienna," I call, looking at my watch for what feels like the hundredth time. "Come on!"

The thought of her picking up another guy today keeps creeping into my head.

I've never caught her having sex or getting close to a guy in the past few weeks. Since I usually take my conquests to my place, maybe she went to the guys' place too. That would make sense, at least in the sense that she wants to bring them to our place from now on. But no, that doesn't make sense. Sienna has always been home when I arrived. No matter what time it was. She was in her bed. I know this because I often checked on her. Whether I was alone or not. Of course, she might have already gone home with the guys or sent them home. But no matter how hard I try to figure it out, I don't want to believe it. Sienna is not the no strings attached sex type. It doesn't fit with the way she talks about sex. Joy, on the other hand, is, and so is my sister, though I don't like to admit it.

"Sienna!" Slowly but surely I grow impatient. "We're going to be late."

I start to have a change of heart, thinking about someone else being allowed to explore her body. With his lips, his hands. And he'll have fucked her. And in all the positions he wanted.

"Here I am!" Sienna comes out of the bathroom and my jaw almost drops. She looks incredible. Her long blonde hair is curly and falls over her shoulders. Her makeup is unusually provocative, her eyes are accented with a bold brown eye shadow, and her red lipstick looks like an invitation to taste. But the hottest thing is the dress! I swallow hard and hope I don't get a hard-on. It's made of black leather, fits her body like a second skin and squeezes her breasts like two ripe melons. As if that weren't enough, the cups of her breasts are molded into the dress to accentuate them even more. Relieved, I notice that at least she is putting on a denim jacket.

"We're good to go!"

"You... you're going like that?" I ask as she puts her iPhone and keys in the pockets of her jacket.

"Yeah?" she replies, narrowing her eyes. "Or do you think I should wear boots instead of pumps?"

"What?" I ask, stunned. I don't care what shoes she's wearing! It's the dress that's driving me crazy. "You ... you think that's my ... problem."

"Well." She giggles and tosses her hair back. This gives me an even better view of her cleavage. Her pale skin is flawless. The thin silver chain with an S pendant flatters her neck. I want to press my mouth to it and give her a hickey to mark her as mine. Sienna would sigh contentedly, snuggle up against me, and -.

"I wasn't sure which shoes were better. But the boots have a thicker heel."

I blink once to come back to the here and now. I can't afford any more lapses like that tonight. The outfit is weapons-grade, and with her threat yesterday at the diner, I need to keep an even closer eye on her.

I say nothing about her shoes and yank open the apartment door, hoping that a blast of cool air will hit me. But it doesn't. Instead, Sienna walks past me, grinning, her perfume wafting into my nose. Tonight, she's going to take me to the limits of my control. And the worst part is it's my own fault that I'm in this mess.

I hope there's someone at the party who wants to have sex with me. I don't care who it is. I have to get Sienna out of my mind. I don't care what it takes.

11

-SIENNA-

I have no idea what I was thinking when I squeezed myself into this skin-tight leather dress. I feel terribly uncomfortable in it. In fact, I hate dresses like this, especially ones that are too short. Joy talked me into it because she thought it would convince Denver of my merits. Her words, not mine. Judging by his reaction as we made our way to the party, I think I succeeded. I noticed that he could hardly take his eyes off me.

After Denver and I clashed at the diner, and I learned that he had actually told his buddies to keep their hands off me, I freaked out inside. Where does he get off? In the end, he is the one who doesn't have the balls to take the final step. He's the one doing all the touching and random gestures. I accept them and wait to see if he will take it further. Kiss me, maybe, but nothing happens.

Besides, I am not the one capable of pushing his nearly two hundred and twenty pounds against the nearest wall and kiss him senseless. First of all, I wouldn't be able to move him if he didn't want to, and secondly, I don't have the self-confidence to do something like that. Phoenix and Joy would do it easily, but I haven't adopted that many of their traits yet. There's still too much of the sheltered Montana girl in me. Besides, I'm not the one constantly proving to him that I have a zillion guys on the side. Denver doesn't seriously think I'm going to join his list of conquests.

One reason I want to go to bed with him is that I find him incredibly hot - no question about that. But beyond that, our relationship has changed in the last few weeks. We like each other and enjoy spending time together. For me, that's just as important, if not more important, than physical attraction. Good looks or not, if you can't connect on a human level, how hot you think the other person is, is completely beside the point.

Denver is not a person who talks a lot, I've noticed that many times. For example, if the conversation turns to his dad, he can barely get a word out, or even the concern about his sisters, which is clearly on his mind, is something he deals with on his own. So, I can't expect him to give me a verbal sign that he wants more than sex. But I don't dare talk to him about it. The fear of rejection is always present.

Getting back to my problem, the dress is pure provocation, not to mention uncomfortable. And now I'm wearing the crappy thing and can barely move for fear of either exposing my butt or having my breasts fall out.

"Why are you wearing that dress again?" asks Millie as I tug at it again. I should have realized after the hundredth time in the last hour that leather is not a stretchy fabric and always slides back into place.

"Provocation!"

"I see," she says, raising her eyebrows. "And you have to walk around like that? Couldn't you do it any other way?"

She talks a good game in her jeans and t-shirt. I'd feel a lot better in them too, but I had to listen to Joy. You should never listen to Joy about something like this.

I shake my head.

"No. You know what Denver did."

Millie sighs and nods. She sips her drink and looks at me intently. She would never say anything that would hurt me in any way. No, instead she thinks about it for a long time until I'm so intimidated by her look that I think about it too and feel bad about it afterwards. But she always means well and I find it remarkable that she always tries to be honest, fair and diplomatic. Not everyone can do that.

"Yeah, but you don't have to sink to his level," she says. "You look great, and most of the guys here can't take their eyes off you. It's not the dress. Is it really worth it to you to take a swing at a jerk like Denver?"

"Millie," I sigh. "You don't understand."

"What doesn't our sweet Millie-mouse understand?" asks Joy, putting her arm around me. She grins at us and I return the look. "You look ravishing."

Sometimes I don't understand how the four of us found each other. Phoenix, Joy, Millie and me. Fate just brought us together and I think we could be friends for life. I even met Phoenix before Denver when she was standing in the doorway. Joy came along as a friend of Phoenix's and eventually I picked up Millie. Now we're a foursome and I think it's pretty cool. It's the first time I've had such a strong friendship.

Still, we are and will always be very different. Millie's and Joy's views of the world, in particular, couldn't be further apart and could end up clashing.

"Do you realize that the three of us and Phoenix are not at all compatible?" I chuckle, and they both agree. "I mean, we're... we're so different and... and yet it just works."

"That's true," Millie agrees. "Somehow, everyone in our group fills a role that complements the others."

Joy nods and points at me again.

125

"So. What's your battle plan for Denver?"

Millie rolls her eyes.

"She doesn't have one. She can't even move properly in that dress."

Joy laughs heartily. "But that's the point of dresses like this. You're supposed to look good in them and get them off quickly for sex."

Joy's frankness really gets to me sometimes and makes Millie blush with embarrassment.

"I don't know what I'd do without your life hacks," I reply wryly, unable to stop rolling my eyes. "And Millie thinks I don't need this dress to take a swing at Denver."

"She's not wrong, he'd be drooling if you wore a potato sack," Joy says with an amused look in her eyes. "But I think it's good that you're showing him what he's missing while he has to use his hand tonight."

Millie purses her lips and I roll my eyes.

"Denver and using his hand." I laugh. My voice brims with irony. "Nice one. He'll find someone to spread their legs for him."

Just then Darren enters the kitchen and I could swear Millie sighs. She's not being very subtle about hiding the fact that she has a crush on him. Darren is way too dumb to realize that someone as wonderful as Millie has lost her heart to him. Which, by the way, I don't understand at all. Darren is nice, but that's it. Nothing about the guy appeals to me. And his southern attitude really bugs me. That's why I'm so surprised that our Millie-mouse, as Joy has been calling her lately, has a crush on him.

"You look hot," Darren says, winking at me. I ignore his words because I don't want to hurt Millie's feelings, but, of course, she gets it. Darren's booty call is everything Millie isn't. In her chaste party outfit that we wear to seminars, there's no way she's going to appeal to him. Intelligent as she is, she knows it, but she can't break out of her shell. She shouldn't change for a guy like Darren. No one should change for anyone just to get their attention.

Millie avoids my gaze and turns away. "I hope Denver told you that already," Darren adds to his compliment.

"No," I reply, looking around, "he hasn't spoken to me since we got here."

Darren nods briefly and smiles at Millie. She smiles back, which makes Joy and I grin. Then he turns on his heel and leaves. It would have been nice if he had said something to her, too. Millie forces a pitiful smile and I can tell by her expression how disappointed she is.

"Well?" Joy grins. "Did he throw you off a little?" She seems to be using the sledgehammer approach again.

"No." Millie gasps. "I ... I was just ... being polite. I ... I didn't mean... to interrupt his compliment to Sienna..." She waves her hands wildly in the air. "You know what I mean."

"Talk to him sometime," I advise her in a quiet voice. "I hear it works."

"Like it did with you and Denver?" she snaps back, slapping her hand over her mouth. "Sienna, I-"

"It's nothing," I say, grinning. "And yeah ... Denver and I should probably talk ..."

"You could also make out," Joy says, giving me a meaningful smile. "That's a form of communication, too."

I roll my eyes, but can't help laughing.

The smell of smoke and alcohol hangs in the air of the frat house we're in. I had planned to get drunk and hook up with

127

some guy so Denver would know - and give him the show I was threatening to give him. But I can't bring myself to do it. I've never had a one-night stand. It's not who I am, and it's not who I want to be. Besides, thanks to my friendship with Denver and the bush radio on campus, I think I'm too well known to let a guy sleep with me in secret so that only Denver would know.

I step out onto the patio into the backyard and can't believe people are still swimming in the pool in October. It's extremely cold in Lincoln and it won't be long before the first snow falls.

"Hi," a deep voice comes from behind me and I jump. "Sorry, I didn't mean to scare you."

A blond guy is standing in front of me. I'd say he's about 6'2" - broad shoulders, a friendly smile and blue eyes - just my type!

"Hi," I say a little startled and smile at him. "Maybe I'm a little jumpy too."

I can't help but return his warm smile. "I'm Tyler," he introduces himself. "I hope it doesn't make you uncomfortable that I'm chatting with you so unexpectedly."

I'm not uncomfortable, but I find it strange. Weird too, to be honest, but that's absurd ... Denver would never set me up with a guy who is exactly my type and looks like him, would he? Wouldn't he? He'd be cutting off his nose to spite his face if he didn't want me to go out with someone else.

"No," I reply with a slight smile. "I'm Sienna."

Friendly, I offer him my hand, which he immediately takes. His hand is warm, but not sweaty. He squeezes it lightly, which makes me smile. Okay, this guy is really more than handsome. Plus, he's already said more than three sentences, and none of the usual college-boy catchphrases have come out of his mouth. No flirty lines to send me running for the hills.

"Hi, Sienna," he says, and I have to laugh quietly.

"Hi Tyler."

A little embarrassed, I raise my eyes to meet his. He's really damn cute. Tyler is wearing jeans, a white t-shirt with a red lumberjack shirt over it, and sneakers. His hair is a little longer on top than on the sides. His blue eyes are framed by thick lashes, and a neat beard lines his cheeks and defines his prominent jaw. Tyler would have definitely caught my eye.

"Are you new?" I want to know and he nods.

"Yeah. I transferred from Ohio."

"Oh okay," I counter with interest. "Why?"

"The football team is better here." He grins and I groan. Oh please no. Not a football player. You've got to be kidding me. "I think I can achieve my goals more effectively with them."

"Possibly." I nod to emphasize my words and smile at Tyler. "What position do you play?"

I can't believe I'm talking football with him.

"I'm a running back," he says. "Do you like football?"

"A little." I keep my answer vague. But it's the truth. Denver and the guys have gotten me into football in the last few weeks. Still, it's not at the top of my list of coolest sports. Less brutal sports like soccer and dancing are there. "I'm starting to like it more and more."

"Oh yeah," he says, winking at me. "So you would come to the stadium sometime under the right circumstances."

I laugh softly and nod.

"Maybe!"

Tyler smiles at me and takes a step towards me. He's a sweet guy and manages to make me forget about Denver for the moment. "I'd definitely be very happy." His voice drops a shade and a shiver runs down my spine.

I lift my head to meet his gaze. Tyler returns it and takes the last step towards me. All the intentions I had just a few minutes ago vanish into thin air. Tyler is insanely nice and sweet and shit, yeah, he's hot. And if he's new, he hasn't yet heard about Denver's flirting ban.

"Maybe I will think about it," I murmur, and place my hands on his chest. The warmth of his skin is palpable and I take another step closer to him. He grins and leans toward me, placing his hands on my hips as he pulls me close. His blue-gray eyes scrutinize me intently.

Fuck, where is this going? This is getting out of hand.

Nervously, I lick my lips, which Tyler interprets as an invitation to lean closer. His breath brushes against my ear, but the expected shiver that runs down my spine with every touch of Denver's fails to materialize.

Why doesn't it happen? Tyler's great and I'm still thinking about that idiot.

"Sienna," he murmurs to me. "I'm going to kiss you now."

My heart races in my chest and before I can say anything, he presses his lips to mine. The kiss is softer than I expected. Tyler doesn't move at first and when I open my mouth a little to say something, he takes it as another invitation and deepens the kiss. He pulls me closer at the waist so that my body is pressed against his. The tight grip of his hands leaves me little room to move.

Tyler's a good kisser and if I could get into it, I'd definitely end up in bed with him, but I can't.

In my head there's only this one guy, I want to do it with. Because in Tyler's arms my heart is beating faster for all the wrong reasons and even the familiar butterflies aren't dancing in my stomach. There is a yawning emptiness.

I want Denver.

I realize now more than ever that he's the guy I want to kiss, touch, and take to my bed.

Son of a bitch! Why did I have to make out with another guy before I finally realized what - or rather who - I want?

I tear myself away from Tyler and push him away from me. He stumbles back a step and opens his mouth to say something, but I immediately cut him off.

"I can't do this." That's all I manage to get out.

Without waiting for Tyler's answer, I storm past him and back into the house. I can still hear him calling for me, but I ignore him. It's all too much for me right now - the party, the people, the dress, Tyler and the kiss.

I have to get out of here.

Joy and Millie come up to me and start to say something, but I shake my head. I don't want to talk to them and burst into tears in front of everyone at the party. It's bad enough that my mood has sunk so low that I have to cry. I struggle to hold back the tears while I am inside. As I cover my cheeks with my hands and start to leave the party with my head down, I bump into someone. I'm already bracing myself to land on my butt on the floor when strong hands grab my upper arms and stop me from falling.

"I've got you." Denver's voice is worried and he holds me close. I feel the warmth of his body and at the same time the kiss with Tyler comes to mind. "It's okay."

"Nothing is okay." I push Denver away and wipe away my tears. I can't hold them back anymore. "Why don't you understand?"

"Sienna, I-" Denver licks his lips and spreads his arms, pulling me back to him. I shake my head, silently begging him not to touch me. When he stops and doesn't make another move towards me, I walk past him.

"Sienna!" I ignore his calls and make my way through the crowd and out of the frat house. "Sienna, wait!"

Panting, I stop at the front door and put my hands on my hips. I didn't realize how out of shape I was, and I'm already gasping for breath. But that could be my high heels.

"Sienna," Denver says and I know he's standing right behind me. "What's wrong with you?"

When Denver touches my upper arms, I turn and glare at him.

"You ask me what's wrong with me?" I yell at him. "Can't you guess?"

"I..." he stammers. My outburst actually seems to take him by surprise. At first he seems to be at a loss for words, but then he continues. "I was looking for you and wanted to talk to you."

"But I don't want to talk to you," I hiss, wiping away the newly formed tears. The salty taste stings my lips and I lick it hastily. "This... this is all your fault."

He furrows his eyebrows, making me even angrier. He must have realized that I don't want to talk to him right now. Everything that happened tonight is something I need to work through first. For me - alone. Without him and his burning eyes.

I fell in love with Denver.

Sometime in the last few weeks.

And now everything is in ruins.

Denver and I blew it. Each in our own way. The fact that I'm so mad at him for letting me get carried away with all this shit tonight makes it even worse. I look terrible, I'm wearing a dress that doesn't even deserve that name, and I made out with a new student to forget about Denver.

"What's my fault?" he asks, taking a step toward me. His expression is pained and I can see the sad look in his eyes. Denver shoves his hands into his jeans pockets.

"Leave me alone, Denver," I whisper, barely having the strength to deal with him. It's just been too much the last few hours. Joy and Millie appear behind him, looking back and forth us.

"You want me to..." He stops and looks at me, confused. "I don't understand you, Sienna."

"I don't care," I hiss. "I don't care about anything ... you ... you ... fuck you."

Joy walks briskly past Denver, while Millie is noticeably more cautious. My friends flank me on both sides as if to protect me.

"Sienna," Joy says quietly, putting her arm around me. "Do you want us to take you home?"

"I ... I guess so ... I don't know."

Denver takes a step closer. "I'll take you home." He looks at me urgently. "Please?"

His gaze is pleading, but I shake my head. I can't bear to be near him today. I want to think without knowing that he is sleeping two rooms away. The distance will do us good to figure out what we want. Although I am already sure what I want - Denver! And not as a casual fling, but for real. As my boyfriend.

"I'm sleeping at Millie's," I decide, turning away from him to leave. Millie and Joy are next to me, so Denver doesn't have a chance to get to me again.

"You can't just leave," he calls after me. "Please come home with me."

12

-SIENNA-

Two days later

I've been avoiding going home for a whole forty-eight hours now, so I've been staying at Millie's. Her dorm room is way too small for both of us, and her annoying roommate Amanda doesn't like having me there either. Two of us in twenty square meters with a small bathroom is not easy. But with three of us, it becomes an ordeal. I don't know the exact reason why Amanda doesn't like me very much. But I am pretty sure it is because of my relationship with Denver. Every time his name or any of the guys' names came up in conversation, she would snort in disdain, to the point where Millie and I had to have our conversations outside the room. With that in mind, it's best that I didn't get that room. If it had been mine. Amanda and I would have clawed each other's eyes out after a few days, I'm sure.

Millie and I squeeze into her small twin bed to sleep because I don't want to go home to Denver. Although there is a full-size bed waiting for me there. But that's not the only thing I miss. Maybe I also miss Denver.

At the party and in the hours leading up to it, everything got completely out of hand. It started with me letting Joy talk me into that hideous dress. It affected Denver, but looking back, it was all a big mistake. So was the kiss with Tyler that capped off my total disaster of a night. The kiss was nice, and under other circumstances I wouldn't have let Tyler off the hook so quickly - but not like that. My mind was constantly on Denver.

He keeps trying to reach me. Calls and messages every hour, but I ignore them all. Since noon today, he has also been calling Joy, Millie and Phoenix.

While Joy and Millie know what happened, I fobbed Phoenix off with half-truths. I told her that Denver and I had a terrible fight about another guy and his constant one-night stands in our apartment. She accepted it and said he'd come around.

Denver is her brother and I still don't know how she would feel about us. I don't want her to look back and think I was hiding something from her. But I also don't want to put her in the middle unnecessarily until things are settled between us.

The realization that I had fallen in love with him also hit me like a ton of bricks! I hadn't planned it. Falling in love with Denver, or falling in love in general, was never the plan.

I thought my new life in Lincoln was going to be so cool, and now everything is totally out of control. I met great new people, just like I wanted to, and I made friends. Why did I have to fall in love with my roommate? Everything was going so well. My best friend lives in the dorm room I could have gotten, and everything else is falling apart. Not to mention my best friend from childhood blocked me because I didn't check in with her enough. Clara's reaction is totally over the top, but I haven't bothered to reach out to her in any other way. If she's ending our longtime friendship because I don't check in with her every day and I'm off to a good start in my new life in Lincoln, I'll have to accept that. She also had the opportunity to go to college in another state, but she didn't want to. I remember Denver saying that she was jealous because she didn't dare leave Helena. Maybe there is some truth to that.

For the past few weeks, I've been suppressing my feelings for Denver, and now they're killing me.

Denver's announcement to his friends made me so angry - and he doesn't take the initiative himself. It still makes me angry because I don't know what to make of him.

On the one hand, he wants to be close to me, but then he never follows through. He tells me that I should find a guy, but at the same time he makes a rule for his friends that I am off limits. Not to mention all of his one-night stands. When he followed me the night of the party and wanted to talk, I just couldn't. That night, any conversation between us would have only made things worse. I was completely devastated.

The reasons why Denver told his buddies, or even the entire football team, as well as every other guy around him, to stay away from me, I can only guess at. It would be wishful thinking to think that he has fallen in love with me, too. Instead, I fear that he sees me as nothing more than Phoenix and Madison. A little sister or a good friend to protect.

God, just thinking about it makes my stomach acid come up.

But it's also coming up because I've just climbed the last few steps in the stairwell and I'm standing in front of our apartment. I know from Phoenix that Denver had practice this morning and is home.

I take the key out of my pocket and open the door.

"Yes," I hear Denver's deep voice and my heart starts beating faster. A discussion is inevitable. "I don't know, Mom!"

I quietly enter the apartment, closing the door behind me

137

before taking off my jacket and shoes. Millie thankfully provided me with clothes for the last forty-eight hours, so I didn't have to walk around in a leather dress and high heels. True, her clothes are a little tight on me, but there was no way around it.

I enter the living room and stifle a scream as I see a young girl sitting on our couch. She looks as startled by me as I am by her.

Who the hell is the Goth in my apartment? She has long black hair, completely black eyes and blood-red lips. She looks like it's Halloween already, even though it's not until next week. She's wearing black jump boots, black tights, of course, a dark red dress to match her lipstick, and a black coat.

"Hello," I say, approaching her. She doesn't take her eyes off me any more than I do her, "I'm Sienna."

She hesitates for a moment, glancing toward the kitchen where Denver's voice can be heard faintly. Then she turns back to me.

"Hi." Her voice is buttery in contrast to her outfit and makeup. Almost anxious. "I'm Madison."

My eyes widen and I look back at the kitchen. This is Madison? Denver and Phoenix's little sister? I can't believe it! They had shown me pictures of her once, but she looked like a younger version of Phoenix. Long blonde hair, light makeup, and a white flowery dress. This is the exact opposite.

"Hey," I say, smiling slightly at her. I'm still too shocked. "Are you visiting Denver?"

Nervously, she clasps her hands and nods. Then my eyes land on the overnight bag at her feet and it slowly dawns on me. The fact that he's in the kitchen talking to her mother can't be good news. How old is she again? Fifteen or sixteen? Looks like she's run away from home.

The kitchen door opens and Denver walks in. His expres-

138

sion is hard, but when he sees me, his eyes widen in surprise and he pauses. "I'll call you back, Mom," he mumbles into his iPhone. "Bye."

Denver ends the call, tucks his phone into his jeans, and looks at me. His mouth is slightly open and his eyes dart between Madison and me. He wasn't expecting me to come home.

"Hey," he says in a raspy voice, seemingly oblivious to his sister. "You're back."

"Yeah," I mumble, crossing my fingers nervously. My heart beats faster as he looks at me so unblinkingly, and I glance at Madison. There's no way he's going to want to do what we have to do in front of his little sister.

"You've already met," Denver says, pointing to Madison. She's still sitting there in a heap, looking at him intently.

"What did Mom say?" she asks, and he immediately cuts her off.

"Not now," he growls. "What do you think she said?"

Madison shrugs helplessly. I really feel sorry for her. He speaks to her in such a gruff tone that she becomes smaller and smaller on our couch. Madison's posture is hunched, her shoulders slump, and she bites her lower lip nervously.

On the other hand, I'm also interested in what she's doing here and, more importantly, how long she's staying.

"That I can stay?" She grins and Denver rolls his eyes and shakes his head. Then he turns to me.

"Can we go to the kitchen for a minute?"

I nod and without saying anything else, he turns and walks away. I take one look at Madison, who is sinking deeper and deeper into our couch. Sighing, I turn away from her and walk into the kitchen with Denver.

He's tense - I can feel it in every fiber of his body - and I'm sure this isn't how he imagined our reunion and subsequent conversation. Denver closes his eyes for a moment and puts his hands on his hips. When he looks at me, it hits me like a thousand bolts of lightning running through my body. His gaze is troubled and he seems helpless. I'm sure it's Madison and not me.

"I thought we'd talk when you got back," he says. "But then Madison showed up and..."

"You don't have to explain." Without thinking, I walk up to him and reach for his hand. He flinches for a second, then pulls me toward him. We stand so close that our upper bodies almost touch. My heart races again and when he looks at me, the butterflies in my stomach start to fly.

Fuck, that look catches me completely unprepared!

"Yes, I do," he says in a raspy voice. "I have so many things to explain, but now..."

"It's okay," I interrupt, even though I want to talk to him. But I understand that he has to take care of Madison right · now. She's his little sister, and our problems have to take a back seat to that. "We'll talk later."

"Okay," Denver says, smiling at me. "Thanks."

I meet his gaze and nod. "Why is she here?"

Denver looks past me, hoping Madison doesn't hear us. "I don't know." He sighs. "I thought it was you earlier when she showed up at the door with her bag. She just said she couldn't stay at home anymore and wanted to stay."

"That's it?" I repeat, slowly turning my head to look at the door as well.

"No," he says, massaging his temples. "She's changed so much in the last year. Look at her ... I showed you pictures of her as she was before. I agreed to let her stay for two nights, but then she has to go home."

"What did she say?" I give him a questioning look. "She brought a huge bag."

"She accepted it," he says with a shrug. "But she wasn't thrilled."

"Okay," I say gently. "I don't mind."

"Thanks, Sienna." Denver surprisingly pulls me close. Smiling, I wrap my arms around his neck and snuggle against him. It feels good to be close to him, even though I know we still have to talk. I breathe in his spicy scent and snuggle even closer. Denver senses this and runs his hands down my back.

"I'm glad you're home," he whispers and I look up at him. There's a smile on his lips that makes the butterflies in my stomach go crazy. My heartbeat must have doubled in a matter of seconds and my hormones are going crazy. We've been this close before, but now it feels even more surreal.

I look back at him as he takes his hand from my back to brush my hair back. I swallow and nervously lick my lips. Denver's eyes dart between my mouth and my eyes.

My heart threatens to explode and I cling tighter to his sweater. The fabric is soft against my skin and even though it is quite thick, I can feel the warmth of his body.

"Denver," I whisper longingly. "I want..."

"Me, too," he mumbles, leaning down to me. "I'm sorry."

I don't respond to his apology but wait. Denver comes closer and I can feel his breath on my skin. He smells of mint and his signature aftershave that I've grown so fond of over the past few weeks. A shiver runs down my spine. Every fiber of my body is tense and I want this to happen now. I don't care whether we've talked or not. I want him to kiss me.

And sure enough! His lips land softly on mine. Immediately I return the kiss and cuddle up to him. Sighing, we surrender to the moment and when his tongue asks for access to my mouth, I grant it. Denver holds me tighter as his fingers dig into my hips. This kiss is even better than I imagined. Much better than...

141

"Denver!" Madison's voice pulls us apart, ending our first kiss. "Can you call Mom again?"

Puzzled, he looks at me and blinks once to regain his composure.

"I, it..." he stutters, gesturing toward the living room with his head. "I should go check on her."

I only manage a nod. Although at this moment, I want nothing more than to pull him back to me. To bury my fingers in the fabric of his sweater and kiss him again.

Without another word, he storms out of the kitchen.

I'm even more confused than before.

Gently, my hand moves to my lips. I can still feel his mouth on mine and the tingling sensation that spreads over my skin is incredible. Grinning broadly, I stand there.

We kissed!

Denver, Madison and I are sitting at the kitchen table eating dinner. I'm trying to act normal, but it's not so easy. Denver and I prowl around each other like two lions ready for battle, but still unable to judge our opponent one hundred percent. Since our kiss a few hours ago, things have gotten even worse. We need to talk so badly to finally know where we stand. Neither of us wants to do anything wrong because we don't want to provoke another fight. His apology meant a lot to me, and I am eagerly awaiting the moment when we can be alone to talk. I want to know what's bothering him and what the deal was with his buddies. I know I was wrong to think that he saw me as a little sister, at least after the kiss.

The longer Denver is around me, the more I need to talk to

him. I need to know where I stand with him so that if the worst happens, I have a plan to deal with my broken heart.

Denver gave up his room for Madison so she wouldn't have to sleep on the couch, which I think is very commendable of him. She thanked him and disappeared into it for a few hours.

Meanwhile, Denver and I tried to get on with our daily lives. I let Millie, Joy, and Phoenix know that I was back home, and then I retreated to my room for a while. I didn't tell them about the kiss. I don't want to freak them out unnecessarily.

Madison is wearing black leggings and a black top. She's also taken off her makeup and doesn't look so scary anymore. What's going on with her that she's changed so much?

"Where are you from, Sienna?" she asks, smiling at me.

"I'm from near Helena."

"Montana," she replies proudly, and I nod. "Why are you studying here?"

"I liked the program at Lincoln the best."

Denver gets up and puts his plate away. I watch him go, watching the play of his back muscles under the thin white t-shirt he wears. I have to stifle a sigh from Madison.

"I'm going to take a shower," he says curtly and disappears from the kitchen. Madison watches her big brother and bites her lip.

"He's mad," she says quietly, poking at her pasta.

"Are you surprised?" I ask, giving her an admonishing look. "You ran away from home and..."

"You're mad too!"

"I'm not mad," I sigh. "You're fifteen, Madison. Something could have happened to you on the way here."

She nods guiltily and continues to pick at her plate. I close my eyes for a moment, trying to think of the best thing to say. She can't stay here forever and I think she knows that.

"Yeah, I know," Madison says, pressing her lips together

143

knowingly. Her fork scrapes across her plate, making that annoying squeak that makes my skin crawl. "Just a few days."

"You'll have to talk it over with Denver."

"If you tell him you're okay with it, he'll take it better," she answers with a smile. "He likes you."

Something flashes in Madison's eyes that make me laugh.

"It's not what you think," I say, smiling. Then I get up and put my plate in the sink.

"What's it like, then?" Madison calls after me, giggling. "I mean, I'm not a little kid anymore. I know what you're doing..."

I turn and look at her with wide eyes. Blood rushes to my cheeks and I hope she doesn't see how uncomfortable I am having this conversation. Because Denver and I aren't doing anything. The first time we tried to do something, she did her best to stop it. Even if unintentionally. Madison stands up and grins at me.

I have no idea what to say. She's Denver's little sister. Yeah, so is Phoenix, but Madison is really young.

"It's not what you think," I say. "It's really not."

"Why not?" She smiles and puts her empty plate next to mine. "The way he looks at you and you look at him...the way you tiptoe around each other and can't keep your hands off each other."

Madison wiggles her eyebrows as if she knows what's going on between Denver and me better than we do. Maybe she does, the way we haven't been able to get our act together for weeks. I groan.

"It's complicated." I struggle to say. "What about you? Do you have a boyfriend?" It can't hurt to switch gears and ask her questions.

Madison's cheeks turn slightly red and she bites her lip.

"So you do."

"It's not what you think!" The red of her cheeks turns a shade darker and she nervously shifts from one foot to the other. My question was a slam dunk!

"I should hope not!" Denver saunters past us, dressed only in boxers, and winks at me. Do we have to do this? In front of his sister? Doesn't he have any idea how aware Madison is of it? Apparently not. "You're too young!"

I stare at Denver for a moment and mentally slap my hand to my forehead. Fifteen isn't too young to have a boyfriend, is it? That's absolute bullshit and could only come from a big brother. I'm really glad I never had a close relationship with Lawrence and that he didn't put me in such embarrassing situations.

"I'm going to bed," Madison snaps me out of my thoughts and I look at her questioningly. "I wish you - no, actually I don't wish you that. Please keep it down!"

"Madison," Denver snarls at her. "Get lost."

She wiggles her eyebrows, clearly provoking her brother. I put my hand over my mouth to stop myself from giggling. This nonverbal conversation between the siblings is hilarious. Eventually, Denver wins the eye contest and Madison leaves the kitchen.

"Oh, by the way," she calls over her shoulder. "There's someone, Sienna. Like I said - please keep it down! I don't want to hear my brother having sex!"

"Madison," Denver calls out, annoyed. "I don't want to see you anymore today."

I never thought that his fifteen-year-old sister could upset him so much. Grinning, I cross my arms over my chest.

"What?" asks Denver, looking at me with big eyes. "She's too young."

"She's fifteen!"

"Too young," he argues again, making me roll my eyes.

"Oh Denver." I laugh and tap him on the shoulder as I walk by. I ignore the fact that my skin tingles when I touch him. Denver's eyes search mine and he licks his lips nervously. Before he can say anything, I continue. "You were on the prowl when you were her age, weren't you?"

"Right," he growls, throwing his hands in the air. "And that's why she's too young."

Laughing, I look at him again before leaving the kitchen.

13

▪DENVER▪

There's light coming from the street into the living room, so it's not completely dark. Which annoys me more and more because I prefer to sleep without any light at all. For the umpteenth time tonight, I flop down on the couch and hope to finally get some sleep. Of course, I let my sister have my room and my bed. I do not have the heart to let her sleep on the couch. Even though she deserves it. After all, she ran away from home and scared our mother. The uncomfortable couch would have been minimal punishment for her.

I still don't really know what's wrong with her and why she ran away from home. Mom couldn't explain it either and I don't care about John's opinion. I can't stand the guy and I'd rather have him out of our family.

Since Sienna agreed, I agreed that Madison could stay with us for a few days if she told me the truth tomorrow. Although I highly doubt that she will actually do that. From what I overheard of the conversation between Sienna and her, she has a boyfriend. I didn't know that and I don't think Phoenix and our mom know either. Madison is fifteen, she's still a child to me. She always will be. The six years between us is very different from the two years between Phoenix and me.

Madison is usually very outgoing, smart, and really pretty with her blonde hair and fair skin. Of course, I would never call my sisters sexy, but before this transformation, I would definitely have said that Madison was going to break some boys' hearts. With her blonde hair and subtle makeup, she was an eye-catcher.

Since going Goth, she's changed completely. One of her reasons for joining the movement is the music. My fear that her boyfriend is also a Goth is no coincidence. I can't believe that the guy is dragging her into his dark world.

Sighing, I tuck my right arm under my head and close my eyes. I'm glad Sienna is home. I've missed her the last two days and I finally want to talk to her. I know I went too far with my ban on flirting with the guys. But I couldn't risk one of those idiots hitting on her and breaking her heart.

I didn't even need them for that because I probably did it best myself. The hurt look on her face at Josh's party went right through me. Not only was she angry with me at that moment, but it seemed like everything that had gone wrong between us in the weeks prior had boiled up inside her.

So, I was all the more surprised when she cuddled up to me when we kissed for the first time today. Shit, it was a hell of a kiss. I wouldn't take it back for anything. If Madison hadn't interrupted us, I'm sure I would have gotten more from her.

Until now, I've ignored my feelings for Sienna because I wasn't sure if they were real or if I was just trying to get laid. There's no denying that Sienna is incredibly good-looking and that I've been hot for her for weeks. But that kiss confirmed my feelings for Sienna.

I am in love with Sienna!

There's no point in avoiding the inevitable. I can't ignore

148

these feelings she's arousing in me. When she snapped at me at the diner and made it clear that she was going to find another guy, I almost lost it with jealousy. At the time, I would hardly have called it jealousy. All I ever wanted to do was protect her.

But did I really want to? Hardly.

From day one, I wanted Sienna. First physically, then more and more in every way. She's incredible. I love being with her, sharing our lives and looking forward to coming home every day because she's there.

My heart speeds up in her presence. As unmanly as it sounds, there are these butterflies in my stomach and the tingling on my skin when she touches me and smiles at me. Now it seems like I've finally blown it with us. Her hurt look at the party and the radio silence that followed nearly drove me crazy.

So here I am, staring at the ceiling, doing nothing again.

I straighten up and look at her room door, which is closed, of course. Even though it's probably a stupid idea, it almost magically draws me in. I could argue that the couch is uncomfortable. On the other hand, I also know that going to her room is a bad idea. We still haven't talked. So I can't get into her bed and...

Yeah, what am I going to do? Sleep with Sienna?

I jump at the thought and my heart starts to beat faster. Sex with Sienna must be heavenly. My cock feels the same and slowly begins to rise in my shorts.

"Fuck," I growl, clenching my hand into a fist. "You've got to be kidding me."

Because I suddenly see myself standing up and walking to Sienna's room door. I can't be stupid enough to actually go to her. But apparently, I am.

Inside I'm already laughing at myself because Sienna won't put up with it. She's not like the other girls I've been able to wrap around my finger with my charm for years. Sienna will demand a discussion before we can finally kiss again and get closer. It's not just the physical attraction that draws me to her, I've come to realize. Sienna makes me feel at home. She doesn't see me as a quarterback and NFL prospect, but as the guy I am. No status, no sports, no slogans can win her over. I like that.

I stop at her door, raise my hand and knock. As expected, I hear nothing from inside. Taking a deep breath, I open the door. "Sienna," I say quietly. "Are you still awake?"

"Yes," she whispers, "what is it?"

"Can I come in?" I hear something rustle and then the light on her bedside table comes on. She blinks a few times before looking at me.

"What's wrong?"

"I... well, I am," I stammer and step inside. Hopefully, she won't kick me out once I'm inside. "The couch is so uncomfortable."

"Now what?" she retorts, eyeing me critically.

Yes, it was a good idea to sleep in just a pair of shorts because the sight of me embarrasses Sienna. I always get around her like that.

"I ... I thought..." But now I'm the embarrassed one and I feel like a total idiot. I don't usually have a problem landing in bed with a girl, do I? "I thought maybe I could sleep with you."

I continue walking towards the bed.

"You want to sleep with me?" she asks, "In my bed?"

"Yes."

Her mouth clearly forms an "oh" and I have to grin. From the looks of it, she wasn't expecting this. "I don't know if that's such a good idea."

"Why? What's going to happen?"

Admittedly, it's a very stupid question. We both know what will happen if I get into bed with her. Sienna has the hots for me, and I have the hots for her. She tilts her head slightly and raises her eyebrows, making me sigh.

"I can leave if you want," I start to back away, getting the feeling that she doesn't want me here. Knocking on her door wasn't a good idea. "I'm sorry. Sleep well."

I look at Sienna a moment longer, waiting for her to stop me, but to my disappointment she doesn't say anything.

What was I expecting?

Everything that could have gone wrong between us did. Even the kiss in the kitchen didn't change that. A late-night visit on my part is the absolute wrong way to convince Sienna of me - of us. Finally, I turn and head for the door.

"Denver," her soft voice calls out. "You can stay if you want."

I stop abruptly and turn to face her. Smiling, Sienna looks at me and taps the empty side of the bed next to her.

I don't need to be told twice and I'm with her in two quick steps. I pull back the covers and crawl under them. Sienna lies back down and pulls the blanket up to her chin. Grinning, I turn to her and raise my eyebrows.

"That shy?" I nod at the blanket. "That's new to me."

"Shut up," she hisses, "just be glad you're not sleeping on the couch."

I laugh softly and lean over to her. Sienna pulls away, but I still lean forward. We're so close now that I can feel her erratic breathing on my face.

"I'm extraordinarily grateful to you," I reply, finally coming to my senses to have a sensible conversation, even though my body, and especially one part of my body, has something completely different in mind. "Sienna, we... we should talk."

Her previously cheerful expression freezes, as if I'd poured a bucket of water over her.

What did I do wrong now? I'm just trying to show a little common sense.

151

"Now?" she replies and I shrug.

"Why not? It would be a start, I … I'm sorry for what I did. I … I just thought that … that it would be better if … if I protected you from them."

I am satisfied with my answer without giving too much away. First, I need to know what Sienna is thinking before I continue. It's hard for me to reveal my feelings to her, even if I have to at some point. I can't beat around the bush forever.

"Protect me?" Sienna asks, shaking her head. "Who are you protecting me from? I'm old enough, Denver."

"You're not," I reply, and she tears up in indignation. "I mean, I… I want to protect you like … like I would for … for Phoenix and Madison."

Sienna's look becomes even more stunned and in one leap she pulls backs the covers and jumps out of bed. I sit up and look over at her.

Fuck, she's only wearing one of those short shorts and a tight top. But that should be the least of my problems right now, although my dick, of course, sees it differently.

"You see me like that?" she exclaims, pressing her lips together to keep her voice from getting too loud. "You … I … I mean a sister?"

"What?" I exclaim, hurrying across the bed to her, "No!"

Sienna backs away and takes a few steps back. I follow her until she bumps into her dresser and looks at me with wide eyes. I meet her gaze and clench my hands.

What on earth have I done now?

"What do you see?" she asks, looking at me. Uncertainty resonates in her eyes. Her arms are now crossed over her chest, her posture becoming increasingly defensive and aloof. "You just made yourself perfectly clear, and if that's the case, you might as well sleep in your own bed with Madison."

"Sienna," I growl, pushing her further back against the

dresser so she's wedged between it and my body. I untangle her arms and take her hands in mine. Her skin is warm and as I run my thumbs over the backs of her hands, she looks up at me. Her look is angrier and more defiant than I expected. Sighing, I place my left hand on the dresser next to her and touch her cheek with my right. She immediately shudders as I run my fingertips over it. "I'm sorry."

"You said that already."

"I-" I murmur, cupping her cheek completely with my hand. "What do you want me to do? Kiss you again?"

"That would be a start," she replies bitchily. "At least then I won't feel..."

I swallow the rest of the sentence with my lips on hers. Sienna moans longingly into the kiss as I beg for access with my tongue. Her arms wrap around my neck and I lift her up. I deftly set her down on the dresser and wrap her beautiful legs around my waist. The kiss feels even better than the first one in the kitchen. Moaning, I lean against her so that her center is pressed against my cock. Sienna's tongue plays with mine and her breasts press teasingly against my torso. The feel of her lips on mine is far too good. My heartbeat slowly returns to normal. Carefully, I push her off of me and pull my lips away from hers. She looks at me with wide eyes and I have to stifle a grin.

"And just to be clear once and for all," I say, placing my hand on the back of her neck to tilt her head slightly. I like this position. "Afraid of what I'm going to say?"

"Don't try my patience, Jones!"

"After that kiss, do you still think I see you the way I see Phoenix and Madison?" I ask. "I don't and that ... I never did. From the moment you walked into my apartment, you blew me away, Sienna."

"Really?" she replies, smiling at me.

I can't believe she's still having doubts.

"Hell, yeah," I say, pressing my lips to hers again. "I didn't want the guys flirting with you and... making eyes at you because-"

It can't be true that I can't speak again. I'm terrible at this. I've never had to say I'm in love before because I've never cared enough about anyone. But with Sienna it's different.

"Because?" she asks, stroking the nape of my neck with her fingertips. A shiver runs down my spine and I lean back into her. "Come on, you can do it."

I let my head hang for a moment as Sienna increases the pressure on my neck, forcing me to look up again. I'd rather kiss her than tell her how I feel.

"Can I show you too?" I try to talk my way out of it, but she shakes her head.

"Actions speak louder than words."

"Not when your name is Denver Jones."

She grins. "You... you take those actions with... with all the girls, but..."

"That's not true," I cut her off, "I'm trying to tell you that I like you."

Suddenly she grins broadly and pulls me even closer.

"You like me?" Sienna giggles and the flash in her eyes tells me she knows she's won. Now she has me right where she wants me. "You like your sisters too, don't you?"

"Sienna!" I close my eyes for a few seconds, carefully considering my next words. "I like you more ... I mean, I ... fell ... in love ... with you."

There, it's out! I've told her!

I hold my breath and wait for her reaction. If she doesn't feel the same way and pushes me away laughing, I don't know what I'll do. I've never felt like this before. Never said it before. Likewise, I wouldn't know how to deal with being rejected.

My heart races in my chest and I press my lips together tightly, waiting for her answer.

"Good," she whispers, "I've fallen in love with you too."

Relief washes over my body and I feel myself collapsing inside. Longingly, I press my mouth to hers, pleading with my tongue for entry. We both moan as she grants it. I pick Sienna up and turn around with her in my arms to lay her down on her bed.

14

-SIENNA-

The morning after our reconciliation, our apartment was in absolute chaos. Jones against Jones. Denver yelled at Madison and vice versa. It was hard to calm the siblings down. Phoenix joined in at some point. At first, she took Madison's side because Denver was really going overboard with his attitude and accusations. But then the balance of power shifted drastically and Phoenix sided with Denver because Madison had lied to her about staying with us as well.

I finally packed my things and left. Since I don't have any siblings, there was nothing I could say about their feud and instead I left before either of them could get me on their side.

That was four days ago.

I have hardly seen Denver in the past four days. He wants to deal with his sister's behavior on his own, and I have to accept that. No matter how hard it is for me and how little I understand. Denver is mad at Madison and mad at himself for not being able to get her to go back to her mom. He went to practice and to his classes and seminars. He also met with his boys yesterday. I feel like he is doing everything he can to avoid talking to me. About us and whether we are together after our confession, or about Madison, which he excluded me from completely.

I close the apartment door behind me and drop my bag on the floor. Then I take off my shoes and jacket. I hang the jacket on the coat rack next to Denver's. It's funny, the first time I stood in this apartment I thought a girl lived here. I didn't even want to believe it could be a guy. Especially one as hot as Denver.

He is attractive, no question. On our night together, we cuddled and made out. We didn't do anything else. No sex, no fondling - nothing. There's absolutely nothing wrong with that, because I didn't want our first time to be with his little sister in the apartment.

"Hey!" I jump and look up. "How was your day?"

Denver is standing in front of me, completely unfazed, smiling at me. It's as if the last few days never happened. Over the past few weeks, whenever we've had a disagreement, he's always acted like nothing happened after a few days.

So far it hasn't bothered me. Things were different between us, and our disagreements used to be over trivial things like the dishwasher not being emptied or his boxer shorts in the bathroom. Today, however, I'm not ready to forgive him right away. He needs to learn that he can talk to me - and more importantly, that he can trust me.

"Hi," I say as I approach him. "Pretty good, and yours?"

"Me too," he says, shoving his hands into his jeans pockets. "Can... can we talk?" He sounds hopeful, and I can't help but smile.

"Are you talking to me again?" I ask anyway, playfully amused. "How gracious."

Then I walk past him into the living room, but I don't get far before he grabs my wrist and pulls me toward him. I could resist, but I don't.

"I'm sorry," Denver says with a sigh. "I shouldn't have ignored you the last few days. That was shitty of me."

"Yeah, it was," I reply. "Why did you shut me out?"

"I'm not used to discussing family matters outside the home. I'd rather play sports and distract myself."

"Uh-huh." I'm angry with him. He thinks it's so easy. A confession here, an apology there, and everything is fine. But it doesn't happen that fast. What does it mean that he doesn't want to talk about it outside the house? The fact that I am still someone outside the home for him after all that has happened between us is more than hurtful.

"I thought this was more than friendship between us," I tell him clearly. "You told me you were in love with me, and I told you the same. Isn't it still true, Denver?"

"Of course it still is," he exclaims in near panic and I have to grin broadly. Denver takes a deep breath and walks over to me. He grabs my hand again and pulls me to the couch. We sit down together and he links our fingers. "What I said to you ... the night I came into your room. It wasn't empty words or anything ... I really meant it."

My heart skips a beat and the butterflies in my stomach come alive again. At least those little buggers had fled his supercool demeanor of the past few days - well, for a while. Denver pulls me close and plants a shy kiss on my forehead. I have to smile and cuddle up to him. He could have kissed me properly, but in this moment such an intimate gesture means everything to me. He can kiss anyone, but he wouldn't just kiss them on the forehead.

"It hurt me," I admit honestly, looking into his eyes. "You could have talked to me. Anytime."

"I know," he says dejectedly, lowering his eyes. He stares at our hands, drawing little circles with his thumb on the back of my hand. "Do you still want to talk to me, or did I... blow it?"

I smile at him. "You're going to have to bring out the big guns to scare me off, and you know it. What about Madison?"

He groans, as if he can't believe I'm bringing it up. But I don't give him the chance to put me off again, or worse, ignore me. I want to know what's going on.

"She wanted to go to a Goth festival in Tennessee," Denver sighs. "Mom and John wouldn't let her, of course, so she took off."

"Typical reaction," I reply and he laughs and nods.

"Probably. I don't understand what's wrong with her. Her whole style, her clothes, and now trying to run away and put pressure on our mom."

"She's fifteen," I say, squeezing his hand. "Don't worry, she'll be fine."

"I am worried," he blurts out again and I roll my eyes. "You don't understand."

"And why not?" I want to know. "Because I don't have any brothers or sisters?"

"No," he whispers and leans over to me. "I shouldn't have said that, I'm sorry. Since our dad left, Mom doesn't have anyone to help raise Madison."

"What about her boyfriend?" I ask carefully. By now I know he's not high on Denver's list of favorite people. "I mean, if they've been together for three years, Madison would have been twelve."

"He's not our dad, and he's not in charge," Denver snaps at me. "He's not raising Madison."

"Denver," I mutter, leaning in slightly. "He's your mom's partner, and they live together. With Madison. Of course he's raising her. How else do you see them - living together?"

"John is not our father," he clarifies again. "Mom can take care of us. She always has, because our dad was rarely home."

"Okay," I whisper, realizing that I'm fighting a losing battle

160

here. Denver will never admit that he would be doing his mother a huge favor by reaching out to John. He'll never replace his dad, but that's not the answer either. Even though I don't know John or his mom personally, I know this can't be good.

"Can we talk about us?" he suddenly changes the subject and grins at me.

"Us?" I repeat and return his grin. Denver bridges the last few inches between us and gently presses his lips to mine. "Okay, let's talk about us, but next time you talk to me."

"I promise," he relents, and I'm still not one hundred percent sure he really feels that way. For the moment, I don't care, because I prefer this Denver much more.

"At first I just thought you were hot," he starts to tell me and I have to laugh. "The more time passed, the more you meant to me. At first, I admit, it was just platonic, friendly feelings. I wanted to protect you from the boys because I didn't think they were good enough for you - like I would have done for my sisters. I know them - especially Jake, Darren, Julien and Dan - and I know their ways with girls. Denver takes a deep breath and my mind wanders to Phoenix and Jake. He really can't figure out that something is going on. "Then I told them you were mine."

"Wow," I reply sarcastically. "That doesn't sound possessive at all."

"I can tell you it probably wasn't the smartest thing to do." He smiles. "Jake got a big kick out of flirting with you whenever he could. I think he knew I had feelings for you long before I did. At the diner... I don't know what happened, but I finally had to tell him off. By then we were closer than a purely platonic friendship would allow. But neither of us took the final step."

I nod in understanding and meet his gaze. He wants me to believe him and forgive him. I do, too.

"I was so mad at you at the party..." I hesitate, thinking of Tyler. But I decide never to tell Denver about it. Even though I'm afraid it will blow up in my face. Then again ... why should it? Tyler and Denver have nothing to do with each other and if Tyler knows that I belong to Denver, he won't say anything about the kiss. He's not stupid enough to mess with Denver, Jake and Darren. The captains of the football team. "I wanted to provoke you with the dress and ... and prove to myself that I ... I didn't need you and to get you out of my head."

"Didn't work?" There's no mistaking the mischief in his eyes, and Denver can barely keep from grinning.

"No," I say, putting my hand on his neck and massaging it. "So, have we settled once and for all that neither of us has covered ourselves in glory these past few weeks and that we could have saved ourselves a lot of grief if we'd talked?"

"We have," he answers, kissing me gently.

I enjoy the feeling it gives me. Much better than arguing or discussing his family situation.

Denver pulls me astride his lap and moans softly into the kiss as my core rubs over his cock. He slides his hands under my sweater and runs his fingers down my sides to the waistband of my bra. Goosebumps spread across my body and I moan softly as he slides his hands under the cup. Gently, he slides them over my skin and teases my nipples, taking them between his index fingers and thumbs.

"Denver," I gasp into the kiss. "More."

Gasping for breath, we separate. He smiles at me and removes his hands from my breasts to pull my sweater over my head. Denver's eyes slide down my body and linger on my breasts. Luckily, I decided to wear a black lace set this morning. To think I could have worn a cotton bra and panties that didn't match. Denver, at least, seems more than pleased with my choice. He leans over and kisses my neck. I sigh with pleasure and press myself closer to him. My center brushes over his cock again and he moans as I slide my hand between our bodies to touch him. I remember Joy's words that guys like to be touched there. My ex-boyfriends were more concerned with the actual act, so they didn't have time for extended foreplay.

"Sienna," he moans and puts his hand on mine. "Don't."

"Don't?" I ask, not sure how to interpret his reaction. Doesn't he like it? I shouldn't listen to Joy. I pull my hand back immediately. "Why not?"

"Because..." He cuts me off and pulls me even closer. "I don't want to jump the gun."

I giggle and press my mouth to his again. Denver kisses me back and cups my breasts with his hands. He massages them gently and I continue to let my pelvis circle over his, which only turns him on more.

"Denver," I whisper, pulling away from him. He grins at me as I push off and stand up. He doesn't take his eyes off me as I unzip my jeans and pull them down. I don't know where I found the courage to undress in front of him. I've never been the type to do it before, but Denver makes me feel safe. His eyes glide over my body and he pulls me to him with a tug after I have taken off my jeans and socks.

"You're so sexy," he murmurs against my stomach, planting soft kisses on it. "So incredibly sexy, baby."

A shiver runs down my spine and I bite my lip as he digs his hands into my thighs and his mouth travels down my stomach to my mound. I gasp as he reaches for the waistband of my panties and pulls them down.

"You've done this before, right?" he wants to know.

Nervousness spreads through me and I don't know how to answer him. I've had sex, yes, but beyond that I'm very inexperienced. My ex-boyfriends never took the time for foreplay and were of the quick type when it came to finishing the act. On top of that, there's a guy sitting in front of me who has laid half the campus and probably half his high school. Trying to impress him with experience can only go wrong. No matter how many times I did it, he would still be more experienced than me.

"What do you mean?" I ask carefully to buy myself some time. I'm sure I'm blushing because I'm not used to talking about sex so openly. "Had sex?"

I need Denver to believe me when I say it. Because somehow, I don't think it's going to sound very sexy when I tell him that my experience with oral sex is zero.

"I know that," Denver smirks and kisses my hip, giving me goosebumps. "I mean, have you ever done it before?"

Confused as to what he means, I'm about to ask when he pulls down my panties and presses his mouth to my shaved pubic area.

"Oh God," I gasp, my body slumping forward at being caught so off guard. My fingers dig into his muscular shoulders. "No."

"No?" Denver pulls away and looks up at me. As you'd expect, he's grinning smugly because it turns him on that he's the first. "You've never been fingered and licked by a man before?"

Again, heat shoots up my cheeks. Over the past few weeks, I've heard far too much about how talented he is with his fingers and tongue. The girls he's been with have been impossible to ignore - as loud as they've moaned and begged him to let them come.

Suddenly I feel like a bucket of water has been poured over my head and I push Denver off of me. He looks at me with wide eyes and wants to say something, but in the end he doesn't and grabs my hands instead. Without comment, he pulls me back into his arms.

164

"What's wrong with you?" he wants to know. "Did I say something wrong?"

"No," I whisper. Because he really didn't. "It's just that I... I've never done this before."

Denver looks at me and I look away.

I should have just lied and pretended that I had all the experience in the world. Instead, I just admitted that I had no idea and want to crawl away. I feel so ashamed in front of him. I have nothing to offer him. Again, all those girls appear in my mind's eye.

"Sienna!" Denver's voice snaps me out of my thoughts and before I can answer, I sink forward again, groaning. He has slid his right hand between my legs, under the bridge of my panties, and is running his fingers through my labia with relish. "Do you like it?"

I answer him with a vague nod, enjoying instead the incredible sensation he is causing inside me. I've never felt anything like this before. My whole sex life seems like a farce now. What he's doing to me feels far too good to have missed out on the last few years. Denver circles his thumb around my clit, making me moan loudly, only to bite my tongue the next moment. "Denver, please," I gasp, "That's... that's..."

"Good?" he helps, sliding two fingers inside me.

"Yes, good," I whisper and close my eyes. "Fuck ... yeah."

Denver continues to circle his thumb over my clit and penetrates me deeper with his fingers. A storm of sensations spreads through me, making me want to explode. My fingers claw into his shoulders, causing him to thrust his into me even faster. Is it always so fast to get to the edge? Usually, it takes time to reach the climax. At this moment, however, it feels like only his finger is making me come without any movement. He places soft kisses on my hip bone and his tongue licks over my heated skin.

"You're almost there," he whispers. "Come for me, Sienna."

The climax builds more and more inside me and I cling to his shoulders. When he curls his fingers lightly inside me, I explode. He holds me by the waist as the orgasm sweeps over me and spreads kisses on my stomach.

"That ... that ... it was ... incredible."

Denver pulls his fingers out of me and pulls me by the waist onto his lap. I look at him and smile back. "I'm glad I was able to expand your sexual horizons."

"Denver," I almost squeal, my cheeks heating up. He just grins and brushes a strand of hair behind my ear. "Don't say that."

"What do you want me to say?" he wants to know. "Thanks for letting me be your first finger fuck?"

"Not that either," I give in indignantly and sigh. "Stop it. Don't say anything, please."

Denver smiles and presses his lips to mine so gently that I let myself fall into the kiss with a sigh.

"You don't like dirty talk, do you?" He grins and kisses me again. "Too bad, because I'm relatively fond of it."

"Stop making fun of me," I retort, "I'm not like the other girls you..."

"Sienna," he cuts me off, digging his fingers harder into my hips. "I don't want another girl either, okay? There's no malice in this at all. Loosen up."

I'm not sure I can relax the way he expects me to. Without answering, I snuggle up against him and press my lips gently against his.

Denver stands up with me in his arms, letting me wrap my legs around his waist. He carries me across the living room to my room and opens the door. He kicks it shut with his foot and sets me down in front of my bed. Uncertain, I look behind me at the mattress and then back at him. He smiles at me and pulls me close. Denver's lips press against mine until he moves down my chin and neck to my cleavage. I tilt my head back and close my eyes.

"Is this what you really want?" he murmurs, meeting my gaze.

"Denver," I whisper, summoning all my courage as he pulls away and meets my eyes again. "Take off your clothes."

He raises his eyebrows and looks at me with a grin. Then he nods and reaches for the hem of his shirt to pull it up over his head. I bite my lips when I see him standing there, bare-chested, and walk towards him. Carefully, I reach out and run my fingers over his chest and six-pack.

"Do you want me to take more off?" he breathes and I look up at him. His blue eyes meet mine and something flashes in them, like a little boy who has just unwrapped his best present.

"I did ask you to," I reply with a grin.

Denver meets my gaze and unzips his jeans. He pulls them down and kicks them away from him, along with his socks, just like I did with mine earlier in the living room. "Now what?"

I look at his body, which I've seen like this a few times before.

"You like it, don't you?" He grins and pulls me close. "From day one you've been into checking me out in boxers or a towel."

"Maybe," I admit mysteriously, running my fingers over his six-pack. "The view is worth it every time."

"You wouldn't believe how rewarding my view is," he murmurs, pressing his lips to mine. I wrap my arms around his neck and we stumble back two steps before landing on my bed together.

15

-DENVER-

Since I haven't exactly been in Sienna's good books the last few days, I'm glad she hasn't dumped me. But since she has forgiven me for my behavior with Madison and we have made up, anything seems possible.

Sienna looks beautiful, lying in front of me in nothing but her black underwear, looking at me half aroused, half shy. I lean down and press my lips to hers. Sienna immediately wraps her arms around my neck and snuggles up against me. Her body is pressed against mine and we both moan as her center brushes against mine. The kiss becomes more passionate and when she opens her lips slightly, I take the opportunity to slide my tongue into her mouth. To illustrate my desire for her, I let my pelvis gyrate against hers. She is so incredibly hot and doesn't even know it. In the living room earlier, I noticed that she has absolutely no idea what kind of body she has and what she radiates with it. Sienna drives me crazy with all her sexiness combined with the innocence she still has. I would never have guessed that she has never been fingered or licked. What kind of idiots was she with that didn't want to explore this paradise? It was unbelievable to feel her around my fingers and to see how she let herself go more and more.

I pulled my lips away from hers, causing her to sigh in frustration. "All in good time," I explain with a grin, sliding my right hand under her back to feel for the clasp of her bra. Sienna returns my gaze. The little hooks come off after I pull them together and the clasp opens.

"May I?" I ask anyway, meeting her gaze.

I usually don't ask my conquests if they really want it at this point. Once they are under me, there is no hesitation. But with Sienna it's different. She's important to me and if she's not ready to sleep with me, that's fine with me. I'll wait for her. God, I must sound like a wimp.

"Yes," she whispers, giving me an irresistible smile. Sienna slides the straps of her bra over her shoulders so damn sensual that I think I'm going to come right in my boxers. I'm not sure she knows how hot she looks as she slides her bra completely off her body and I see her breasts for the first time. Sweet pink nipples reach out to me so I can't help but encircle them with my lips. Sienna moans immediately as I circle her nipple with my tongue until it is completely hard. I do the same on the other side. It's a good thing I've already given her extensive foreplay in the living room, so she's more than ready for me. I'm just not up to the task of getting her more ready without cumming myself first.

Her nipples get even harder as I slide my hand inside her panties to spread her moisture. Sienna pushes her pelvis towards me as I slowly insert my fingers inside her. It turns me on beyond belief that she's never been pleasured like this by a man before. That she has never come because of the fingers, lips and tongue of another man before me. Sienna is no longer a virgin, but her level of experience is so low that it feels like she is.

"God Denver," she moans, "that feels so good."

"Of course it's good," I reply arrogantly and see her eyes flash as I look at her. I slide my fingers deeper inside her and press the heel of my hand on her clit. Sienna presses her lips tightly together to keep from moaning loudly. I repeat this little game a few more times and let my lips circle around her nipples.

"Denver please," she whispers, "I ... I'm almost ready."

I lean up to her and press my lips to hers. Sienna returns the kiss, thrusting her pelvis toward my fingers, eager for her orgasm. Just before she's ready, I pull my fingers out and grin at her. Her eyes narrow to slits, making me laugh. I kiss her again and pull back from her. She follows my every move with wary eyes. Her cheeks are flushed and her chest rises and falls excitedly.

"Why did you stop?" she wants to know, and I return her gaze.

"Because I want to be inside you when you come again," I say and plant a kiss on the corner of her mouth. Sienna turns even redder and bites her lip. Then I move away from the bed and strip off my boxers.

I kick them away from me, along with the rest of my clothes, and grin at her. Sienna doesn't take her eyes off my cock, which makes me grin. I climb back onto the bed with her and grab the waistband of her panties. Without resisting, she lets them slip off and I groan as she presents her wet pussy to me. How many times have I imagined exactly this and just how much it exceeds all my expectations. Sienna is beautiful - inside and out.

I then reach for the back of her knees to pull her closer to me. "Oh baby," I whisper and press a kiss to her right knee, making her giggle. "I've imagined this so many times."

"Me too," she confesses, and if my cock wasn't already fully erect, it would have swollen even more. "There are condoms in my nightstand. First drawer."

I nod and lean over her to rummage through it. It is on the tip of my tongue to ask her why she has condoms stashed in her room, but I let it go. I know Sienna hasn't been with anyone else, or at least I've successfully convinced myself that she hasn't. Still, the thought of it drives me crazy. Even though I have no right to, considering the number of girls I've fucked in the last few weeks. So, I save the questions about condoms. It would ruin the mood.

"Joy gave them to me," she says, as if she can read my mind, and kisses my chest. Her fingers run gently down my stomach to my pubic area and back up again. I press my lips together to keep from groaning in frustration at being denied her touch. "I know what I told you ... and I ... I thought that I ... I could." Sienna stops and I look at her. Now I'm the one who knows what she means, even if she doesn't say it. I place the condoms on the blanket next to her head.

"Hey," I say quietly, putting my hand on her cheek. "I know that and ... and even if you did - I don't care." It's not that, but anything else would be inappropriate right now. I almost burst with jealousy when she threatened to pick someone up at Josh's party. "What happened before me - before us - doesn't matter. I want you and only you."

Sienna smiles and leans over to me. She puts her hand on the back of my neck and pulls me into a soft kiss. Moaning, I surrender to her and press my cock against her wet pussy a few times. "Denver," she moans, clawing her fingers into my upper arms. "Let's do it."

I swallow as her lustful gaze meets mine and reach for a condom. I open the wrapper, take the condom out, and toss the empty wrapper on the floor. Without taking my eyes off of Sienna, I put it on, checking twice to make sure it's on. Her eyes dart between my face and my cock. Her nervousness is obvious. Gently, I reach for her thighs and wrap them around me. Sienna moans as I lower my pelvis.

"Denver," she gasps as I place my forearms next to her head and gently brush back a few strands of her hair. "It's been a while... I mean, I..."

Sienna averts her eyes, but I place my hand on her cheek, forcing her to look at me again. The blush on her face betrays how uncomfortable she is with the situation, but I say nothing. Instead, I press my lips to hers and kiss her, pushing myself into her inch by inch. Sienna arches her back and closes her eyes. She's even tighter than I expected. What did she mean by "it's been a while"? How many men has she slept with? It feels like I'm her first. I give her plenty of time to get used to me and don't move until I'm one hundred percent sure she's fully adjusted to me.

"Denver," she breathes, suddenly opening her eyes. "You can move."

Her eyes meet mine, and I am completely taken aback. The way she looks at me - with so much grace, excitement, devotion and ... and love. It's too much for me. I've never had a girl look at me like that before, or I've never noticed it before. I don't know, but with Sienna it's different. She is turning my sex life upside down. Even though we haven't done anything exciting yet. I moan loudly as I pull out of her, then push in harder. Her tightness surrounds me. I reach for her hands, still clawed into my upper arms, and intertwine our fingers above her head.

"Can I..." I force out. "Can I move faster?"

I've never asked a question like this before. I've always intuitively known what to do. I basically know with Sienna too, but I want it to be perfect for her. I want her to remember this sex for the rest of her life.

"Yes," she answers, "and kiss me - please!"

Smiling, I comply and place my lips on hers. My heart threatens to explode as I kiss her in the same heated rhythm as I thrust into her. Not only is it incredibly hot, but there's an intimacy to it that I've never experienced with my one-night stands. Sex with Sienna is beyond anything I've ever experienced.

Our tongues immediately fall into a passionate game while I move my hips back and forth faster and faster. Having Sienna underneath me feels perfect and the way she accepts my thrusts while blowing my mind with her kiss makes me want to come.

"Fuck," I moan, burying my face in the crook of her neck. I suck on the thin skin, marking her as I claw my hands into her hips.

I thrust harder into her, taking her completely. Her moans tell me I'm doing it right and she doesn't mind my harder thrusts. Since I'm about to come at any moment and I'm desperate to come with Sienna, I slide my hand between our bodies and rub her clit. "Oh God," she gasps, arching her back as I press the heel of my hand harder against her pearl. To drive her even crazier, I pick up the pace again and feel her muscle walls slowly but surely tighten around me.

"I'm close," I let her know, pressing my mouth to hers. "Come with me, baby."

Sienna nods and I pull out of her once more. As I do, she looks me straight in the eye and just as she's about to say something, I thrust into her one last time, gently taking her clit between my index finger and thumb.

That's when we both jump over the cliff. Moaning I collapse on top of her and the contractions of her pussy rob me of my last shred of sanity. Jerking I release my load into her and for the first time in my life, I regret that we used a condom.

Even though it was absolutely the right thing to do. She feels so incredibly good, though, that I wish I could have felt her without any barrier between us. To prolong her orgasm, I rub her clit a few more times.

"Oh God," I murmur, kissing her shoulder before burying my head in her neck again.

Sienna strokes my neck and I feel her slowly release my cock so I can pull out of her. I don't want to bury her under my body. But when I try to roll off her, she holds me tight.

"Don't," she whispers, "I want to feel you for a moment."

"I'm too heavy," I whisper, falling to my side. Before she can protest again, I pull her onto me.

Her eyes are closed and she rests her head on my shoulder as our bodies take time to settle. The last few minutes have been insane. Sex with Sienna was beyond anything I could have imagined. I hope she felt the same.

We are silent for a few minutes, during which I stare at the ceiling and hold her in my arms. Until slowly some life returns to me and I want to get rid of the condom.

"Sienna," I whisper and kiss her hair. Something I've never done after sex before. I'm mutating into a wimp because of her. "I want to get rid of the condom real quick."

She mumbles something I don't understand and slowly starts to move. Eventually she pulls herself together and lets me stand up. Smiling, I look at her and put my hand on her cheek. Sienna nestles her face into it and I lean over and kiss her gently.

"I'll be right back," I say. "Shall we order some food? I'm hungry."

I look at Sienna for a moment and start to get up when she grabs my hand and stops me. "Is that what you do?"

"What?" I ask, raising my eyebrows. "Order some food?"

"I don't know," Sienna mutters, suddenly embarrassed and

looking around as if she needs to find something to cover up. "I've never had sex in the middle of the day before."

"Oh," I retort with a grin. "And whatever you're thinking - forget it. The sex was fantastic and now I'm going to take off the condom and we're going to get dressed and eat and lounge and talk."

"Okay," she says hesitantly, grinning. Sienna leans in and kisses me. "Well, hurry up. I have a lot of talking to do."

"And then we have to work off the food." I grin and wiggle my eyes. "Are you good at riding?"

Sienna instantly turns bright red and slaps my chest. "Go now," she cries, "I'll get dressed."

Laughing, I plant another kiss on her lips before disappearing.

16

-SIENNA-

A few days later

I feel like I'm on cloud nine. The problem with Madison is also solved. After talking to her mom, she went home with her. Things are going well with Denver, almost too well, I can hardly believe it. After we slept together for the first time, we actually ordered a pizza, talked, and had sex again that night until we fell asleep exhausted. It went on like that for the next two days until I had to stop because I was so sore. I'm not used to having such an exuberant and fulfilling sex life. Denver, on the other hand, seems to be made for any kind of sport. Just thinking about his firm muscles and the movement of his hips as he thrusts into me makes me hot. It's not just the sex that makes him perfect. We are also incredibly compatible as people, and our pre-existing friendship seems to have become even stronger as a result of our relationship. We laugh a lot together, but also talk about serious things like the future or our parents. Denver still hardly talks about his dad and also avoids the topic of Madison. He's still mad at his little sister and I can tell that it bothers him a lot, but I can't force him to talk to me about it. Still, I hope he will open up to me soon.

The Lincoln Tigers are playing today and we are on our way to the stadium. Phoenix, Millie, Joy and me. My friends don't know about Denver and me yet. I want to tell them in person, not in a text message. Denver and I haven't talked about making it official. After all, it's only been a few days and a hell of a lot of sex. For us, the lines between friendship, sex, and relationship got blurred at some point, so we didn't say on day X that we were dating as of today. We just are.

Due to the rapidly dropping temperatures in Illinois, we are all wearing thick jackets. Phoenix is the only one who has a specially made jacket with Denver's number ten and his name Jones on the back. I'd like to ask her what Jake has to say about her not wearing his, but I won't. Joy would take advantage of the situation to ask me about Denver and why I don't wear a jacket with his number on it.

I have no idea how to tell Phoenix that I am in love with her brother and he is in love with me. Our friendship is important to me, but so is my relationship with Denver.

"Earth to Sienna!" Joy snaps her fingers in my face, making Millie and Phoenix laugh. "Your ticket!"

"Oh, sorry," I say, holding it out for the ticket inspector to scan. "Thank you."

I follow the others through the checkpoint and meet grinning faces. I roll my eyes and avoid their stares. I can't hide for much longer that something in my life has changed dramatically.

"What's wrong with you?" asks Millie as we make our way to our seats. "You're absent-minded, and you're grinning all the time like a ... "

Surprised, I stop and look at them. No doubt they've noticed. I quickly glance at Phoenix, who gives me the same questioning look. I'm finished, but for now I feign ignorance. Maybe Millie is just being friendly and I'm stressing over nothing.

"I ... I'm grinning?" I mutter. "How ... how am I grinning?"

Joy laughs and puts her arm around me. "What do you mean?" she says, "You're grinning like someone who's had really good sex grins!"

"Joy," Millie shrieks immediately, giving me time. Still, I feel the heat rising inside me and my cheeks flush. "Do you always have to be so ... blunt?"

"Yeah?" she says dryly. "Seriously, Sienna ... who dusted you off down there to put you in such a good mood?"

Can't she shut her smart mouth for once in her life? Just once, damn it, so that I don't have to explain myself. Especially in front of Phoenix. After all, it was her brother who dusted me off.

"You're impossible," Millie exclaims and turns on her heel. I look back at Phoenix, who just nods and follows Millie. Either she hasn't noticed, or she doesn't want to, because she can't stand the thought of Denver and me. Again, I imagine the worst. Phoenix will end her friendship with me and think I'm a conniving bitch for sleeping with her brother.

"It's Denver, isn't it?" asks Joy quietly as we start to follow Millie and Phoenix. I look over at her and purse my lips. What the hell am I going to do? Yes, it's Denver and you can't keep something like that a secret from Joy. She has a sixth sense.

"Not a word to Phoe," I hiss. "I'll have to break it to her gently."

"I'm so happy for you," she screams and hugs me. "Did that idiot finally get it right?"

Phoenix and Millie turn to us and raise their eyebrows. I wave them off and push Joy away, who looks at me apologetically. "Sorry," she says, "I'm really happy for you."

"Thanks." I chuckle and a broad grin creeps across my lips. "He really dusts me off in an exemplary manner."

I wink at Joy and before she can say anything back, I run over to Millie and wrap my arms around her. "Is Darren happy that his personal coach is coming to the event?"

As expected, my best friend blushes and fends off my question. I almost feel sorry for her that she's in love with Darren because he doesn't even notice her. Except when she talks about football, then they can't stop talking. That Millie knows so much about football and is such a strategist is really amazing. Coach Flanders can learn a lot from our friend. Sometimes the guys even ask her how she would have called the plays. When it comes to football, she forgets her shyness and really gets going. Unfortunately, Darren is too much of a jerk to take Millie seriously. The fact that she's head over heels in love with the macho guy is a total waste. She deserves so much better.

I sigh quietly. Maybe we're all wrong and Darren is the one for her, but his lifestyle is so opposite to Millie's that it can't work.

"I don't know that much," she deflects, causing all three of us to roll our eyes. "And Darren doesn't care about me."

"Oh, Millie-mouse." Joy giggles. "Darren's a jerk."

"Definitely," Phoenix agrees. "He's friends with my brother, so he must be a jerk."

"Denver's not an idiot," I blurt out in my friend's defense, causing his little sister to raise her eyebrows.

Oh wow, Sienna, you can't put your foot in it any deeper.

"So, Denver's a jerk?" Joy saves me. "And what about Jake?"

This question immediately silences Phoenix and I form a silent "Thank you" in Joy's direction. Still, I know I have to tell Phoenix and Millie.

The game is competitive and we're down by a field goal, which is a disaster. Three points is nothing. Florida State has the ball with only two minutes left on the clock. They are on fourth and goal and can either go for it or kick a field goal. But they are still too far from the end zone to try. Nervously, I rub my hands together and keep looking over at the bench where Denver is sitting with Jake, conferring. Tyler is standing a few feet away from them.

I haven't seen Tyler alone since the kiss at Josh's party, so we can talk about it. I know that he and Denver have become friends, which is not a good thing. If Tyler mentions to Denver that he stuck his tongue down my throat, he's going to freak out. I told him there was no guy. As far as sex goes, that's true. Tyler and I kissed and it was a good kiss. He knew what he was doing and how to use his tongue. Nothing compared to Denver's kissing, but that is partly because of how I feel about Denver.

Florida's offense sizes up and I look down the field, mesmerized. The center hands the ball to the quarterback, who takes a few steps back. I'm surprised they're still going for it, but I have no idea. "Why didn't they go for the field goal?" I ask, turning to Millie.

"They're too far from the end zone," she replies, as Darren suddenly rushes in from the left and knocks the Florida quarterback to the ground. "That was amazing," my friend exclaims, "that tackle was insane."

"Yes, absolutely," I reply, hoping desperately that it won't happen to Denver. I hate it when he gets knocked down. I always suffer double and triple with him. He makes fun of it and

181

thinks it's going to be like this for years to come. In the NFL, it will be even worse than it is now in college because he'll be going up against a whole different caliber of defensive players.

"Now Denver's going to come back on the field," Millie says, as if I don't understand even the basics. "It has to work, even though the ball could still go back to Florida."

I nod and look at Joy, who is uncharacteristically distracted, staring intently at the sideline. "What are you looking at?" I ask her, but she brushes it off and looks down at the field.

"They're going for it now."

I get the feeling she's avoiding my question. One of the players has her preoccupied, but who knows who she's been having sex with again - and we haven't even noticed.

I refocus on the action on the field and cheer loudly as Denver high-fives Jake and throws his hands in the air to get the crowd going again.

"Why don't you just print it on your forehead *Denver, fuck me*," Joy whispers to me and I roll my eyes.

Denver calls the next play and the offense gets into position. He counts down as the center throws him the ball and he takes a few steps back to pass to Jake. Unfortunately, he only gains a few yards. It is still a long way to the next first down. So, it's back to square one. On the second try they get a first down and make up a few yards, but after that they don't get much going. Denver passes the ball to Tyler, but he doesn't get a first down either. When they go for it on third and goal, the stadium erupts in cheers. The play starts over again, but this time Denver decides not to pass to one of his teammates, but to run it in himself.

"Is he crazy?" screams Millie next to me. "He's never going to make that run."

I look at Joy, who is speechless for once, and then at Phoenix, who covers her eyes. But Denver runs and runs until he's stopped two yards from the end zone. "Oh my God," Phoenix exclaims, jumping up. "That's my brother."

I can't help but laugh and look over at Millie, who has gone completely pale. It looks like she's never seen a quarterback run like that before. Denver gets his offense back together and calls the play. I have no idea what he's going to do, but I have a sinking feeling he's going to try it again.

"He's running again," I say, and Millie looks at me in disbelief.

She shakes her head. "I think they're going for a quarterback sneak."

"A ... quarterback sneak?"

"Yeah," Millie says excitedly. "They're close to the end zone, and they're going to try to push Denver over the line with the ball."

"It might work," Joy interjects. "If Denver makes a long run. Is he good at that?" She looks at me and I shake my head. Damn, that minx must really be daring everyone to notice.

"Going long?" Millie repeats, looking first at Joy and then at me. "Oh my God ... Denver and..."

I cover her mouth before Phoenix can interrupt our conversation and nod. "Yeah," I whisper, "I'll tell you later, but Phoe-"

"Point taken," Millie says with a grin. "She doesn't know or suspect anything."

"Right."

"Like she doesn't suspect," Joy says, rolling her eyes. Fortunately, we can't talk any further, because the boys are doing the play. Sure enough, exactly what Millie predicted happens. They run a quarterback sneak and win the game.

We cheer and, of course, hug each other afterwards. It's absolutely awesome. Florida is a good team and we beat them. The chants of "Denver Jones" go on and on and I'd like to blow him a kiss. Most of all, I'd like to make it clear to all those stupid bimbos two rows behind us that he's mine. Denver Jones has a girlfriend, and those chicks can keep saying how great they think he is a hundred times over. He's in good hands.

"Let's go downstairs," Phoenix says, and we nod.

After every final whistle, the players' families are allowed on the field to celebrate the victory. Today is no exception. My heart is pounding with every step I take because I have no idea how Denver will greet me in front of our friends and the entire college. This is his stage, the place where all eyes are on him. He looks relaxed and laughs with Jake. I'm sure he's not worried. It's always me overthinking and not knowing how to handle a situation, even if it's ridiculous. Eventually things will come out about us. Phoenix is a few steps ahead of us and jumps into her brother's arms, laughing. Denver hugs his little sister before letting her go, and she hugs Jake.

Joy and Millie walk over to Darren, who is immediately sought out by Tyler. I look at them for a moment because Joy seems to be ignoring Tyler. Hopefully, she hasn't slept with him. If she has, she must never know that I made out with him.

"Hey!" I jump and turn around. Denver is standing in front of me, grinning. He's sweaty and has several blades of grass stuck to his temple. "Can I have a few minutes of your time?"

"Of course," I reply with a smile. "You played really well."

Unsure what to do, Denver makes the decision for me as he pulls me to him and kisses me. At first, I don't know what's happening because I wasn't expecting such a public display of our relationship. We're not officially together, we haven't announced it to the others yet. The fact that Denver is doing it now after the game in front of a packed stadium destroys all my plans to tell my girlfriends in person. But after a few seconds, I don't care and even manage to tune out Phoenix as I wrap my arms around his neck and snuggle up against him. A

184

comforting shiver runs down my spine as he pulls me as close as he can despite his pads.

"You played amazingly," I say as we pull away from each other. "I'm so proud of you."

"Thanks, baby." Denver kisses me again. Grinning, I remove the blades of grass from his temple. "And finally someone is getting rid of them."

"That's better." I laugh. "Otherwise, you'll go over badly with your fans." I look behind me where the girls from the bleachers are standing indignantly, eyeing us like an attraction at a carnival.

"I have to go see my fans," Denver says, stealing another kiss before leaving me there and actually saunters over to them. Annoyed, I look away and turn to my friends instead. They look at me, though, and grin so broadly that I prefer the chicks.

"You and Denver?" Darren breaks the silence. "Had to happen sometime."

He shrugs so casually, as if there's absolutely nothing surprising about it.

"Uh yeah," I mutter, ignoring him. I have nothing against Darren, but I often find that his lifestyle and the way he treats Millie are not okay. Maybe he really doesn't realize that she adores him, but he could still show her a little courtesy. He also keeps a very low profile when it comes to his family, and gets easily irritated when asked something he doesn't want to be asked. I don't do well with that. In that respect, Denver is more like him than I would like, unfortunately. He also has some issues, especially with his dad that he doesn't like to talk about.

What Darren thinks about Denver and me is none of my business. I don't care what Jake, Millie and Joy think either. The only opinion that matters to me is Phoenix's.

"Phoenix?" I say hesitantly and look at my friend. "Are you... well ... are you okay with this?"

"Me?" she wants to know and I nod.

"He ... he's your brother and I'm your friend."

Phoenix raises her eyebrows and seems puzzled by my statement until she suddenly bursts out laughing.

What's going on now?

Denver comes to my side again and puts his arm around me, pulling me close. Immediately I feel safer in case there's a confrontation with Phoenix.

"Well," she says and my heart skips a beat. "I was looking forward to gossiping about your sex life with you, but I'm afraid that's out of the question now." Her mouth puckers as if she's eaten something disgusting. Denver rolls his eyes and the others laugh. "But, of course, it's okay with me. If you want to do that to yourself."

"Yes, I do," I answer with a grin, putting my hand on Denver's chest and looking up at him. "Absolutely!"

He meets my gaze and gently places his lips on mine.

17

-SIENNA-

Grinning, I leave the seminar room and make my way to the cafeteria to meet Millie and Joy for lunch. Denver is still at practice and is planning to join us afterward. As for Phoenix, Jake and Darren, I don't know. Maybe Phoenix and Jake are secretly seeing each other so Denver doesn't find out about it.

Since Denver made our relationship public last weekend and our friends now know, things are going even better than before. At least that's how I feel. Maybe it's my imagination because of my infatuation with the guy.

We made his room into our bedroom and mine will function as a guest room and office. I still think it's weird, after having slept in separate rooms for so long. Still, I like that we go to sleep together at night and wake up together in the morning. During the day we don't see each other that much, but in the evening, we eat together and sit on the couch afterwards. By already living together, we skipped a few steps in the early stages of our relationship. This way, we didn't have the rude awakening after a year or two when we wanted to move in together.

"Sienna!" I jump when I'm called and turn around. Tyler is standing a few feet away, leaning against the wall and eyeing me. "You got a minute?"

So far, I've avoided talking to him. I'm a little afraid of what Tyler might say. Even though I don't think it's possible, I dread the thought that he might have feelings for me. My heart belongs to Denver and it will stay that way.

The thing with Tyler was a stupid mistake at a party. Especially at a party where I was trying to prove to myself and Denver that I didn't need him. Which is why I got carried away with the - admittedly good - kiss. Tyler is a good kisser, no question. Beyond that, though, I should have gotten to know him better to judge whether he would be a good match. Besides, he's damn good-looking. The superficial pluses definitely do not diminish.

Still, I have no interest in him, and anything he might feel for me would only cause major problems not only for us personally, but also for our group. Because, let's face it ... Denver won't ask Tyler out for a beer again if he knows that he has a crush on his girlfriend. I look around again to make sure nobody is watching us. Then I turn to Tyler.

"Hey," I say. "Sure I do."

He nods and takes a step towards me. When I raise my eyes, he's as close to me as he was in the backyard at Josh's party. The kiss and the way he spoke to me that night made me feel good. They flattered my ego, and the jab at Denver was perfect at that moment. But now I would rather step back and not be seen with him.

"Okay," he says. "Let's talk about what happened between us."

I nod slowly and close my eyes for a moment. He makes it sound like we did something else. Much more than a meaningless kiss.

"It was nothing," I say directly, meeting his eyes. Tyler meets my gaze and the corners of his mouth turn up slightly. "I wasn't feeling well, Tyler. I ... I'd been stressed out about... about..." Damn, it can't be that hard to tell him. He must have known that we had been having problems for a long time.

"Denver?" he helps me and I nod.

"Yeah, with Denver," I admit reluctantly, "things didn't work out the way they were supposed to."

"Okay," he says, straightening his shoulders as if the words to come require a firm stance. "I'd like to explain myself, if you'll give me the chance. I like you, Sienna."

And there it is - the sentence I definitely didn't want to hear come out of his mouth.

Fuck!

I'm in love with Denver. If Tyler likes me, it would just complicate things unnecessarily. We're friends.

"Tyler, that's nice, but I..." I stammer. I have to let him down. He was at the stadium and saw what happened between Denver and me. "Denver is my boyfriend and..."

He looks at me for a moment and then suddenly bursts out laughing.

What the hell does that mean? Even though I don't want him to have feelings for me, it's still very humiliating.

"I don't want anything from you," he reassures me, holding up his hands. "At least not like that, don't worry. I don't even like blondes."

"Well, thank you," I grumble, but I can't help smiling back at him.

"It was my first party in Lincoln, the guys asked me if I wanted to come," he tells me, smiling at me. "I didn't really know anyone and had barely made any contacts. When I saw you in the garden, I just had to talk to you."

"And stick your tongue down my throat?" I ask with a

chuckle, because in retrospect I can laugh about the situation. I should be relieved that I'm not his type and don't have to worry about him.

Tyler doesn't say anything. Quite the opposite. All color has drained from his face. He's as white as a sheet and before I can say anything I'm pushed aside and Denver slams Tyler against the wall behind us.

His right forearm is pressed against Tyler's throat and I almost scream the image so surreal.

"Is it true, you bum?" he yells. "You stuck your tongue down my girlfriend's throat?"

Jesus. This can't be happening. Denver is going completely crazy. Without hesitation, he hits Tyler, who doesn't take it lying down. He pushes him away, drops his gym bag and swings at Denver's temple. The punch lands and Denver is going to have a nasty black eye. I stand there helplessly watching my boyfriend beat up his buddy over a stupid kiss. They fight violently. But Tyler refuses to be reduced to a victim.

"Stop it," I yell, about to intervene when I'm pulled back.

"Are you out of your mind?" Phoenix yells at me, appearing out of nowhere with Jake. "They're going to punch you in the face."

"But someone has to do something!"

Panicked, I turn around to look at Denver and Tyler, whose faces are now quite battered. It's not just that they're actually friends and couldn't handle this like two grown-ups. It's about a crappy kiss that happened when we weren't even dating. Denver is totally overreacting.

"Darren," Jake's voice suddenly rings out and he looks over at his buddy who has just joined Millie and Joy in the crowd.

Meanwhile, there's a crowd of people, including some of the football players, who could easily separate Denver and Tyler, and no one has the guts to intervene. "Help me before they get really hurt."

Darren drops his gym bag and grabs Denver while Jake grabs Tyler. As you might expect, the two of them fight back as hard as they can. They don't even think about stopping.

"Denver," Darren yells. "Stop it!"

"Let go of me," he retorts, trying to break free. "He was hitting on Sienna behind my back."

I roll my eyes because he just never listens, preferring to jump to conclusions.

"He didn't," I say and Denver looks at me with wide eyes. "He didn't ... hit on me." I don't want to get into it with him right now. "Just listen, please!"

"What?" he asks, and if looks could kill, Tyler and I would both drop dead. Denver is pissed. "You said that..."

When he notices how many people are standing around us, he falls silent. Maybe that's for the best, because we don't have to discuss this in front of the whole college. I suspect that by now just about everyone who happened to be on campus today is standing here. Every single one of them is interested in the quarterback's relationship problems. They'll be talking about us - me - for weeks or months to come. In the end, I'll be the bitch who broke up the football team.

"What's going on?" Coach Flanders' angry voice makes us all jump. He makes his way through the crowd, looking back and forth between Denver and Tyler. "What's going on?"

His presence seems to at least reassure Darren and Jake that Denver and Tyler won't go for each other's throats again. Cautiously they let go of them. But they remain ready in case of another attack - probably by Denver.

"Nothing," Tyler replies, reaching for his gym bag. "Denver's jumping to conclusions."

He snorts, also reaching for his gym bag and shouldering it. His gaze shifts to Coach and then back to me. I look at him pleadingly and hold out my hand, hoping he'll take it and we

191

can work this out at home. But Denver swats it away with his upper arm and disappears in the opposite direction. Jake follows, shaking his head. Darren seems to think for a moment, then follows him as well.

"Nothing to see here," Coach calls in a thunderous voice, and the crowd slowly disperses. He snorts again and looks at me with such an accusatory look that I want to sink into the ground in humiliation. I wonder how much he would have liked to give me a moral lecture about splitting up his team and what I was thinking when I hit on two of his players. Then he turns and disappears.

Still stunned by what has happened in the last few minutes, I pause. None of this would have happened if I had just pushed Tyler away, or if I hadn't lied to Denver when he asked me if there was someone else. This is all my fault.

"What happened?" asks Millie, coming up to us with Joy. "Why were they fighting?"

"I screwed up," I whisper. "I ... I don't know either, but ... but I couldn't tell Denver."

"Tell Denver what?" pokes Phoenix. "The way he freaked out, it must have been really bad. Did you cheat on him?"

I turn and stare at Phoenix. "Are you out of your mind?" I hiss. "I would never do that."

"I'm sorry," she whispers apologetically, immediately avoiding my gaze. "What happened?"

"Come on, let's sit down," Joy says, pointing to a nearby bench. Phoenix puts her arm around me and pulls me behind her while Millie carries my bag.

I plop down on the bench like a wet rag. Phoenix sits on my right, Millie on my left. Joy crouches down in front of the bench. She gently places her hands on my knees.

"When Denver asked me if there was someone else, I said no," I confess to my friends, looking at them. "We were about to make love for the first time and saying anything else would have ruined the moment. You know how jealous Denver is ..."

They nod immediately. After all, they overheard him forbidding any guy in college from asking me out.

"Just before I left Josh's party, I ran into Tyler in the backyard," I continue. "He was new and approached me. We exchanged a few words and then ... then we kissed."

Phoenix, Millie and Joy's eyes widen.

"You kissed Tyler?" asks Joy incredulously, the first to find her voice. I nod and look at her guiltily. I wait for her to make a snide remark, but it doesn't come. Instead, she just stares at me. "Okay ... wow. Who started it?"

"Tyler," I reply. "He kissed me first, but I kissed him back."

"Oh wow," Phoenix remarks. "I didn't even know that."

Of course she didn't, because I didn't tell anyone. It would have only caused problems. I didn't think it was necessary because after that everything worked out between Denver and me. My priorities were elsewhere. I didn't care about the kiss at all.

"It was just a stupid kiss," I continue. "It didn't mean anything ... to us ... to either of us. But Denver completely lost it."

"I have to go," Joy suddenly exclaims, jumping up. My eyes widen and I look at her. What's going on now? I have never seen her like this before. Normally she always has some advice for me in situations like this. Which would probably be that I should give Denver a blowjob and the whole thing will take care of itself. It's not the worst advice. But this behavior is completely out of character for my friend.

"Joy, wait," Phoenix calls and runs after her.

I look at Millie who just shrugs her shoulders.

Sighing, I rest my head on her shoulder and close my eyes. "What's gotten into everyone?" I sigh, "Denver's beat up Tyler, Joy's not giving me any meaningless advice. I don't get it."

Sighing, Millie puts her arm around me and pulls me close. "I don't know," she sighs. "Maybe everyone's starting to freak out because it's getting close to the holidays. Thanksgiving is right around the corner."

I don't think that's it, but I don't disagree with her.

18

- DENVER -

Jake, Darren and I went to our favorite bar on campus because I didn't want to go home to Sienna. I know she's sitting there waiting for me. But I can't talk to her right now.

That's why I asked my mates to keep me company. If I had known it would end in a lecture, I would have stayed away.

"Now calm down!" Jake glares at me, leaving no doubt that he is anything but pleased with my behavior. Darren puts three beers on the table and sits down with us. Wordlessly, he slides one over to me.

"It was just a kiss."

I stare angrily at my best friend and sip my beer. Just a kiss. Don't make me laugh. Acting like my best friend, Tyler is trying to make out with my girlfriend behind my back. Jake can't just brush it off like it was just a kiss. He heard the bum talking to Sienna, too. I'm not an idiot. I saw the way he looked at her. No one, I mean no one, and certainly not someone who calls himself my friend, does that. He can say a lot of things, but the fact is that he's pushing his way into my team, into my group, and trying to wrap my girlfriend around his finger behind my back.

195

That's exactly what Tyler did, but maybe that was his plan. Playing the good friend, finding out my weaknesses and then using them against me to get to Sienna. I never thought he'd be so devious. I liked him from the first day Coach Flanders introduced him to us. We all hit it off and accepted him into our group. I can't believe I was so wrong about him.

"Just a kiss?" I ask, looking at Jake. "How would you feel if someone stuck his tongue down your girlfriend's throat?"

"I don't have a girlfriend and I would listen to her or him, especially if he's my friend. Before I punch him in the mouth on campus."

Annoyed, I avoid Jake's gaze because he's right. I completely overreacted and shouldn't have hit Tyler like that. Especially as I took quite a beating myself and now my temple is burning like fire. The guy's got a pretty good right hand.

"What were you thinking, Denver?" Jake continues.

"I blew up when I saw them together," I reply meekly. "You understand that... don't you?"

To be honest, I don't think Darren and Jake understand. Jake always makes himself scarce when it comes to his love life, let alone relationships. We used to talk about how many girls we'd been with and how they were in bed. For a few months now, those conversations have stopped. As far as I'm concerned, it's none of my best friend's business how I fuck Sienna, what sounds she makes and how well her breasts fit in my hands. She's my girlfriend, it's disgusting. He'll end up getting off on it. Not that I'd put it past Jake, but I can't talk about Sienna like she's one of the countless girls I've been to bed with.

Meanwhile, Jake is still getting it on. So why doesn't he ever say anything about it?

And Darren? Darren shags everything, literally everything that comes his way. Sometimes even several girls in one evening or at the same time. He is a Casanova and lives it to the full. Sometimes I'm not sure he even notices how much he's screwing around. I'm sure he doesn't even realize that there is someone out there who has lost their heart to him. Millie has a crush on Darren, everyone can see that. Everyone except Darren himself. She adores him, but he thinks she's a frigid virgin and would never be interested in her. Since she's Sienna's best friend, I've gotten to know her well over the past few weeks and I like her a lot. Darren doesn't realize how lucky he would be if he finally noticed Millie.

"We didn't hear where or when they kissed," Jake says, and he's right. All I heard was Sienna telling Tyler that he'd stuck his tongue down her throat and I snapped. How horrified she looked at me when the boys finally broke us up. God, she'll never speak to me again. She made me swear to God I would talk to her if something was bothering me. Again, I didn't.

"Denver," Darren admonishes me, and I give him an annoyed look. "You went ballistic and didn't even know what was happening."

"They were kissing, that's all I needed to know," I reply angrily, closing my eyes for a moment before continuing. I have no idea why the following words come out of my mouth, because I'm not usually like this. "Just before we had sex for the first time ... there ... there I asked her if there was someone else. I had to know, and she said no."

Darren groans and takes a sip of his beer. He exchanges glances with Jake as if they have to decide who is going to talk next. Finally, Jake speaks.

"You've been after Sienna ever since she walked into your apartment. At first you just wanted to get her in the sack, then when neither of us were allowed to even look at her, let alone hug her or tease her in a friendly way, we knew you wanted more."

"That has nothing to do with it."

"Of course it does," Darren interjects. "She knew you were jealous and ... and would react the way you did if you found out about the kiss. Sienna's not stupid. She knows you better than you think. Sorry, mate, but you punched our buddy in the face because you overheard a few words. Yes, they kissed, but you don't know when or where. Sienna's smart enough not to rub your nose in it. Especially considering the position you were in when you asked her about it."

"So she lied to me!"

"Denver," Jake growls, "you've fucked just about anyone who's willing, and if Joy and Millie hadn't objected and her friends, you'd have mounted them too. Sienna overheard it all and didn't say a word, at least not that I've heard. And you're totally freaking out over a kiss."

"I never hid anything from her and she told me..."

"I guess you didn't have to when she could hear everything."

"Whose side are you on, anyway?" I go into defense mode because I'm running out of arguments. "Both of you?" I look at Darren, who just shrugs his shoulders. He says nothing, instead taking a sip of his beer.

"We're on your side," Jake says diplomatically. "Sienna's and yours. You love her and she loves you. Don't get mad at me, but the idea that she cheated on you with Tyler is the biggest load of bullshit I've ever heard. That's not who Sienna is. I mean, how many guys did she have sex with before you? One or two?"

I keep quiet, because the longer our conversation goes on, the more I feel like an idiot. But it is eating at me that Tyler and Sienna kissed. I can't wrap my head around it. *I love her.*

It's the first time I've admitted it so clearly. Of course, I've known for a long time that I have stronger feelings for Sienna.

Feelings I've never had for a girl before, but today has shown me that I love her and I'm terrified of losing her. Knowing that there could be another man in her life makes me almost desperate. I don't want to lose her - not another person I love and feel absolutely powerless to stop it. You're always powerless when you lose someone. I know that only too well.

"Hello!" My head jerks up and when I see Tyler, I want to stand up and punch him in the face again. How dare he speak to me? Darren pushes me back into my chair and gives me an annoyed look.

"Don't you dare move," he growls. "You know, I'll take you down with ease."

There is no doubt about it. I'm relieved he's on my team every time he tackles the opposing quarterback to the ground. In practice, he's often put on the other team so he doesn't hurt me. He then takes it out on our rookie quarterback, who always ends up in the physio's chair with a few bruises, even though he wears pads. This season, though, I should be playing with Darren more. In the NFL, I have to deal with much bigger defensive players. Plus, Darren is my friend - he would never hurt me in a tackle. Of course, it's never intentional, but in a real game, with an opponent to stop, it happens faster than in practice with your own quarterback.

I focus on Darren again and give him an annoyed look. Is everyone conspiring against me? Tyler has a beer in his hand and his face looks as bruised as mine. We haven't done each other any favors.

"Can we talk?" He looks at me hopefully, but I brush him off immediately.

"No," I say in a hard voice. "Fuck off."

Tyler sighs and sets his beer down on the table. He pulls out the chair to my right and sits down.

"I told you to fuck off!"

"And you should listen," he retorts, pointing at our faces. "Then we can save ourselves the coach's lecture tomorrow."

Of course, I got the message from Coach Flanders that he wanted to talk to us about it. It's understandable that he's angry because two of his star players are fighting in the middle of the day. If we'd been seriously injured, especially if I'd hurt my right hand, it would have been a disaster for the next few games.

"Listen to him, Denver," Jake intervenes. "For the team and for your relationship."

I snort contemptuously.

"Thanks," Tyler says. "I really mean it."

"Start talking," I demand, wrapping my hands around my beer so I don't hit him again. Tyler is handsome and a girl magnet. I don't even blame Sienna for weakening. Even though it tears me up inside that she kissed him.

"First of all, I don't want anything from Sienna."

"How reassuring," I reply sarcastically. "It was enough to stick your tongue down her throat. I'm not listening to this."

I start to get up and again Darren pushes me back into my chair. This time it doesn't take any more words from my friend to keep me seated.

"You bet you will," Tyler hisses, looking at me angrily. "You've got one hell of a woman. I haven't known you long, but from what I've heard you used to jump from bed to bed before Sienna, or should I say until a few weeks ago, and you didn't give a shit about how she felt. But she loves you, there's no doubt about that. Even if I wanted her, I would never have a chance. For Sienna, there's only you."

I actually have to smile when he says that. Tyler seems to pick up on my emotion and continues. "Now can I keep talking and explain or are you going to continue not listening?"

"Go on," I mutter and take a sip of my beer.

"As you know, I had just transferred from Ohio and didn't know anyone in Lincoln," Tyler tells me. I hope he's not going to tell us his whole life story. "It's not easy coming into a new team and possibly bumping other players from their spots." He looks at Jake, who is also a running back. My best friend has nothing to fear from Tyler. They are both our strongest players at that position and have secured their places in the starting line-up. "I was all the more pleased when you invited me to the party. But I quickly felt like the new kid on the block. That's not an accusation, it's a fact. You have known each other for years and have already found your groups. Now I know I don't have to worry about that, but I've been in a new team before. Back in high school, I didn't make any new friends because they saw me as an enemy who wanted their starting place."

We listen to him in silence. Even though I'd rather he got to the part about Sienna. But the more I listen to Tyler, the more I have to admit that I was completely wrong to get so freaked out.

"I went to the garden and now we're getting to the part you're interested in," he says, looking at me. "There I saw Sienna and approached her. She seemed somehow ... well, lost ... alone and I wanted to cheer her up."

"And you couldn't think of anything better than to kiss her?" I interrupt him. No doubt he was watching her, and then he hit on her when Sienna was alone. Disgusting asshole!

"Denver," Tyler hisses. "Will you listen and shut the fuck up? It's annoying."

I nod and drink my beer instead. Might be better to keep my mouth busy.

"Sienna didn't say anything about being with anyone, and as far as I knew, you two weren't together at the time." He looks around questioningly and we all nod.

"They weren't," Jake agrees. "Go on, please."

"Sienna and I got to talking and then I kissed her."

"So you did," I shout, wanting to jump up again, but I can't even react that quickly, Darren's hand is already on my shoulder. The guy's got reflexes, it's crazy. "You kissed her!"

"I kissed her," he admits, fixing me with his gaze. "And do you know what happened next?"

"What?" I growl, already steaming again because he's stopping me with another pointless question. I want him to finish the story.

"She pushed me away," Tyler says. "She mumbled something about how she couldn't and left. I was confused and followed her. All I remember is her storming out of the house and you, Joy and Millie following her. I left too, before things got out of hand. That's all there is and ever will be between Sienna and me."

We are silent for a moment, drinking our beers. A sigh escapes me. I know it is now up to me to explain myself. I don't know yet if I'm going to apologize to Tyler. He deserved it when I punched him in the face. He could have come to me and told me a lot sooner. Although I have to admit that if the roles were reversed, I probably never would have.

"Sienna and I had a fight the day before," I tell him. "I went a bit overboard. I'd been telling the guys for weeks not to date her - especially the ones on the team. I'm sorry, Tyler. I'm not usually like this, but Sienna... I ... I - she means a lot to me." I can't say I love her in front of my friends before I tell her. It wouldn't be right. "That's why I completely lost my temper and went off on you."

"Let's just forget about it," he says, and I look at him in surprise. "Maybe I shouldn't have cleared it up with her in the campus hallway."

"Hm," I think, not really knowing what to say. "Maybe."

"I just wanted to tell her that the kiss meant nothing to me and that I'm not interested in her," he says with a shrug. "And I'll tell you again, I'm not interested in Sienna."

"Got it." I hold out my hand to Tyler in reconciliation. "Friends? Because I still fucking like you."

"Friends," Tyler agrees and takes my hand. "And I really hope you know how lucky you are to have her, you idiot."

"Actually, he does," Darren grins, massaging my left shoulder. "Sometimes his brain upstairs stops working and it's just the one in his trousers."

I roll my eyes, which makes the guys laugh out loud.

19

-SIENNA-

A few days later

Denver completely overreacted with his jealousy towards Tyler, and when he came home drunk that same night and fell into bed next to me like a drunken corpse, my jaw dropped. Does he really think getting drunk with his mates is the way to go? We had a long talk just before that about how he needs to talk to me. That it's part of a relationship and he's doing the exact opposite. Once again Denver shuts me out to deal with it himself. It's not the same situation as with Madison, but it still hurt me that he didn't talk to me. Even more so when I found out from Jake that Denver had spoken to Tyler the same evening when he went to pick him up for training. I understand that I need to apologize too. I lied to him about seeing another guy. But the fact that he freaked out like that and ignored me afterwards instead of coming home with me to sort it out, I can't forgive him for that either.

It hurts like hell that he'd rather talk to anyone other than me.

Of course, I'm also glad that he went to the bar with Jake and Darren and that they set him straight. I am also glad that he was able to make up with Tyler.

Because apart from that one kiss, that brief moment, there was nothing between Tyler and me. If I'm honest with myself, I've been infatuated with Denver since day one. I even think I love him. All the more reason for me to get an apology and talk to him. According to Phoenix, even his coach has received one.

Phoenix was trying to protect her brother. I wouldn't have expected anything less. Millie tried to mediate, which softened me, but her words didn't make me forgive. She said that Denver was stubborn and preferred to avoid conflict - but that I was still important to him. I agree with her - I know I am important to him. He told me so that night. As well as the fact that he had forgiven me. He could still get that much past his lips. What's the saying? Drunks and little children always tell the truth. As if that wasn't enough, my parents announced that they were coming to spend Thanksgiving with me. Actually, I was going to fly to Montana and try to talk to Clara. I still don't understand why she blocked me. I mean, it was to be expected that we would have different lives at college.

Mrs. Jones, Denver's mom, also wants to have us over for Thanksgiving dinner. So, I put my parents off until Christmas. But that didn't seem to stop them from wanting to visit their little girl and her lovely roommate, Denver. In front of Denver, I only mentioned that they were coming, but didn't give an exact date. By doing so, I've probably caused another argument with him. And rightly so this time. I should have told my parents weeks ago.

I might go mad.

When the doorbell rings, I jump and put down the milk I opened earlier to prepare my parents' meal. I walk to the front door and open it. Joy is standing opposite me, smiling weakly.

She has her black hair tied up in a high braid, with only the blue tips touching her shoulders. She is wearing a thick down jacket, black leggings and UGG boots. She looks unusually timid, as if she's actually afraid I'll send her away.

She hasn't checked in on our girls' chat for a few days and has ignored my private messages. I am all the more surprised to see her here now.

"Hi," she greets me. "Can I come in?"

Ever since Denver went off on Tyler and it became public knowledge that we had kissed, Joy has distanced herself from me. So, I assume her behavior is related to Tyler and the kiss. But it doesn't really make any sense because Tyler's only been in Lincoln for a few weeks.

Of course, I let her in. Joy is still my friend.

"Hi," I say, confident that we can clear up whatever is bothering her by talking. "Sure, come on in. Denver's not here."

I step aside and let her in. Joy takes off her winter jacket and boots and leaves them in the designated place in the hallway. She is wearing a loose-fitting sweater that hangs over her right shoulder, giving a glimpse of her skin, which is tanned even in winter.

"My parents are coming for Thanksgiving," I say. "I'm baking pies. Would you like to come into the kitchen?"

"Sure," she replies and follows me. Joy sits down at the kitchen table while I clear it and look at her. "Do you want something to drink?"

"No," she says, shaking her head. Then she folds her hands together - again, unsteadily by her standards. "Just talk."

"Okay." I join her at the kitchen table. Joy looks at me for a moment. She looks sad. Sadder than I've ever seen her.

"What do you want to talk about?" I finally ask when she says nothing.

"Tyler."

"Tyler?" I ask, raising my eyebrows. Even though I suspected as much. Nothing else had happened to come between us like this. "What about him?"

"Did you really just... kiss?"

Surprised, I looked at her and opened my mouth, only to close it again the next moment. I hadn't expected that question. What does Joy have to do with Tyler? As far as I know, they've known each other for as long as I've known him. Unless they were having sex before I met him at the party. Joy has a very open and casual sex life, I know that. So, I wouldn't be surprised.

"Of course," I say indignantly. "If it wasn't, I would have told you."

"Okay," she says, nodding briefly. "Cool."

I look at her and knit my eyebrows together. There's more, isn't there? Joy would never ignore me for days if she was having casual sex with Tyler. She's far too open about such things.

"Joy," I say in a firm voice. "That's not all, is it? You left without a word when you found out about the kiss. You usually give me some stupid advice that I end up following every time, don't you?"

She actually grins, but immediately nods again.

"Tyler and I... we... we have a history."

My jaw almost drops. I was expecting a lot of things, but not that she and Tyler knew each other.

"We went to high school together until he moved to Ohio with his parents."

"Oh, wow," I groan. "That ... that surprises me. Were you ... in love with him?"

I never thought I would say that word to Joy. I am in love, Phoenix is in love, Millie is in love, but not Joy. She doesn't even know the word, even though it sounds harsh.

"Maybe," she says, and I raise my eyebrows. "Yes, okay, I was in love with him. Very much, but he didn't want me ... not like that ... I don't know." Joy throws her hands up in the air and paces the kitchen. "He was my ... my first."

"Oh!" I look at her in astonishment. "What ... what happened then?"

"I was ... fifteen and ... and it was our last summer together. Tyler went to the same high school as me and we also knew each other through our parents. His dad was a doctor on the army base and my dad worked in the hospital. The badly injured soldiers who couldn't be treated in the barracks were taken to the hospital to see my dad. Tyler and I had known each other for years. That summer was the first time he really paid attention to me. You know how it is with boys who are two years older and ..." I raise my eyebrows. "Well, maybe not. Whatever. I was in love with Tyler and we spent almost every minute together that summer. We slept together just before the new school year started."

Joy presses her lips together and looks up at the ceiling for a moment, as if she can't show any weakness. To be honest, I have never met anyone as distant as her. How badly must Tyler have hurt her? Cautiously, I approach her and reach for her hands to unclench them.

"Joy," I whisper. "It's me... you can cry if you want."

"We made love," she whispers, "and the next morning he was gone. I thought... I thought he went to get breakfast, we... we were at my parents' boathouse, but Tyler didn't come back. I went home and my mom told me that his family had moved to Ohio. The world just came crashing down on me. Tyler was ... he was just using me to ... to fuck me."

"Oh, Joy!" I pull her into my arms and stroke her back. "I'm so sorry."

I'm honestly appalled by Tyler. I never thought he was capable of something like that. He never seemed like the asshole he apparently is.

"And here he is," she sniffs, "five years later, acting like everything's fine. At first, he didn't even recognize me... and... and he's making out with one of my best friends. You and I... we... we're the exact opposite." I nod slowly. "Apparently, you're his type. I got my hopes up for nothing."

"No," I say firmly, pulling away from her. "He told me he doesn't like blondes."

"What?" she asks, looking at me in confusion. "He doesn't like... blondes?"

"No," I repeat. "He doesn't. I don't know who he's into or what type he prefers. So, when did he notice you?"

Joy sighs and leans against the kitchen table.

"A few days after the party, he came up to me and asked if it was really me," she says, grinning at my surprise. "The last time we saw each other, my hair was still black, not blue, I wasn't wearing as much make-up, and I was dressed differently. Tyler didn't recognize me."

"Did you talk about it?" I probe carefully.

"No," Joy says. "And we're not going to. It's done and we can't undo it. Nor will Tyler want to talk about the fact that he stole my virginity."

"Stole?" I ask. "Oh, Joy... do you really think he did, or are you just mad at him?"

"Of course I'm mad at him," she hisses and I have to laugh. I'm only laughing because now she's back to the Joy I know and I can honestly deal with her better than the lost creature she was for the last few minutes. Seeing her hurt like that was and still is damn unusual. On the other hand, it's nice to know that even someone as confident as Joy has weaknesses. But I would never have thought it would be Tyler Connor.

"You're so confident and experienced with boys ... aren't you?" I ask, fearing for a second that she was only pretending to be a man-eating vamp.

210

"Of course I am," she says, and once again the Joy we all know comes out. Confident, experienced and always ready with a witty remark. "A few weeks after Tyler, I met Anthony, my first boyfriend. I was with him for three years. We still get on well, but we both wanted to go to college unattached. After that, I went for it. Believe me, I've tested, checked and approved all the advice I give you."

"That's reassuring," I chuckle. "But seriously, Joy. Are you still in love with Tyler?"

"No," she says firmly. I believe her too. "You... you don't know what it's like; at least I hope you don't. It was my first time, I was scared and it hurt. Tyler was careful, but it was still uncomfortable." I nod in understanding. "We fell asleep and the next morning he was gone. There was nothing to remind me he was there except the used condom and then he moved to Ohio. He should have told me."

"I understand that," I agree. "Talk to him and sort it out. Tyler will give you answers."

"We'll see," she says, avoiding my gaze. I know she won't talk to him about it. But that is for her to decide. If she doesn't want to talk, that's her decision. "I just wanted to tell you because I don't want it to come between us. I'm not angry with you, Sienna. In fact, I don't even care... I mean, no, I don't. But I'd be just as pissed if he'd made out with Phoenix or Millie."

"It's okay," I say and hug her. Joy squeezes me and I feel the relief flood through both of us as we hold each other. Something like this shouldn't come between us. Especially when it meant so little, especially to Tyler and me. "Thanks for telling me and for being a little bit romantic."

"Oh, please!" She laughs. "Don't you dare tell anyone! My reputation..."

"I get it," I chuckle, pretending to lock my mouth and

throw away the key. A silly child's oath, but it has its validity. "No one will find out from me."

"Thank you." She grins. "How are things going with Denver?"

I sigh and pull away from her.

"Instead of coming home to talk to me a few days ago, he went to a bar with Darren, Jake and Tyler and got drunk."

"With Tyler?" Joy asks, stunned, and I nod.

"Yes, with Tyler." I can't help laughing. "He listened to him, he got to explain himself, but he didn't come home. He says he's not mad at me anymore, but that's not what's bothering me. Denver hates confronting me about things. It was the same when Madison was with us. He shuts me out and doesn't understand that he can share his worries with me. I'm his girlfriend.

I shake my head and blink my tears away. I don't want to cry about it anymore, but now my feelings are overwhelming me.

"I know I messed up too," I continue and look at Joy. "I should have told him I kissed Tyler. But as they became better and better friends and ... and we were finally together, I was afraid I would lose him over it. He was so jealous before we got together. How would he have reacted if I told him I had kissed his friend?"

"I understand, Sienna," Joy says, giving me a hug. "But I also understand Denver. You didn't cheat on him, but it feels like it to him."

"Of course it does," I sigh. "Why does he talk to everyone - even Coach Flanders - but not me?"

"He had to talk to the coach to avoid suspension and you know it." Sullenly, I press my lips together and nod. Of course, I know. And a suspension over this is the last thing we need right now. "Denver is stubborn and, from what Phoenix once told me, especially when it comes to her father's death, he's also pretty quick to react when it involves people he cares about."

"I know," I say quietly. "I just wish he would include me more and talk to me."

"He did come home that night, didn't he?"

"Yes, of course," I reply, running my fingers through my hair. "He got in really late that night, after I had waited for hours trying to reach him. His battery was dead. Jake and Darren didn't answer, either. He could barely speak that night. He was completely drunk and fell into bed next to me. Just before he fell asleep, he mumbled that he forgave me for the kiss. The next morning, we had a terrible argument, I went back to my old room and we haven't spoken since. I can't get through to him. He hurt me, not I him."

"Don't you think you're making it easy on yourself?" Joy raises her eyebrows and I pull a face. Lips pressed tightly together, arms crossed across my chest, I look at her. "You've both made mistakes, obviously, but if you know what he's like... why don't you reach out to him?"

"Are you serious?" Horrified, I look at Joy. "He's..."

"Denver hasn't lied to you about his intentions, Sienna!" I flinch at her caustic tone. "Did he fu- have sex with all those girls? Yes. Did he lay it all out in front of you? Yes. I understand that you're angry with him because he didn't want to talk to you about it, but went out for a drink instead. You wouldn't do that, of course, but you knowingly lied to him."

"I just didn't want to ruin anything," I snort. "Things were finally going well between us. The kiss could have..."

"It did, and maybe worse," she cuts me off. "What did you hope to gain from a discussion that night? Don't you think Denver made a choice - albeit the wrong one - when he didn't come home? He let Jake and Darren calm him down instead of coming home and letting your argument boil over."

"He forgave Tyler and..."

"Sienna, please!" Joy runs her fingers over her forehead and looks at me admonishingly. "He didn't make the right choice that night, but he was here the next morning. He wanted to talk and you went at him again. You did, didn't you?"

"Maybe," I mutter and my friend rolls her eyes. "Yeah, okay, he came into the kitchen and wanted to talk. I freaked out and blamed him. Denver finally just waved it off and left."

"And you're surprised he doesn't want to talk?" Joy raises her eyebrows and shakes her head. "He doesn't stand a chance if you keep telling him off like a stupid schoolboy. When it should have been up to you to explain yourself and apologize. More than Denver."

I let Joy's statement sink in and sit down on the kitchen chair behind me. She's not wrong that Denver avoided a much worse confrontation between us that night. Jake and Darren seem to have calmed him down. The next morning, I freaked out without even giving him a chance to explain. Even though I was the one who screwed up.

"Oh, man." That's all I could bring myself to say. "I didn't mean to."

"I know you didn't." Joy smiles at me and squeezes my hand. "You're going to be okay."

"I hope so," I sigh and look at Joy with big eyes. "And to top it off, my parents are coming tomorrow."

Right now, I don't know what's more upsetting. The fight with my boyfriend or the visit from my parents, who still don't know that Denver is Denver and not Phoenix. I'm such a mess.

"They think Phoenix is Denver and Denver is Phoenix," I add meekly.

"You're not serious?" Joy starts to laugh out loud. "And they don't know you're sleeping with one of them."

"You're back," I exclaim, jumping up and wrapping my

arms around her. Grinning, I plant a kiss on her cheek. "I missed this."

Joy returns the hug. "It's going to be okay," she whispers into my ear. "He loves you. And your parents will get over it, too."

I say nothing and grin to myself.

I hope so.

20

-SIENNA-

Joy has gone home and I still haven't fully digested the conversation. That she was in love with Tyler really took me by surprise. It's not like Joy to be in a situation like that. She has always seemed so tough and confident that I would never believe a guy could have such an effect on her, even years later. I'm sorry that her first time and her first crush were such a disappointment for her. Maybe that explains her current attitude towards life. Why she is the way she is and why she is so resistant to falling in love and having a real relationship.

I still like Tyler and the more I think about it, the more I think they are a good match. They seem to have a lot in common, even if they don't realize it at the moment.

I shake off the thoughts of Tyler and Joy and focus on my own problems instead. I have enough of them. Denver said goodbye to me this morning. There is silence between us. Living in silence with each other is almost more unbearable than fighting. The talk with Joy did me good, although she was very hard on me. Millie probably wanted to say the same thing to me, but her polite manner prevented her from doing so. I also made mistakes and should have given Denver a chance to explain himself the next morning. The fact that he left after I hurled accusations at him again was to be expected. He has a late practice today and I hope when he returns we can finally talk.

I put the last of the baking utensils back in the drawer, set the timer on the oven, and walk into the living room just as the front door opens. Denver enters holding a huge bouquet of flowers and smiles at me.

"Hi," he says carefully. I immediately return the smile. It's the first time he's approached me in days, and it does my battered heart a world of good. It skips a beat when I realize the flowers must be for me and part of his apology. Denver kicks the front door shut with his foot and throws his gym bag on the floor. He sets the flowers on it and I don't take my eyes off him for a second. After taking off his shoes and jacket and putting them on the coat rack and in the shoe closet, he reaches for the flowers again and walks toward me.

"Hey," he greets me again, looking uncertain as he stops right in front of me. "Can we talk?"

I look at him for a moment, squinting again at the beautiful flowers in his hand. Then I nod, but say nothing.

"Thanks," he says, taking a deep breath. "I'm an idiot, no, that doesn't really cover it ... I ... I'm a complete idiot."

I grin at him and bite my lip.

"I'd sign off on that."

"Sienna," he whispers and reaches for my hand, but I pull it away. "Okay, that wasn't right. What I did a few days ago, my lashing out at Tyler, that... I shouldn't have done that."

"It's not about that anymore," I say, turning on my heel. Does he really think I'm still mad about the fight? It's about everything that happened - or didn't happen - between us after that.

218

"Sienna," he calls after me, and the rustle of paper around the flowers reaches my ear. He must have put them down. "Wait, please! Can you just give me a chance and listen? What else do I have to do to get your attention?"

He grabs my wrist and turns me around. I stare at him and lift my head to meet his eyes. Denver looks sad, and his eyes don't have the usual slight arrogance and cockiness that I know and kind of love about him. Instead, he is hurt and at a loss.

"I want to apologize and start over," he says, loosening his grip on my wrist. "Please listen to me."

"Okay," I say quietly, letting him pull me to the sofa. We sit down together and Denver closes his eyes before continuing. He seems tired and at a loss as to how things could have gone so completely wrong between us again. I want to snuggle up to him, but something inside me resists meeting him halfway.

"I felt like I'd been hit over the head when I heard you two had kissed. My fuse blew. I was afraid I was going to lose you and ... and I lost it. Especially since Tyler is my friend."

He lets go of my wrist to rest his forearms on his thighs and intertwine his fingers. I immediately miss the physical contact and it's like he's putting up a wall between us. An uncomfortable shiver runs down my spine. I remind myself not to call him on it, but to give him his space.

"I know all the things I've done ... with other girls, but ..." He takes a deep breath. "It was never with any of your friends, Sienna."

"Tyler and I kissed-"

"It's not about the kiss," he snaps at me, immediately forming his lips into a silent "sorry."

"It's about what happened before. He's my friend and I asked you if there was someone else. You said no."

"I know." Guiltily, I bite my lip. "And I'm sorry. But I

pushed him away because I was thinking of you. That kiss didn't mean anything." Carefully, I reach out and place my left hand on top of his. I wait to see if he pulls away, but he doesn't. Relief and hope flood my body. "Denver, I... I told you there was no one else because there was no one serious. We were going to make love for the first time ... how would you have reacted to such a confession at that moment? I'm so sorry that I didn't tell you afterwards. I messed up and I ... I wish I can take it back. But I can't."

A tear breaks out of the corner of my eye and runs down my cheek to my lips. The salty taste makes my mouth curl. Denver looks at me.

"It's okay," he says, squeezing my hand. It's a small gesture, but it means a lot to me. "I should have controlled myself ... and ... and not punched Tyler in the face. I'm so sorry, baby."

"You never should have hit Tyler like that," I correct him.

Denver leans in and I feel his breath on my face. "I'm sorry, Sienna," he whispers. "For the way I acted. For getting drunk with the guys instead of coming home when all I could think about was you."

My lips curve into a smile.

"I know," he says. "And all I can say is I'm sorry. So incredibly sorry, but I ... I'm not good at this. I was afraid to confront you. Here." He reaches for the flowers and holds them out to me. "These are for you. It's not much, but my dad used to get my mom flowers when he messed up. And when he came home after months on the job."

He tries to smile at me but doesn't quite manage it. I take the flowers from him and smell them. They smell heavenly. Smiling, I put them back on the table and look at him.

"Denver," I whisper and lean toward him. I can only imagine how much hope he has put into this gesture, how much he looked up to his father. He misses him, more than he would ever admit. I think he wants a relationship similar to the one his parents had and hopes that using the same gestures his father used will have the same effect on me as it did on his mother. I place my hand on his cheek and caress it. "They're beautiful."

"You really like them?" He looks at me in awe.

"Of course I like them - even if they were weeds," I whisper. "It's the gesture that counts, Denver. You put some thought into it."

"I ... I-" He falters. "I love you."

My heart stops for a moment, only to explode in my chest the next. Those three words turn my world upside down. *I love you.* Denver looks at me unblinkingly, his lips pressed tightly together as if he's holding back, giving me time to process his confession. And I do. I never expected his feelings for me to be so strong. Especially after we fought so hard again.

Fresh tears run down my cheeks because the whole situation has thrown me for a loop. I always thought it would be very romantic. After a movie or one of his good games. When we are pumped up on adrenaline and feeling good, but not when we are busy making up. I even expected it from Denver after make-up sex. I am really surprised by this situation. Still, the words hit home. I love him too.

"You haven't said anything," Denver's brittle voice sounds, and I look up. I didn't realize I'd been silent for so long. "You... you don't feel the same way about me, do you?"

Panic spreads across his eyes and his breathing accelerates. His chest rises and falls violently.

"What?" I gasp. "No... I, of course, feel the same way about you."

I shake my head and close my eyes for a moment. I think I've completely ruined his declaration of love. Of course, he is annoyed by my reaction. But when you don't expect it, you have to let it sink in.

I love Denver.

I feel his hand on my cheek and look up at him. He gently brushes away my tears and smiles - albeit pained.

"I love you too," I breathe, unable to stop myself from sobbing. "Of course I love you too."

Denver exhales audibly and his shoulders slump. The relief that floods his body is clear to see. I place my left hand on his cheek. His stubble scratches my palm.

"Hmm," he whispers, moving even closer. "Can I finally kiss you again?" I chuckle and lean into him. The butterflies in my stomach come alive again and all I can manage is a nod.

Denver wastes no time in pressing his mouth to mine. Sighing, I lean into the kiss. I'm so happy to have him back. Overjoyed, I snuggle up against him. My tongue brushes his lips and Denver opens them. With a quick movement, he lifts me up and pulls me astride his lap.

Our tongues begin an erotic game - teasing, entwining, tantalizing each other. We both try to get the upper hand in the kiss until I pull away from him. Denver looks at me with wide eyes as I stand up and take a step back. Which isn't easy considering the coffee table is right up against my calves.

Denver doesn't take his eyes off me as I reach for the hem of my sweater and pull it over my head. I don't know where I'm getting this courage from, but going days without sex seems to have taken its toll on me.

The sweater falls to the floor and Denver looks at me intently. He immediately licks his lips and glances down my body. He desires me, I can feel it. And I desire him as well, because I'm not only madly in love with him, but also damn hot for him.

"Do you like what you see?" I rock my hips back and forth as I hook my thumbs into the waistband of my leggings and slowly slide them down. The more skin I expose, the greedier his gaze becomes. Without Denver, as well as Joy and Phoenix, I would never have become this. My Montana self would never have stood here and undressed in front of him. I was a young, inexperienced girl who had had some bad sex - compared to now. My Lincoln self, on the other hand, is confident. But there is one thing I haven't done yet. I look at Denver's crotch. The bulge is visible despite his sweatpants and boxers. I've seen his penis enough times that what I'm about to do shouldn't intimidate me. But it does because I've never had it in my mouth before. My experience with blowjobs is lousy. I've only done it once and it went completely wrong. My ex-boyfriend had no regard for me and shoved it in my mouth way too hard. So much so that he touched my uvula without any problem. To make matters worse, he had my ponytail wrapped around his hand so I couldn't pull back. I coughed my guts out afterwards and managed, with a lot of effort, not to puke in front of him. I never tried it again. The panic that gripped me every time I even thought about my partner ruthlessly ramming his cock down my throat was just too great.

I pull my leggings off my legs and toss them onto my sweater next to me. My socks follow. Then I kneel down between his legs and look up at him.

Denver continues to watch me with lustful eyes as I stroke my thighs and look up at him. "You don't have to do this," he whispers and puts his hand on my cheek. He strokes it gently with his thumb. "You know that, right?"

"But I want to," I reply. "I ... I want to try."

"Okay," Denver whispers and gives me an irresistible smile. This gives me another boost of confidence and makes the memories of my past experiences disappear. My hands run down his thighs to the waistband of his pants. Denver stands and pulls them down along with his socks and boxers. When he's finished kicking them to my clothes, he sits back down and looks at me lovingly. I return the look and then look down at his cock. It hasn't swelled to its full size yet, I can tell. I take a deep breath and gently close my hand around it. Denver moans and closes his eyes. Smiling, I look at him as I move my hand up and down. His skin is warm and soft. I feel him continue to swell and rise to his full height.

After a few minutes of caressing him with my hand, I lean forward and lick the small notch in his glans with the tip of my tongue. Denver moans loudly and I repeat what I'm doing. "Take it in your mouth," he instructs me impatiently. "Please."

I look up at him and my heart starts to beat faster. The moment I've been putting off for so long has arrived. Uncertainty spreads through me and I hesitate. Denver doesn't miss my change of heart and gently strokes my cheek with his fingers. "Trust me, Sienna. It's okay, you can't go wrong."

"I know," I reply. "It's just... I ... I've only done this once before and ... and it was a disaster."

My cheeks glow with shame, but he smiles lovingly at me. Denver leans over and plants a kiss on my lips, probably tasting himself. Just like I've done a few times after he's spoiled me.

"You can't go wrong," he repeats his words, looking at me lovingly. "If you don't want to and you don't like it..."

Sucking him off can't be that hard - Phoenix and Joy can handle sucking someone off. I gather my courage and slide my mouth over his head. Denver moans again. But before I let him slide any deeper, I look up at him again. "Please keep your hands where they are," I say with a pounding heart. I can only imagine how much he'd like to run his hand through my hair, to be in control. The fact that he's the more active, dominant party during sex doesn't bother me. But with this blowjob, I need to be in complete control. "And don't push my head down."

"Promise." Denver looks down at me, a smile on his lips.

I turn back to his erection, now swollen to its full size. Then I lower my mouth back to his cock and begin to move it forward. Inch by inch I take his penis deeper into my mouth. It's thicker and longer than my ex-boyfriend's penis.

"Oh baby," Denver moans as I release it and lick along its length before taking it back into my mouth. "Suck my cock, Sienna, like you..."

I comply with his request and wrap my lips around his cock as he asks. Denver moans louder and harder. Out of the corner of my eye, I see how hard it is for him not to bury his hand in my hair and take control of the blowjob. I'm trying harder than I ever thought possible, and I'm grateful that he's so patient with me. It's not something I take for granted, especially with a guy who has so much sexual experience. He will have had more than a few blowjobs in his life. Certainly better than mine.

I let Denver's cock slide deeper into my mouth and then I feel the gag reflex. My fingers claw harder into his thighs and I notice the first tears in the corners of my eyes, but I want to do it. For him and for us. Denver moans, and when I pull away again and move my head forward, his pelvis jerks. I tear my eyes open, tears running down my cheeks, and all I can feel is that his shaft has penetrated my mouth so deeply that I'm gagging. In addition, his hand is now on the back of my head. However, he does not push his fingers into my hair, as I expected, so that he can use my mouth as he pleases, but instead he gently strokes it. As if he wants to calm me down and it helps.

"Breathe through your nose," he presses, and I do, "That's right, and ignore your gag reflex. I'm going to pull back a little and push again, okay?"

A strained "hm" escapes my lips and I concentrate on my

breathing. Denver pulls his pelvis back and I keep breathing through my nose. In and out. Then he pushes forward again. He repeats this a few times.

"You're doing great, baby. Do you want to swallow my cum?"

Disgust spreads through me and I have to force myself not to stop. While I didn't swallow my ex-boyfriend's cum, he did come shortly after I pulled my head back, hitting my face as well as my breasts. This made the blowjob experience even worse for me because not only did I feel sick from the gagging, but I also felt dirty from his cum.

I shake my head and Denver pulls his shaft out of my mouth. I take a deep breath and look up at him. Denver grabs my hands and pulls me onto his lap. I moan as his hardness rubs over my pussy. "You were amazing," he whispers, planting a kiss on my lips. "Did you like it?"

Denver's fingertips brush tenderly over my upper arms and he looks into my eyes.

"Yes," I whisper. "Thanks for giving me time and ... and a little food for thought at the end."

I wink at him at the double meaning of my statement, which makes him laugh. "Sienna Gardner, who the hell turned you into a depraved hot lady?"

Chuckling, I throw my head back before wrapping my arms around his neck and pressing my mouth to his. "I love you, Denver. And either we do it right now, right here, or you take me to the bedroom."

I add a wicked note to my voice and it works. His penis gets harder again, partly because I'm gyrating my pelvis. My hands move over his chest, sliding under his sweater to feel his bare skin under my fingertips. Tracing a trail of kisses from his lips to his ear, I lean forward and run the tip of my tongue over the shell of his ear. He moans again.

"Tell me where you want it!"

Surprised at myself, I push even closer to him. My fingernails run over his six-pack and I kiss his neck.

"Where do you want it, baby?" Denver slides his hand between my legs and presses the heel of his hand against my core.

"Oh," I gasp, and a moan escapes me as he pushes the web of my panties aside and runs his finger through my cleft.

"I vote we do it right here."

"Right here," I confirm.

Denver pushes me off him to free me from my briefs and takes off his sweater himself. I free myself of my bra. Then I climb back onto his lap.

His hands run down my hips to my breasts. He pushes them up and leans forward. His mouth runs over my pale skin and takes my nipples, one by one, into his mouth.

"Without a condom?" he wants to know because we've never done it before. There's always been a layer of latex between us, but I've been on the pill for over a month. Contraception is guaranteed. When I was prescribed the pill, my gynecologist checked me out and I am - as I expected - healthy. Denver is also constantly tested because of football.

"Yes," I confirm. "Without a condom."

Relieved that neither of us has to go to the bedroom to get a condom, he grins at me. He positions his tip at my entrance and presses down on my pelvis.

For the next few minutes, I feel like I'm in a frenzy. Denver is more than willing to give me everything. My foreplay has done a good job because it doesn't take long for him to start twitching under me. "Fuck," he moans and leans back. "I ... I'm already coming."

"Hold on," I gasp, reaching between us to bring myself to a climax as well. I desperately want to come with him.

"Fuck, Sienna." Denver's penis starts to twitch inside me.

227

"How can you do this to yourself when I'm already at the edge?"

I have to laugh and press my lips to his again. I claw my left hand into his neck while stimulating myself with my right. My pelvis bobs up and down. This is definitely the best sex I have ever had. I love it when he gives me lengthy foreplay and then makes prolonged love to me, but this is just as good.

"I'm ready," I gasp a few minutes later, my body rising above him. "Denver!"

He moans too, jamming his cock into me with one last violent thrust and orgasming loudly. That finally pushes me over the edge. My body collapses forward and I lean my forehead against his. Denver's hands run down my sweaty back and I feel him cum inside me.

"Wow," I gasp. "That's how we're going to do it from now on."

"Whatever you want," Denver replies and pulls out of me. His cum runs out of me and down my legs. I look at him a little startled, which makes him grin. He presses his lips to mine and pulls me against him. "Give me a few minutes and we'll continue."

I shake my head in amusement and cuddle up to him.

21

- DENVER -

The next morning, I am awakened by the sun shining through the window into Sienna's room. We forgot to close the curtains last night and now it's payback time. I blink and have to adjust to the brightness. Grinning, I turn to my still sleeping girlfriend.

She is lying on her side, her face turned towards me. Carefully, I reach out so as not to wake her and brush a single strand of hair behind her ear. Her skin is velvety soft. Sienna purses her lips and wrinkles her nose, looking incredibly cute. But she continues to sleep as if nothing has happened. Which I can understand - after all, we made love until the wee hours of the morning. After the make-up sex in the living room, we showered and went to her room. There I thanked her at length for the wonderful blowjob. Sienna was insecure and I noticed how difficult it was for her to take my cock in her mouth. It was incredible for me to feel her like that and I'm glad she was able to overcome her fear. I would have understood if she had stopped. But that wouldn't have been like Sienna. When she sets her mind to something, she wants to see it through. The first time without a condom was also a new experience for both of us. I've never done it without a rubber before. Sharing that experience with Sienna brought us even closer. Still, the times after that we didn't do it without the extra protection. Neither of us wants a baby. Even though the pill is very safe, we didn't want to rely on just one form of contraception at this time - Sienna at the beginning of her studies and me in the penultimate and decisive phase of my future.

Without waking her, I pull back the covers and get out of bed. Sienna mumbles something but remains in slumber land. She turns over on her side and smacks her lips in her sleep.

With a smile on my face, I leave her room naked and go to the bathroom to shower and freshen up. I am so relieved that I was able to break the ice of the last few days with the flowers and my apology. After all the silence, I was afraid I had blown it. When she came at me again, the morning after I got drunk with the guys, accusing me of not opening up to her and not caring enough to talk to her, I shut down. There is no other way to put it. Something inside of me froze and wouldn't let Sienna get close to me. I didn't want to be blamed for any-thing. Until I realized that if I didn't reach out to her, we'd be living separate lives for days, weeks, maybe months to come. And I really missed her. It was terrible not to talk to her, not to hold her, not to kiss her. To go to bed at night without pulling her to me, and to have breakfast in the morning without telling her about my day and asking about hers. So, I buckled down and got flowers.

Darren and Jake said that even with flowers I wouldn't have a chance with Sienna. But I wouldn't listen. Besides, it always worked for Dad. Mom didn't forgive him right away, even with flowers - which I expect with Sienna - but she was more for-giving. Then they usually talked and made up. It was the same with Sienna and me.

I haven't introduced her to my mom and John yet. I don't get along with him very well, and even though Mom is trying, our relationship has suffered more and more. When Mom introduced us to him, she, Phoenix, and Madison had just finished family therapy, which I had refused to go to. Suddenly having a new man by her side, after she had been seeing a psychiatrist on a regular basis, threw me for a loop. It was clear to me that John was taking advantage of my mother's grief and sneaking up on her through my sisters. I have since realized that this is total bullshit.

I still find it incredibly hard to give him a chance, even though he has proven time and time again that he loves mom and us. He treats Madison as his own daughter. He is always there for her, driving her everywhere and spending time with her whenever he can. John is a real estate agent and travels a lot. He is also always nice to Phoenix and they have a very good relationship. I would even say that he will walk Madison down the aisle when she gets married. He has taken on the role of father. I'm hesitant to make that statement about Phoenix, but I'm sure about Madison. John doesn't have any children of his own, so it's all the more remarkable how much he enjoys family life with us. He is divorced and also from Chicago. Until he gave up on me six months ago, he always accompanied my mom to the stadium, even though I made it very clear to him more than once that I didn't want him there. That he shouldn't be there next to my mom, cheering me on like he was somebody important - like he was my father. On top of that, he always checked on me - I'm sure he still does - and whenever he was needed, he was there. He never made me feel like I wasn't part of the family.

Since my mom invited Sienna and me for Thanksgiving dinner, she will be meeting my girlfriend soon. I'm really excited about this and I think they're going to get along really well. Sienna is the first girl I'm going to officially introduce at home. I have to admit that makes me more nervous than I'd like to admit. Since none of my friends are in committed relationships either, I can't even ask them for advice.

I also want to make an appointment to go to the Army Cemetery in Chicago to visit Dad's grave with Sienna. It's important to me. I would have liked to introduce her to him - properly - and tell him that I think she is the one for me. I love Sienna the way he loved Mom, and I'm sure she will walk with me on my path. Just like Mom did with Dad. I really hope she will join me in a year and a half when I find my NFL club.

I'm in a good mood this morning and I don't want to ruin it by thinking about my dad. He's not coming back - ever - and I'm finally coming to terms with that after five years. That's what Mom, Madison and Phoenix have done.

John will never take his place and he knows it. He makes Mom happy and that should be the most important thing. None of us want her to be alone for the rest of her life.

Sighing, I step out of the shower, dry off and grab a fresh pair of boxers from the bathroom shelf. Sienna thought it made sense to put underwear there for me, because otherwise, she said, I'd be walking around the apartment naked all the time. After putting on a pair of shorts and a t-shirt in my room, I go to the kitchen to make breakfast for us.

Before I get to the kitchen, the doorbell rings and I furrow my brow. It's not even ten in the morning and we already have visitors? If it's Darren and Jake, I'm going to rip their balls off.

I open the door and feel like slamming it again. Sienna's parents are standing in front of me, grinning at me. Way, way back in my head I remember my girlfriend mentioning that they were coming to visit us. And even further back in my mind is the knowledge that they don't know about us yet and still think I'm my sister. Which pisses me off, but Sienna didn't know how to tell them. Coming clean would have been the right thing to do and would have saved us a lot of trouble now. Especially me, because I'd like to formally introduce myself to my future in-laws.

"Mrs. Gardner, Mr. Gardner," I stammer. "Well, this... this is a... surprise?"

Jesus, what am I supposed to say? Sienna is putting me in an impossible position. Especially as her mother glances down my body, leaving no doubt that she can't understand why I'm standing in front of her at this hour in shorts and a t-shirt.

"Good morning, Phoenix," Mrs. Gardner greets me, and Mr. Gardner pats me on the shoulder as I let them in.

"Sienna's still sleeping."

"And what are you doing here?" her curious mother wants to know immediately. I'd like to answer that I fucked her daughter into nirvana last night, but I think she'd pass out.

"I slept in Phoe-Denver's room because ... because we have water damage in our shared apartment and ... and Denver is out of the country right now." I feel so clueless, and when Mrs. Gardner's eyebrows furrow, I don't know if she's buying it. Mr. Gardner certainly doesn't, as he grins at me, amused and knowing at the same time.

We weren't together the last time they visited, but his reaction isn't what I expected. "We brought breakfast," he tells me, putting his hand on his wife's shoulder. "Phoenix should wake Sienna, and we-"

"I can wake Sienna!" Mrs. Gardner looks at me, completely flustered. Her eyes sparkle, and I can't blame her for being eager to see her daughter again. Still, there's no way she can wake Sienna. The clothes we took off in the living room yesterday are still in her room, all of them, and I'm sure she can't handle a trash can full of used condoms.

"I'll take care of it," I say. "You can go ahead into the kitchen."

Mrs. Gardner starts to object again, but Mr. Gardner pulls his wife behind him. I pause for a moment and take a deep breath before I move to Sienna's room. At least we were smart enough to use her bed; otherwise this would be even weirder.

I enter the room and walk over to the bed. She is still sleeping peacefully and I am reluctant to wake her.

"Sienna," I whisper. "Wake up."

Gently, I stroke her cheek first, and when she doesn't stir, I shake her shoulder until she opens her eyes, her lids fluttering. "Morning." Her voice is hoarse and impossibly sexy. Slowly, she begins to move, sitting up so that the blanket slides off her body. As she does, I get a perfect view of her gorgeous breasts, which I want to pounce on again. I could swear that her nipples are still tender and would immediately stand erect if I touched them. "Are you coming back to bed?"

Sienna pulls me toward her by the hem of my shirt and forces me to bend over her. I'd love nothing more than to get back into bed with her, but her parents are waiting for us in the kitchen. "I'm afraid not," I reply, and she pushes her lower lip forward. I give her a kiss and pull away completely, "Your parents are here."

Sienna's eyes pop open and she instantly goes white as a sheet.

"Shit," she exclaims and jumps out of bed. It takes her a moment to realize she's completely naked. I clench my right fist in front of my mouth to keep from bursting out laughing. Her face is priceless.

"Don't laugh," she hisses, "you'd better distract them until I get dressed."

I take a step towards her and pull her to me. Wrapping my arms around her, I press her body against mine and put my hands on her sexy ass.

"And if I don't?" I ask with a knitted brow and kiss her.

Sienna kisses me back and wraps her arms around my neck. Smiling, I look at her and stroke her butt. "Are they going to kick me out?"

"You think this is funny?" she snarls and I shake my head.

"No," I say seriously, pushing her off me as I find a pair of pants. "Because by now you should have told them that I'm Denver and that I'm your boyfriend, too. It's not funny at all."

"I know..." Sienna is now the one who wraps her arms around me from behind and presses her body against mine. She stands on her tiptoes to plant a kiss on the back of my neck. Sighing, I give in and intertwine our fingers, resting on my stomach. We stand there for a moment. "I'll tell them. Don't be mad."

"I'm not mad," I answer, turning to face her. "Nor disappointed, as you women are so fond of saying."

"Are we?" Immediately her eyebrows shoot up and she looks at me questioningly.

"You are," I grin and kiss her again. Then I pull away and give her a smack on the bottom. Sienna yelps, which makes me roll my eyes. It wasn't that hard. "Go take a shower and put some clothes on. You smell like me and sex."

She immediately turns bright red, which makes me want to pull her against me again, even though we don't have time for these games.

Fuck, her parents are sitting in our kitchen about to have breakfast with her and the only thing I can think about is fucking her and slapping her ass again.

"I would love to take you back to bed," I murmur to her while my mouth is on her neck and my hands are massaging her ass. "And then I'd spoil you and fuck the shit out of you."

"Sounds tempting," she replies, "We could be quiet."

I abruptly pull away from Sienna and look at her in mock shock.

"If there's one thing I don't want, it's quiet sex with you."

"Neither do I." She laughs brightly, warming my heart. Sienna has me by the balls more than I ever want to admit.

"I'll distract them until then," I decide, pulling away from her to finally leave the room. She nods at me with a smile and I finally leave her room.

In the hallway I can hear her parents talking in the kitchen. Her mother is talking excitedly about how she's not sure if she should have packed some food and homemade pies. Her voice is high, almost a little too high. Her father, on the other hand, seems relaxed and asks when I'll be back.

I enter the kitchen and find Mrs. Gardner standing at the counter, pulling a full pot of coffee from the coffeemaker. "Coffee, Phoenix?" I nod and sit down beside her husband.

"Did you find everything?" I ask when I see that the table is set as well.

"Of course," Sienna's mother says proudly, smiling at me. "I remembered where everything is."

Of course, she knew because she had rearranged our kitchen during her last visit to create a more organized system. Sienna's words, not mine. We left it that way because we found that her mom's system was actually better.

Sienna's dad gives me a still amused look. "Sienna's taking a shower," I mutter. "She... she'll be right in."

I'm really uncomfortable with this situation. Sienna better hurry. I don't know what to talk to her parents about.

"So, where's Denver?" asks Mrs. Gardner, sitting across from me. Great, that's where Sienna should sit.

It takes me a moment to answer. "In Europe."

"Europe?" she prods. "Europe's big."

"She's in England." I don't know how I came up with that. Probably because a few days ago, when I couldn't sleep, I saw a documentary about it on TV. "And what is she doing there?"

236

"Studying," I mumble, reaching for the full coffee cup in front of me and pouring another sip of milk into it. I keep glancing at the door, hoping Sienna will finally show up. "I'm... sorry... you... you must have been looking forward to seeing her."

"Of course, we were," she pipes, "what's she studying again?"

"Economics, like Sienna and..."

"Esther," Mr. Gardner interrupts his wife with a grin. "Now leave the poor boy alone."

"Why?" she asks, raising her eyebrows. "I just want to know as much as I can about our daughter's roommate. There's nothing wrong with that."

I avoid her gaze. It makes me uncomfortable to look at her while she wants to know something about Sienna and Phoenix's lives that doesn't even exist.

"We know," her dad suddenly slams the table and I jerk hard, staring at him. My heart stops for a moment and I take a deep breath. "Denver Jones!"

My jaw drops and I want to say something, but no sound comes out of my mouth. I consider jumping up and going to the bathroom to warn Sienna, but that seems ridiculous. What am I going to do? Nervously, I bite my lip and look back and forth between Sienna's parents.

"How did you find out?" I finally ask. There's no point in getting caught in more lies, and somehow I'm glad they already know that part of the truth.

"After you told me you were playing football, about a month later, I checked to see how things were going. On the official website of the Lincoln Tigers."

The Internet, of course.

"But there was no Phoenix Jones listed at quarterback, just a Denver Jones, and when I clicked on the player profile, there were pictures of you."

"Oh man," I mutter, running my hands over my face. "I'm sorry."

"I followed the team for a while, hoping Sienna would tell us the truth on one of our phone calls, but she didn't," he continues. "And after one of the games, I found a picture of you in the gallery. What do you think was in that picture?"

"I don't know," I mutter, avoiding his gaze. I want Sienna to get her pretty butt in the kitchen right now and save me.

"A picture of you kissing my daughter!"

Now my heart stops and I could swear it's so quiet in the kitchen you could hear a pin drop.

'Mom, Dad!' Sienna walks in smiling. She's wearing black sweatpants and an orange hoodie with the Lincoln Tigers logo on it. 'You're early, but it's good to see you. What's the...' Seeing my still-shocked look, she pauses. "... Going on?'

'Sit down, Sienna,' her mother says sternly, pointing to the chair next to her. Without saying a word, she sits down and crosses her fingers. 'Did Phoenix tell you anything—'

'They know,' I cut her off before she can continue talking out of her ass. 'Everything.'

Now it's Sienna who can't make a sound. Within seconds, all the color drains from her pretty face. I want to sit next to her and take her hand, but it would look weird across the table. Her parents' eyes dart between us.

'But ... but ... how?' Shock is still written all over her face. Her eyes dart back and forth between her parents. 'I... I mean, I... I never ... hinted at anything, did I?'

'You didn't,' her father replies. 'The Internet did.'

'Shit,' she mumbles, 'I'm sorry. Mom, Dad... I'm really sorry.'

No one says anything for a moment, until Sienna's mother puts a hand on her shoulder, forcing her daughter to look at her.

'Why didn't you tell us?' she wants to know, looking at her daughter with disappointment.

'Well, at first I was shocked that Denver wasn't a girl,' she says, looking at me with amusement. I smile back at her, remembering our first meeting. I thought it was a joke, too. 'But there was no other room available and we got along well. The first time you came, Phoenix was here by chance.'

'The girl's name is really Phoenix?' her father asks, bemused, and now I'm the one nodding in response to his question.

'And she really is my little sister, too,' I add. 'I had no idea that day that Sienna wasn't telling you the truth.' I shake my head and laugh at the same time, thinking about that day and what I had gotten myself into for her. I nod and point at Sienna. 'She asked me to pretend to be Phoenix.'

'I didn't want to,' my girlfriend cries in near panic, as if she's really afraid her parents are going to cut her off and take her back to Montana. 'I really didn't, but the more time that passed, the less I dared to tell you the truth.'

Sienna slumps her shoulders and nervously bites her lower lip. I wish I could sit next to her, give her a hug and offer her support. I don't think her parents are going to do anything extreme, because I get the impression that they've taken everything very well–especially her dad. But still, in the coming months, depending on how far we get in the league, I'll be getting new and higher paying sponsorship deals. I'll be able to pay our rent and buy food and whatever else we need. She could either go to work or take out a loan to pay her tuition. But like I said, I don't think her parents would do that. Also, their body language is not defensive or tense. Mr. Gardner, in particular, remains upbeat and relaxed. Mrs. Gardner still seems to be considering how to respond to the truth she already knows.

'Sienna,' her mother says, stroking her back. 'We...' When her husband raises his eyebrows, she groans and immediately makes amends. 'I didn't approve of you studying in Lincoln at first, it's true. I was afraid for you and thought that if you were in Helena, we could be there for you. I was wrong, I see that now.'

'The room is a lot more expensive than the dorm, and...'

'It's okay, honey,' she says gently. 'Your dad and I just want you to be happy, and it looks like you are.' Mrs. Gardner's eyes meet mine, and she smiles at me sincerely. I return it. It's a relief to know that she understands that her daughter is happy here.

'And ... and it just kind of worked out for us.' The corners of Sienna's mouth turn up. 'At some point, we realized that we were more than just friends.'

Minus all our ups and downs, that describes it perfectly.

At some point, we realized we were more than just friends.

22

-SIENNA-

One week later

An uneasy feeling spreads through me as Denver's car approaches the large gate behind which the largest military base in the northern United States is located. Behind the cast-iron gate with the U.S. Army crest is an Army cemetery. Denver told me that at the time, his mother had the choice of burying his father in the military cemetery with an official funeral and full honors, or in one of Chicago's many city cemeteries. Mrs. Jones chose the official burial for her husband, knowing that this would have been his wish.

Now the visit to the cemetery is like an official state visit. The grounds are completely sealed off, and the gate is opened only with a visitor's pass and an interview with a gatekeeper. Denver has not said a word since we left home. A few miles back, he took my hand. We intertwined our fingers and I kept stroking the back of his hand with my thumb. It's very hard for him to come here with me.

Denver looked up to his father and had a special relationship with him. He tells me all the time how terrible it was to lose him. He doesn't, however, talk about what exactly happened.

He stops at the gate and rolls down his window. Then he holds up his visitor's pass to the guard.

'Are you alone?' the guard asks Denver, and he shakes his head.

'I'm here with my girlfriend,' he replies, pointing at me. 'Sienna Gardner, born 5/23/2003 in Helena, Montana.' With that, he shows him my ID, which the guard accepts with thanks and hands it back to Denver.

'Thank you,' he replies and opens the gate. Denver rolls up the window again, tosses the visitor's pass back into the center console, and hands me my ID.

I like the white brick Civil War-era houses, contrasting with the late 20th-century ones that give the barracks its distinctive look. Somehow the place scares me, and I'm glad I'm not alone. Denver doesn't handle this place well. Still, it's important to him that I visit his father's grave – with him.

Otherwise, I don't think he would have come here for Thanksgiving. It is the most important holiday in the USA. The most important family holiday – more important than Christmas. To be in a military cemetery on that day to visit your father's grave is terrible. Especially if you're as young as Denver.

Denver parks his car a few yards away in the cemetery's visitor parking lot and turns off the engine. Silently, we get out of the car and I take the little flower I got this morning from the back seat. There is another car in the parking lot next to Denver's. It's an old Honda, past its prime.

Denver didn't say anything about me buying a flower, but I didn't want to go to his dad's grave empty-handed. It felt wrong.

I walk over to Denver, who locks the car and reaches for my hand. He interlocks our fingers and smiles at me. His smile doesn't reach his eyes. It's the rehearsed smile he gives the press and fans when all he wants to do is leave after a game. Usually after defeats. His eyes are empty. It tears my heart to see him like that.

Together we make our way to his father's grave. It's freezing in Chicago and I can feel it. When I exhale, my warm breath forms little clouds. With each step we take toward the grave, Denver squeezes my hand tighter. I can only imagine the pain he must be feeling, and I wish I could take just a fraction of it away from him. After about ten minutes of walking, we reach the grave.

A nondescript white stone with a black inscription rises from the ground in front of us.

It says 'Lieutenant Colonel' and below that his unit and his name 'Franklin Jones' followed by the dates of his life 'October 16, 1973 – October 27, 2016'.

There is absolutely nothing personal about the grave, which I think is a shame. It would not be a place for me to mourn. But I also understand that Mrs. Jones wanted to pay this final tribute to her husband.

Carefully, I step away from Denver and place my flower on the ground. I stare at the stone for a moment before rising to stand beside my boyfriend. Denver and I stand still and silent until I reach for his hand and squeeze it. Suddenly he pulls me to him and presses me so hard against his body that I think my lungs are being crushed. I know Denver has strength, but damn – this really hurts. I wrap my arms around him and stroke his back as a jolt goes through his body. At first, I can't place it, but then I clearly hear a sob. Denver is crying.

I press myself closer to him, which is hardly possible. He sobs louder and louder and I shed a tear too. I can hardly stand to see him like this and not be able to do anything but hold him in my arms.

I never saw Denver cry about his dad. Of course he was sad, but he was always incredibly proud and remembered the good memories. I didn't expect him to be so overwhelmed by his feelings. I feel even more helpless now. Standing here, stroking his back and just being there for him feels inadequate. But it is all I can do for him.

'There were three days left,' he says suddenly, pulling away from me. His eyes are glassy and tears keep falling from them, which I carefully wipe away with my thumbs. 'He was supposed to come home after almost seven months. We had everything set up. Mom had planned a welcome home party.'

It tears my heart to hear these words, but it's important for him to tell me.

'And then ... then I came home from school. There was an Army vehicle outside our door, and I knew something bad had happened. I... I knew he was dead. Why else would there be an Army vehicle outside our door so close to his coming home? I ran up the driveway and into the house. My mother was in the kitchen with my grandparents. Colonel Preston, who was also a very close friend of my dad's, was sitting at the table with them. He had taken off his cap was pale, and when he saw me, he lost even more color.'

'I'm so sorry, Denver.' The first words out of my mouth and the lamest sentence of all. But it's the truth. I am so, so sorry. 'Do you know what happened?'

'I only know what Mom told me, and honestly, I don't want to know more,' he replies, moving away from me. Denver gets down on one knee in front of the gravestone and wipes the traces of winter from the stone with his jacket sleeve. 'Dad was on patrol, securing the area. His vehicle was attacked by partisans and blown up.' An icy shiver runs down my spine. 'They died – all of them.' I put my hand on his shoulder and squeeze gently. 'Dad always knew what he was getting into, and so did Mom. At least I think so,' he whispers. 'They had been together for twenty-five years and married twenty years at that point. My father was about to be promoted to colonel. All that was missing was the swearing-in ceremony, which would have taken place in Washington in December of that year. That's why he has a headstone of comparable size.'

I look around and indeed: Most of the gravestones are much smaller. Carefully I crouch down next to him and snuggle up against him. Denver puts his arm around me and pulls me close. 'In her early forties, my mother was a widow, alone with three children. I was sixteen, Phoenix was fourteen, and Madison was ten. Fortunately, my grandmother helped us a lot in the early months. Thanksgiving, Christmas and birthdays were the worst. Maybe that's why I can't bring myself to give John a chance. To me, he's not a part of our family.'

'Because you wish your father was here.'

'Yes,' Denver says, 'I haven't made it easy for John the last few years, I've made sure he knows he's not my dad.'

'And him?'

'He resigned himself to it about six months ago, I think,' Denver mumbles, now resigned as well, as if he doesn't know how to save the relationship with his stepfather either. 'He says hello and goodbye to me, but otherwise avoids all communication.'

I can tell that Denver is actually starting to question what's going on between him and John. Not just today, but for several days now. But I also realize that we can't fix it here and now. They have to start over. They have to get to know each other again, and Denver in particular has to interact with John. I think for a moment about what to say and decide to change the subject. It might not be the right thing to do, because I can tell there is a lot left unsaid about John, but we are not going to get anywhere here. We need to discuss this at home, not at his father's grave.

'What do you think your father would say about us?' I ask him, and sure enough, Denver smiles. He pulls me closer and plants a kiss on my forehead.

'He'd like you, but he wouldn't approve of my life before you. Mom and Dad met when they were teenagers and were together ever since. But I think he'd be happy and he'd know you're the one, too.'

I fall even more in love with Denver at this moment. It's so sweet the way he says it and how sure he is that we belong together. Because I am too. The last few weeks have not been easy for us, but we are getting through it together. We're still very young and don't know where life will take us, but I see my future at his side, too.

'I know your dad would be proud of you,' I whisper and kiss him. 'You're great, Denver, someone who loves and respects the people around him. You take good care of your sisters, even if you sometimes go too far.'

'Thanks, baby,' he whispers, slowly relaxing. 'We should get going. It's cold.'

'It sure is,' I say, intertwining my hand with his again. 'We should come back soon.'

'Maybe,' Denver says absently as we head for the exit.

Denver parks his car in the driveway of his parents' home, and I look up at the front of the small single-family house. Smiling, I squeeze his hand and look up at him. He looks back at me and gives me a soft kiss. 'Thanks for coming to the cemetery with me.'

'You don't have to thank me,' I say, looking at him hard. 'It is only natural that I accompany you. I have to thank you. I know how hard it is for you to include me, Denver. It meant even more to me that you took me to your father's grave. And if you don't want to go alone, I'll go with you whenever you want.'

'I'm not used to taking someone with me,' he whispers, smiling shyly at me. As if he's ashamed of it, because he doesn't like to show that side of himself. 'My sisters go a lot. Jake goes with Phoenix all the time, as far as I know. He's known my dad since he was seven. I haven't been to his grave with my sisters or my mom since the funeral. Jake went with me once, but I could barely stand to be around him. I ran away after he said a few words. You were the first...' He swallows and looks away. When he raises his hand to wipe his eyes, I bite my tongue to keep from saying something. Finally, he looks back at me. 'You were the first person I could stand to be near me there. I shouldn't have stopped the family therapy. Maybe then I would have dealt with his death better.'

Instead of answering, I kiss him. Despite everything we've experienced today, I'm looking forward to the next few hours. I'm looking forward to meeting his mother and John. For days, I've been alternating between worrying about meeting his parents for the first time and visiting the cemetery. I really hope they like me and think I'm a good fit for Denver. I especially want to hit it off with his mom. Phoenix said she'll love me, but who knows if she was just trying to reassure me. Madison will be there as well, and for the first time she will bring her boyfriend Fynn. Denver immediately railed against him and said he'd take the guy to task. I immediately tried to talk some sense into him and let him know how embarrassing it would be for Madison. Denver just said he was going to check him out anyway. Check yes, embarrass no. I hope he got the message. Fynn is her first boyfriend and I can only imagine how embarrassing it will be for Madison.

'And remember not to embarrass your sister,' I remind him. Denver rolls his eyes, but I just give him a warning look. He opens the door and gets out. 'Denver!' I call after him, but he's already slammed the door behind him. Annoyed, I get out and look at him. 'Denver,' I repeat his name again.

'Sienna!' As expected, he imitates my voice, which is the last thing I need.

'Phoenix!' My friend gets out of the car next to us and grins at us. 'Are you guys fighting?'

'No,' Denver replies in a good mood. For me it's more like playful good humor, but I don't say anything. 'We were just discussing that I'm going to take a closer look at this Fynn.'

'You're not going to do that,' Phoenix scolds, putting her hands on her hips. I look at Denver in agreement and take the salad I've prepared from the back seat.

'You didn't really bring a salad?' Phoenix looks at me in surprise and then at her brother. 'You're too perfect.'

'That's her,' Denver agrees with his little sister and puts his arm around my shoulders. Grinning, I look up at him and he leans in and kisses me. I return the kiss and snuggle up against him. Together with Phoenix we make our way to the front door, which she unlocks with her key and lets us in.

I look around the hall with interest. Opposite the front door, a staircase leads to the upper floor. Photos hang on the wall. From a distance, I can make out the Jones siblings. To the right of the front door is a coat rack and a dresser with a mirror above it. On it is a bowl with car keys. I pass the salad to Denver to take off my jacket and shoes.

'Phoenix?' a female, light voice sounds. 'Is that you?'

'Yes,' my friend calls, 'Denver and Sienna too.'

The next moment, a woman appears who looks like an older version of Phoenix. She's definitely her mother. The hair, the mouth, the eyes–all Phoenix!

Mrs. Jones' blonde hair is cut in a trendy short style. Her makeup is light and she's wearing jeans and a light blue blouse.

'Hi Mom,' Phoenix says and gives her a hug.

'Hi honey,' Mrs. Jones replies, coming up to us.

'Mom.' Denver clears his throat and hands the salad to Phoenix, who carries it into the kitchen without comment. A man in his fifties appears behind Mrs. Jones. It must be John. His dark hair is already graying. He seems outgoing at first glance, and his build is similar to Denver's.

'Hello John,' Denver greets him with a nod and puts his arm around me. 'Let me introduce you. Mom, John, this is Sienna, my girlfriend. Baby, this is my mom Lori and her boyfriend John.'

'Hello,' I say with a smile and shake their hands. 'Thank you for inviting us.'

'We're glad you came,' Lori replies, and her partner just gives me a friendly nod. I take Denver's hand and squeeze it. He squeezes it back, confirming the good feeling that has been building up inside me. Everything has gone well so far, and his mother and her boyfriend seem very nice.

'Madison and Fynn are waiting for us in the living room.'

We nod and follow them. When I see Madison sitting there, I can hardly believe it's her. A few weeks ago on our couch she looked completely different. Her hair is dark brown now, her makeup is friendly and light. There is nothing left of the gothic style. Instead of the black dress, tights and heavy Doc Martens, she is wearing a light sweater, jeans and light brown ankle boots. Fynn sits next to her. He has light brown hair that he wears longer on top of his head, forming little corkscrew curls. Like Denver, he wears a hoodie and jeans.

'Mad.' Denver grins. 'So colorful today?'

I ram my elbow into his stomach, making him groan and rub the spot. Then I walk over to Madison and hug her. 'Hi,' I hug her tightly and she hugs me back. 'And please don't listen to him. He's an idiot.' I wink at her, which makes her grin. Then I turn to her friend. 'Hi, I'm Sienna, Denver's girlfriend.'

'Hi,' he replies excitedly, shaking my hand a little too vigorously. Immediately his eyes go to Denver. 'I'm Fynn.'

'I'm Denver!' My boyfriend pushes past me and takes Fynn's hand in his. You can see from Fynn's expression that Denver is squeezing his hand unnecessarily hard and that he's intimidating him as well. Madison and I roll our eyes, but Denver doesn't care. 'Actually, I wanted to give you a little squeeze and...'

'Denver,' I hiss and grab his arm. He doesn't move an inch. It would be ridiculous if I could move over two hundred pounds. 'Don't do that.'

'And get on your case,' he says with a smile. 'But finally my little sister looks like my little sister again. You must have done something right.'

Madison grins at Denver and wraps her arms around Fynn. She seems happy with him, and that's the most important thing.

'Dinner's ready,' Mrs. Jones' voice rings out, and I grab Denver's hand and pull him behind me to the table. He follows me, smiling, and pulls my chair back so I can sit down. Denver sits next to me.

Mrs. Jones has laid out quite a spread. There is a roast with potatoes and salad, but also lasagna. I can't decide what to eat first.

Mrs. Jones inquires about my studies and I also have a good conversation with John, whose last name I don't know. He seems very open-minded and interested in my studies. So is his mother, much to the annoyance of Phoenix, whom she

250

keeps looking at. Denver is getting more relaxed by the minute. He loves his mom, you can see that right away. He keeps looking over at her with a smile and responds lovingly to everything she says. But he also becomes concerned about her when he thinks she's overdoing it in the community. 'Sienna and I went to visit Dad,' Denver suddenly speaks up, and the conversation around the table falls silent. Everyone looks at him in surprise. Since he told me he hasn't been to the grave with his family since the funeral, I guess they think he never visits. 'We ... we laid a flower,' he continues.

I reach under the table for his hand and intertwine our fingers. 'I know I haven't always been fair over the years.' He raises his head and looks around the table. His voice shakes and I squeeze his hand again, wanting him to continue. This is so incredibly important to Denver and his family. 'Especially to you, John.'

'Denver,' he says immediately. 'It's all right.'

'No,' Denver interrupts. 'It wasn't all right. I... I didn't want a new dad, I had one dad and he ... he was perfect – for me. I would like you to give me another chance to do better in the future. We ... we can start over. If that's what you want?'

Denver looks lost as he looks at John and squeezes my hand tighter. John looks back at him and smiles.

'Of course,' he says. 'I'd love to.'

I look over at Mrs. Jones who, with tears in her eyes, stands up without saying a word and hugs her son. It must be incredible for her to hear those words come out of his mouth. Denver stands up to give his mother a proper hug.

John also stands and walks over to Denver. He hugs him too and whispers something in his ear. Denver nods and looks at me for a moment. Then he turns back to John and says something else to him. He smiles and pats him on the back. John, Mrs. Jones and Denver sit back down. My boyfriend reaches under the table for my hand and leans over to me. Gently, he presses his lips to mine, which makes me uncomfortable at first. His family is at the table and I don't know if this is for their eyes. But then the thought strikes me as silly. We're a couple – of course we're kissing.

'I also have something to tell you,' Phoenix suddenly speaks and looks around the table. We look at her tensely. She glances around the group and seems to think about her words again. Has she finally gotten it together with Jake?

I doubt it. They are still sneaking around each other. They won't become a couple that fast. Besides, she would have told us – Joy, Millie and me – to find a way to tell Denver.

'Well?' asks Mrs. Jones, interested, on the one hand, and confused on the other. 'What is it?'

'I've decided to put my studies on hold,' Phoenix drops the bombshell, and while Madison and I grin broadly at her, Mrs. Jones, John, and Denver's faces drop. They weren't expecting this. I, on the other hand, am pleased because Phoenix has hinted more than once that she had other plans for after high school and hasn't given up on them yet. 'I don't enjoy it and ... and I'm not good at it,' she adds as an explanation.

'And ... and what do you want to do?' her mother picks up, looking at her daughter closely. She looks far from enthusiastic. She doesn't like this decision, it's plain to see. Denver and John also put down their cutlery and look at Phoenix. I think it's very brave of her to take this step and announce it in front of everyone at such a big table. It's short and sweet, so everyone knows.

'I want to work and travel in Europe,' Phoenix says. A gleam comes into her eyes. 'And honestly, I have it all set up.'

'Excuse me?' blurts out Denver. 'You got it all set up? Flights booked, jobs found, and we're just being notified or what?'

He clenches his hands into fists, and the way he looks at Phoenix, she should drop dead. It was to be expected that he wouldn't be thrilled, but such a dismissive attitude surprises me. After all, it's Phoenix's life and her decision what to do with it.

On the one hand, I'm sad that she chose to work and travel, but on the other hand, I admire her courage and determination to defy her family and supporters. I hardly had the courage to change states.

'I guess so,' Phoenix murmurs. 'You guys would have tried to talk me out of it. I wanted to do this after high school, but you guys wanted me to go to college.'

'Because it makes sense, Phoenix,' Mrs. Jones says forcefully. 'We talked about it.'

'I'm not good at it, Mom!' Phoenix's voice grows louder with each word. 'I don't like my studies. Ask Sienna—' She points at me and I widen my eyes. I don't actually want to get involved in this conversation. I haven't been part of this family long enough for that.

'I don't understand any of this.'

'I think it's a good idea,' Fynn says suddenly, and Madison nods. 'My brother went to Australia for a year. He really liked it, and we got to go visit him.'

I give him a grateful smile. I admire his courage, because I'm still sitting here, not saying a word, even though Phoenix has actively encouraged me to.

'We could visit Phoenix, too,' Madison chuckles. 'I think it's good that you're doing it, too.'

'Thanks Mad,' Phoenix mutters, looking hopefully at her brother. 'Denver?'

My boyfriend puffs out his cheeks and finally nods hesitantly.

'I'm going to miss you a lot, though.' He sighs heavily. 'But

I could tell you didn't like college. And you'll only be gone for a few months, okay?'

'Well, sure,' Phoenix says, visibly relieved. 'My visa is until May.'

'Then I guess I'll have to relent,' Mrs. Jones says, and John puts his hand on hers.

'I agree with Madison.' He winks at the youngest Jones. 'We can go see Phoe.'

'See, Mom,' Phoenix says, raising her eyebrows. 'Listen to the man.'

Mrs. Jones finally nods and asks her daughter for details.

Smiling, I lean over to Denver and kiss him on the cheek.

'I love you,' I whisper. 'And we should think about visiting. I've never been to Europe.'

Denver sighs and plants a kiss on my lips. I return it and cuddle up to him happily. This is definitely one of the most exciting days of my life. Actually, it's been a roller coaster of emotions for both of us. Denver has faced his demons and finally let me into his heart and life. I love him and even though I know he will probably get to the point where he will try to shut me out again, but I will fight for him. We are not perfect and we have both made mistakes in the past.

But today showed me that we can make it together if we want to.

'Which country are you going to?' I ask Phoenix and she immediately starts talking excitedly.

EPILOGUE

⬛ DENVER ⬛

Two Months Later, Minneapolis, Target Field

I enter the home locker room at Target Field in Minneapolis and sit down in front of the locker prepared for me. Normally the Minneapolis Warriors play in this stadium, but this year it's the venue for the college football championship. We're playing Ohio State, which means we're playing Tyler's old team. For the past two weeks, we have been meticulously preparing for this day. We arrived in Minneapolis earlier this week and were cleared for all college events. Now, of course, I want to win this title.

My mom, John, Madison and Sienna with Joy arrived yesterday to be a part of it as well. Phoenix left for Europe earlier this week to start her work and travel. I still can't really wrap my head around it. I know I gave her my blessing on Thanksgiving, but the more I think about it, the more I am against it. She should sit at her desk like everyone else and study for her exams. If she can't do that, she can change subjects, but she shouldn't waste three months of her life. For

Sienna's sake, I'm trying to keep it together and keep my opinion to myself. My girlfriend is excited about my sister's idea and is already looking for hotels in Bristol. Looking back, I feel bad because I don't want to argue with Sienna – especially about Phoenix. We haven't seen much of each other since the Christmas break. My focus has been on football and Sienna has had to study for her exams.

Millie can't come because she has to prepare for her exams. I don't understand this decision at all because she loves football and Minneapolis is her hometown. But we can't force her to come. Sienna is heartbroken that her best friend won't be here, but the players have a limited number of tickets. Since we all get along well on the team, we shuffle the tickets back and forth. I've filled my quota. Each player is allowed five. Since Phoenix is in Europe, I had one ticket left and Joy got it. Maybe I should have asked Darren to add Millie to his quota since his family isn't coming from Texas. His sister Dana is getting married in three weeks and that's the event the Andrews are focused on. Which I think is pretty unfair, because Darren has a chance to achieve the biggest triumph of his career so far today. Jake's parents are here as well as Tyler's.

Jake sits down next to me on the bench and looks at me with a smile.

'Are you ready?'

'Absolutely,' I reply, pulling on my pads. 'You?'

'I can't wait.' My best friend looks determined. 'We're going to take them down.'

'You're very optimistic,' I say, immediately wondering why I'm being so negative. We have nothing to fear from Ohio, and we have one of their best offensive players this year. We deserve to be in this final and none of us has any doubts about it. If my teammates don't, as the captain of the team, I have even less right to doubt it, right? That wouldn't be fair to them.

256

'You don't?' demands Jake. 'We can do this, Denver. We're better than them.'

I nod and pat him on the back. Jake is right, we are better and we will win the championship this year.

Together we continue to change and check our helmets with the staff – and I check my wrist guard.

'Men,' Coach Flanders calls out, motioning for us to join him in the center. We stand in a circle around him. 'Today is a big day. For me, for you, and for the Lincoln Tigers family. It's been two years since we've been to this final, and you know what?' He looks at each of us before continuing. 'It's been too long a break.'

We yell and scream wildly and agree with the coach. 'This forced break ends today,' he continues. 'We have the best defensive end in the college league – Darren Andrews!' We clap and the players standing next to him pat him on the back. 'We stole Ohio's best running back,' he continues, pointing to Tyler. 'And we got Denver Jones! The best quarterback this season.'

Again, there's a noise in the booth and Jake pats me on the head.

'You guys are going to go out there and kick Ohio's ass!'

There are only two minutes left on the clock as I take the field for the last time tonight to call a play for my team. Ohio leads by five points, which means we need to score a touchdown. It's all or nothing now. Win or lose.

'I'm going to play Tyler,' I say after we line up in a circle. 'Jake and Warren will fake a run. We need to try and get a first down. I don't want to take any chances and I want to take as much time off the clock as possible.

A quick touchdown would mean Ohio gets the ball back. We have to prevent that, but still, a touchdown is the only way to win. To me, that means taking as much time off the clock as possible and scoring a touchdown. Because if Ohio gets the ball back and we only get a field goal, it's over. They will still have a two-point lead and their quarterback will not throw an interception. He's been around too long and has too much nerve for that. The guys nod after I call the play and we line up at the line. Our center tosses me the ball and I take a few steps back to survey the field. Jake and Warren have stuck to their running routes and Tyler is on his way. I take advantage of the gaps between two beefy defenders and throw the ball over their heads. Tyler catches the pass but is immediately tackled to the ground.

"Damn," I growl, because we didn't get a first down. "Keep going, guys!"

Once again, we are together and I decide to run the play again, which Jake doesn't like. I can see it on his face, but my best friend isn't the quarterback and we're not in a game where we can argue.

I have to trust that this is going to work and that we're going to get a first down this time. It looks promising at first, but then Tyler is stopped again.

Damn it! You've got to be kidding me!

Jake's look is more than clear. On the next play, I decide to try the running route on the outside. Jake doesn't like it either, but we have some damn quick and agile wide receivers in Phil and Luke. We line up again and I look up at the giant video cube showing my family. I have no idea if the media people are using it to give me another boost because there are people sitting there that I want to win this championship for, or if they are using it to put so much pressure on me that I throw an interception and the ball goes back to Ohio.

Of course, it does the former. I don't look away as long as

258

they're showing it. Mom, as usual, covers her eyes when things get really exciting. She used to do that in high school or send my dad to the games alone. When I think of my dad, I look up at the sky and close my eyes. He would want me to win today. He would be incredibly happy for me. When I open my eyes and look at the video cube one last time, the camera has zoomed in on Sienna. Madison calls her attention and my friend forms a heart with her fingers. I raise my hand to signal that I've seen it.

Then I focus back on the game.

I catch the ball from the center, take a few steps back, fake a throw and pass the ball to Luke. Now all I can do is stand still and watch my teammate.

And sure enough, it works! Luke gets well past the first down before going down.

"Way to go," I yell, high-fiving him as we meet for the next play call.

"Fifty seconds left," Jake says as we stand side by side waiting for the others. "Play me, I'll get to the one-yard line, and then we'll run you over the line with a quarterback sneak on the last play," he says. Logan will take his time with the kick. We've got two timeouts left and Ohio's not going to make a move.

"I know," I say. "But don't you think they'll see through it?"

"Sure," Jake replies. I roll my eyes and start to turn away when he grabs my shoulder. "Do we have a choice?"

"No," I admit and nod at him. "We can do this."

We line up again after I call Jake's play for this drive. I can only hope his idea works and that we're fast enough to slow Ohio down. There are fifteen seconds left on the clock. It's perfect, but it's also insanely risky. It has to be a touchdown. The center throws me the ball again and I take a few steps back until I see Jake. He has broken free and I pass him the ball. Now it's up to my best friend and our players to keep Ohio away from Jake.

259

Jake runs and runs and runs—I hardly dare to look at the clock. The clock is ticking mercilessly.

Eight...

Seven.

Six.

Five...

I lean on my thighs and stare at the grass. I can't watch. Even though my body is pumping with adrenaline.

"Touchdown for the Lincoln Tigers!"

I jerk my head up to see Jake standing in the end zone, and suddenly all the other players land on him. They are burying my best friend under them. Without hesitation, I jump up, rip my helmet off my head, and clench my hand into a fist. My first glance is not to the stands, but up at the sky again.

"I did it, Dad," I whisper, tears of joy streaming down my face. "I won... I won."

"We did it!" Darren pulls me around and grabs the back of my neck to press my forehead against his. We started playing football together in Lincoln almost three years ago and worked our way up to this point. How many losses have we taken? How many lectures from Coach Flanders have we had before tonight? How many times have we been written off by the press? Now here we are! "We won!"

"We won," I repeat his words, grabbing him by the neck as well. "Damn it! We're college champions!"

It's so surreal! But it's true—we won. We are college champions! I can't say it enough.

"I can't believe it," I exclaim, hugging Darren tightly. "We won."

Darren and I separate to greet the first well-wishers from Ohio. They are depressed and sad. There are tears in their eyes. I go over to their quarterback, Mitchel.

"Hey," I say and slam into him. Then I pull him close and pat him on the back. "You played well."

My words are no consolation to him, and I can only guess how bad he's going to feel tonight and probably for days and weeks to come, but I want him to know that he was a force to be reckoned with tonight. Our paths will lead us to the draft in a year and a half. And then, hopefully, we'll see each other again on the big stage.

"Thanks, Denver," he replies. "Enjoy your evening."

"Thanks," I say, strolling over to my teammates to celebrate with them.

"We're champions," Tyler shouts after a long chat with his old teammates. "And there's someone else who wants to congratulate you." I give him a quick hug.

"Who's your best running back?!" I spin around and fall into Jake's arms. My best friend since elementary school. If I've been working on this title with Darren for three years, it's been more than twice as long with Jake. "You're my best running back," I say in return, and we jump up and down like little boys. "We actually did it!"

As we break away from each other, we are asked by a college league staff member to slowly make our way to the awards ceremony. On the sidelines, our families and friends stand in a cordoned-off area. The next few minutes pass in a daze until the league director hands me the trophy and I hold it up to the Minneapolis night sky.

"Give me that thing!" Darren takes the trophy from me. "Your girlfriend wants to congratulate you."

I turn around and see Sienna coming at me. I immediately

open my arms and run towards her. I hadn't even noticed that the families had already been let onto the field.

Overjoyed, she jumps into my arms and I turn us around in a circle. Laughing, she hugs me and her blonde hair flies through the air.

"I'm so proud of you," she says after I stop and let her down slowly. Tears run down her cheek, which I gently brush away. "So, so proud. The way you played and ... and I love you."

"I love you, too," I reply, kissing her again.

Sienna grins broadly at me, and I'm so happy to be able to share this moment of my college career with her. I hug my girl one more time until I finally let her go to accept my family's congratulations as well.

"You were amazing, sweetheart." Mom is the second person after Sienna to reach out to me. "I wish your dad could see you, Denver."

"Thanks Mom," I reply, swallowing my tears. "I wish he could too."

"I'm so proud of you!" She gives me another kiss on the cheek and lets me talk to my sister.

I lift Madison up as well. She plants a kiss on my cheek and grins broadly at me. "Congratulations," she says, "from Fynn too."

"Thanks." I put her down and turn to John. Our relationship isn't perfect, but it's definitely better than it's been in the last three years. We've been reaching out to each other, and as a result, we're talking more. In the beginning, I often thought he was into football to suck up, but no. He played in high school, but then he got a knee injury that cost him his college scholarship. It shocks me that I didn't know that. We like the same action movies and the same cars. We even have a lot in common that I didn't expect. Now it's up to me to explore these things with him and bring us closer. Because he's wanted to do that for years.

"Congratulations," he says, slapping me. "Especially the last passes were really strong from you."

"Thank you," I reply sincerely and turn back to Sienna.

She tilts her head slightly to look me in the eye. Grinning, I look down at her and take her face in my hands. Then I lean down and cover her mouth with mine. Sienna kisses me back and snuggles up against me.

"So, what are we going to do with the trophy?" She wants to know. "The first of many."

"Hmm," I ponder, leaning down so only she can hear. "Unfortunately, there's only one, and I think Darren's going to take it to bed with him, but I have another idea…"

Sienna laughs and looks past me to Darren, who is guarding the trophy like a treasure.

"What idea?" she wants to know, wiggling her eyebrows as if she knows exactly what I'm getting at.

"I heard you're wearing a very special jersey and I thought you'd only wear that jersey when we both celebrate the championship tonight."

Sienna nods and I place my lips on hers. She wraps her arms around my neck and kisses me back.

"Hey lovebirds!" We pull away from each other and look at Darren, Jake, Tyler and Joy who are holding the trophy. "We want to take a picture for Millie and Phoenix. Come here."

I pull Sienna over to our friends and place her in front of me. Jake stands to our right and Joy in front of him. Darren and Tyler crouch in front of us with the trophy in their midst.

At Madison's command, holding Joy's iPhone, we smile for the camera.

The day couldn't be more perfect.

ABOUT THE AUTHOR

Of course, it was sports – specifically ball games – that led Mrs. Kristal to writing. She started writing stories in 2012, and her first attempts at writing about soccer evolved over the years into real stories and eventually books.

From that point on, Mrs. Kristal switched continents and wrote about American football. In 2021, she published her first book about college romance and football. Mrs. Kristal draws inspiration from everyday situations, memories of experiences, and conversations with friends and family.

Her books always focus on love and friendship in addition to sports. What she loves most about writing is being able to immerse herself in other worlds, taking her characters on a long journey, with a happy ending at the end. When Mrs. Kristal is not writing, she spends time with her friends and family and travels the world. One of her greatest wishes is to see the countries, cities, and stadiums she writes about at least once in her life.

Editorial manager: Audrey Puech
Composition and layout: Thibault Beneytou
Interior illustrations: © Shutterstock
Cover design: Keti Spirkoska
Cover illustration: © Shutterstock

Made in the USA
Columbia, SC
06 August 2024